D1011007

Remembering the Dead

Also available by Elizabeth J. Duncan

Penny Brannigan mysteries

The Marmalade Murders

Murder Is for Keeps

Murder on the Hour

Slated for Death

Never Laugh as a Hearse Goes By

A Small Hill to Die On

A Killer's Christmas in Wales

A Brush with Death

The Cold Light of Mourning

Shakespeare in the Catskills mysteries

Much Ado About Murder

Ill Met by Murder

Untimely Death

Remembering the Dead

A PENNY BRANNIGAN MYSTERY

Elizabeth J. Duncan

NEW YORK

Published in the United States by Crooked Lane Books, an imprint of The Quick Brown Fox & Company LLC.

Crooked Lane Books and its logo are trademarks of The Quick Brown Fox & Company LLC.

Library of Congress Catalog-in-Publication data available upon request.

ISBN (hardcover): 978-1-64385-113-6
ISBN (ePub): 978-1-64385-114-3

Cover illustration by Scott Zelazny

Book design by Jennifer Canzone

Printed in the United States.

www.crookedlanebooks.com

Crooked Lane Books
34 West 27th St., 10th Floor
New York, NY 10001

First Edition: September 2019

10 9 8 7 6 5 4 3 2 1

For Carol Lloyd, and in loving memory
of her beloved friend and partner,
B.J. Maillette

Prologue

Wednesday, September 6, 1917, Birkenhead, England

"Fleur de lis!"

In a strong, clear voice, Archdruid Dyfed called out the nom de plume of the poet who was about to be awarded the highest literary honour Wales could bestow.

The National Eisteddfod audience of thousands, including men and women standing three and four deep outside the temporary pavilion that had been set up in the middle of an English field, fell into a respectful but excited silence as they waited for the archdruid to announce for the second time the name of the winner of the festival's most prestigious prize.

"If the poet who competed under the name *Fleur de lis* is here, he should stand!"

Surrounded by dignitaries, including the Welsh prime minister David Lloyd George, the archdruid adjusted the flowing white robes of his costume and touched the gold, torc-shaped breastplate that adorned his chest as he stepped closer to the edge of the stage, preparing to call out the winner's name for the third and final time. The moment had come for the winner of the main prize at this annual celebration of Welsh literature and culture to stand and reveal himself to the assembly, and then allow himself to be escorted to the stage for the chairing ceremony.

After judging that he had waited long enough to allow the tension to rise and the anticipation to peak, the archdruid addressed the crowd in their native Welsh. "Pan genir yr utgyrn a wnaiff Fleurs de lis, a Fleurs de lis yn unig, sefyll, os gwelwch yn dda." *When the Gorsedd trumpeters play the fanfare, would Fleur de lis, and only Fleur de lis, please stand up.*

The assembly held its collective breath as two trumpeters, with brightly coloured embroidered banners hanging from their silver instruments, played a musical flourish.

But no one stood.

Archdruid Dyfed consulted his notes, then rested one hand lightly on the armrest of the ornately carved bardic chair that had been commissioned for today's ceremony. "The winner of this year's chair is Hedd Wyn," he announced, using the poet's bardic name. "That is, Ellis Humphrey Evans, from the village of Trawsfynydd, North Wales."

But where was the winner? Members of the audience exchanged puzzled, concerned looks. Why did he not come forward and present himself to accept the great honour about to be bestowed upon him?

And then the archdruid uttered the most unexpected, most dreadful reason. "The victor has fallen in battle and lies in a silent grave in a foreign field." Hedd Wyn, on the cusp of literary greatness at the age of thirty, had been killed in action six weeks earlier, at the Battle of Pilckem Ridge, the opening attack of the Third Battle of Ypres, which would come to be better known as the Battle of Passchendaele. The chair was to be awarded posthumously. Although the archdruid was well aware of the fate that had befallen the winner, he had followed the traditional procedure of calling out the winner's name three times.

A stunned silence fell over the Eisteddfod field, and the crowd did not at first react. And then, as the archdruid's words began to take hold, a wave of murmured disbelief swept through the audience, the ripples of shock increasing to cries of anguished grief for their lost poet.

Three members of the platform party, dressed in white druidic costume similar to the archdruid's, rose from their seats and stepped solemnly forward to join him.

"Yr ŵyl yn ei dagrau a'r Bardd yn ei fedd—the festival in tears and the poet in his grave," said the archdruid. The druids unfolded a large square of black cloth, and, each holding a corner, they slowly and reverently draped it over the bardic chair, its soft folds shrouding the potent symbol of a generation of young Welsh men whose unfulfilled promise had been sacrificed to the Great War.

Chapter One

Early September 2018, Llanelen, North Wales

"And so you see, Penny," Mrs. Lloyd explained, "that's why the 1917 National Eisteddfod is always referred to as *Eisteddfod y Gadair Ddu*. The Eisteddfod of the Black Chair." She shifted her bottom slightly to settle herself more comfortably in the client's chair and checked the progress of her manicure before continuing. "And the story goes that on the dreary day that the Black Chair, or *y Gadair Ddu*, as we call it in Welsh, was delivered to Hedd Wyn's parents' farm—still draped in its black cloth, mind you—the whole village turned out dressed in mourning. And there was a great storm, with such thunder and lightning, and heavy rain, and the land covered in darkness, that folks had never seen the likes of it before or since." She made a little *tsk*ing noise. "What on earth was our finest poet doing out there in all that Belgian mud? It doesn't bear thinking about. And not just him. What a terrible waste that war was. All those young lives, lost. What was it all for? I ask you."

Penny Brannigan placed a stack of neatly folded white hand towels on the work top in the manicure room of the Llanelen Spa. "Yes, that war does seem pointless now," she agreed, "but then you could say that about most wars, couldn't you?" She turned away to open a cupboard and put the towels away, then turned back to face Mrs. Lloyd and said, "I've never been to a National Eisteddfod. I know what they are, of course, and I've been tempted to go, but in the end, I couldn't quite bring myself to do it. I'm not one for crowds."

"Oh, well," said Mrs. Lloyd good-naturedly, "you'll get crowds at the Eisteddfod, all right. It's only the biggest event in the country." She mulled that over for a moment. "Well, the Royal Welsh Show might give it a run for its money, I suppose." Held every year, usually in August, the National Eisteddfod is a week-long cultural celebration of Welsh music, dance, visual arts, and especially literature and poetry. Filled with colourful pageantry and mystical symbolism, its origins can be traced back to the twelfth century, but the elaborate, modern-day ceremonies date back just a few hundred years, when the concept of bards and druids was introduced. The festival attracts about 150,000 visitors each year, and as many as 6,000 competitors vie for prizes. It has been held outside Wales only half a dozen times, including in Birkenhead in 1917. But because there was a war on, the event was held in September that year, and lasted only three days.

"I remember the story about the Black Chair," said Eirlys, Penny's assistant, who was giving Mrs. Lloyd her manicure. Now in her early twenties, Eirlys had started working at the Spa as a bright sixteen-year-old school leaver and brought a youthful enthusiasm and innovation to her workplace. She had convinced Penny to introduce nail varnish in bright primary colours and cool pastels to appeal to teenagers, and had taken makeup courses so the Spa could offer a complete bridal service. "And Hedd Wyn, the poet, too. We learned all about him, and even visited Yr Ysgwrn—that's his farmhouse—on a school outing. I saw the chair myself. We all got to sit on it. Famous, it is, and incredibly beautiful, too."

"Well, I'm very pleased to hear that," said Mrs. Lloyd. "That you learned all about the history of Hedd Wyn and the Black Chair in school. It's only right that young people learn about our Welsh heritage. And as for that chair, well, it's practically a national treasure. Probably the best-known piece of furniture in the whole country. Anyway, what got me started on all this, an item on BBC Wales last evening said that the chair was taken somewhere to be refurbished or restored, or whatever they do to old pieces of furniture to preserve them and make them presentable, and then it's coming back to the farmhouse where Hedd Wyn lived to be put on display again. And that's not all. They've restored the farmhouse and done up one of the old outbuildings, the cow shed I think it was, and made it into a proper visitor centre with an exhibition space and a tearoom and a shop." She nodded at Eirlys. "That would be the farm you visited, back when it was still owned by the family. Now it's going to be a national historic site where folk can learn the story of our great poet. It's amazing when you think of it. He left school when he was fourteen to look after the sheep on his father's farm and went on to become one of the nation's greatest poets. But according to the news program, the refurbished centre doesn't open for a few months yet."

The conversation moved on as the manicure continued in the Llanelen Spa's bright studio with its display wall of bottles of nail varnish in every colour, from pale pinks to deep blues.

"Well, I'd best be running along," Penny said after a few minutes. "I really only wanted to pop in to say hello to you, Mrs. Lloyd, so I'll leave you and Eirlys to it." And after wishing Mrs. Lloyd good luck at her bridge game that evening, she left the two of them to finish the manicure and returned to her office.

Penny had drifted into Llanelen almost thirty years ago as a backpacking university graduate from Eastern Canada with no particular plans except to embellish her recently earned fine arts degree by visiting the grand museums and galleries of Europe. On her way to Holyhead to catch the ferry to Dublin, she had found herself in the slightly out-of-the-way Welsh market town on a lovely summer's day, just as the afternoon was fading into a soft, golden evening. Although she'd thought she'd stop for just a night or two, she'd met people, one thing had led to another, and she'd stayed on for the next three decades, building a happy, comfortable life for herself. Her roots in her adopted country were deep and strong, and as the years went by, she'd realised there was no reason to return to her homeland.

She entered her office, turned the page in her diary to see what she had on for the day, then checked her watch. She'd be a few minutes early, but it was time for her meeting with her business partner, Victoria Hopkirk. The beauty side of their spa business—the hair salon, manicure and pedicure studio, and makeup service, including makeup for weddings and other special occasions—was thriving, but they'd agreed they needed to do a better job of promoting their other services—massages, facials, and daylong pampering.

The women tried to have lunch together at least once a week, occasionally at a nearby café but usually—to keep any business discussion private—in Victoria's flat on the first floor of the Spa. Against just about everyone's advice, they'd bought the three-storey stone building a few years ago, and given its priceless location beside the River Conwy, with stunning views to the lush, green, wooded hills beyond, and its solid structure, their instincts had turned out to be sound. Following a complete renovation, the once-decrepit building had proved a beautiful, functional investment.

Penny pulled her office door shut behind her and made her way down the hall that led to the reception area. Just as she reached the receptionist's desk, the door to the Spa opened and Victoria Hopkirk herself entered, struggling to cope with the door and manage two bags of shopping.

"It's an absolutely beautiful day," she said as Penny sprang toward her, arms outstretched to hold the door open. "We really should be outside on such a glorious day. Why don't we take a picnic lunch to the churchyard? Just let me drop this lot off"—she lifted the bags slightly—"and we can pick up a couple of sandwiches on the way."

* * *

Victoria was right; the weather was glorious. It was the kind of day that straddles two seasons, starting off slightly cool and then warming as the morning wears on. Now, seated side by side on a bench in the churchyard overlooking the River Conwy, the two women munched their sandwiches, tossing the occasional crumb to a friendly robin who hopped and hovered nearby, hoping for a handout. A pair of white swans drifted by, navigating their way smoothly down the fast-flowing river toward the three-arched bridge that had spanned the river for almost four hundred years. Penny and Victoria leaned back against the bench, lifting their faces to a cloudless blue sky, soaking in the sunshine, and revelling in a moment of shared companionship and a deep sense of well-being.

When they'd finished their lunch, Penny stood up to stretch her legs, and while she was admiring the roofline of the centuries-old stone church, two figures emerged from the covered porch. She waved to them.

"It's Emyr and Thomas," she said. Victoria swung around on the bench and also waved. "It looks like Emyr's coming over to see us."

With a few long strides, Emyr Gruffydd joined them. A gentle breeze ruffled his dark hair, and he raised a hand to smooth it. After greeting them, he sat with his back to the river on the low stone wall that ran alongside the edge of the churchyard. Penny sat down again beside Victoria on the bench facing him, and the three smiled at one another.

"I'm glad I bumped into you," Emyr said. "I was just having a word with the rector about a dinner party."

"Oh," said Penny. "Up at the Hall?"

Emry nodded. "Yes. It's been a long time since we had a proper do, and the time just feels right. It's going to be a rather formal occasion, so I was just asking Thomas if he'd say grace, and he's kindly agreed, so now, Victoria, I'm asking you if you'd agree to favour us with an after-dinner harp recital."

"I'd love to, if I can. What date are we talking about?"

"Oh, sorry. Of course, the date. Thomas just asked me the same question and I wasn't really able to tell him. It'll be in November. Because this year marks the hundredth anniversary of the Armistice and the end of the First World War, I've decided to hold a dinner on the Saturday night before Remembrance Sunday."

Victoria pulled her diary out of her handbag and riffled forward several pages from the blue ribbon marking the current week. "Here we are. Remembrance Sunday actually falls right on November eleventh this year, so your dinner party would be on the tenth. I could do that."

Emyr nodded. "Wonderful. And I'll let the rector know the date."

"Will it be a very large party?" asked Penny.

"Well, besides Thomas and Bronwyn, I haven't really thought about who to invite, but I was thinking around twenty. Maybe a few more. You know how these lists tend to grow. If you invite this person"—he held out his right hand, palm up—"then you have to invite that person." He made a similar gesture with his left hand. "Possibly as many as thirty. But no more than that. Most of the dinner guests will be invited just for the evening, and a few others will be my guests for the weekend."

"Oh, how wonderful!" said Penny. "A proper old-fashioned country house party."

"Yes." Emyr smiled. "We haven't given a black-tie dinner at the Hall, let alone entertained weekend guests, since . . ." His voice trailed off and his dark-blue eyes turned toward the bridge.

Since Meg Wynne Thompson died. Penny silently finished the sentence for him, recalling the terrible time about ten years ago when Emyr's beautiful fiancée had been murdered. Penny looked at Emyr's eyes and then followed their gaze. *A lot of water has passed under that bridge since then*, she thought.

After taking a moment to collect himself, Emyr returned his attention to Penny and Victoria.

"My great-grandmother served as a nurse during World War I, so the war has personal relevance for me, as I'm sure it does for most families. So besides the dinner, I thought I'd put together a small exhibit of items, from the war or to do with the war, for the guests to view after dinner and before the harp recital. Or maybe they would view the exhibit in the library before dinner and we'd have the recital after dinner, in the sitting room." He made a little sheepish grimace. "As you can tell, I haven't really thought through the program."

"Oh, you mean an exhibit of medals, or letters, and things like that?" Penny asked. "I expect Alwynne Gwilt could find some things for you, and she'd probably be happy to help. She organized that exhibit at the town museum a few years ago to commemorate the start of the war."

"Yes, I remember that exhibit," replied Emyr, "but I have enough items. More than enough, in fact. And some very special things, too, including my great-grandmother's nursing uniform. My mother showed it to me once, when I was a boy, and it's up in the attics somewhere."

"Oh," said Penny. "Is it the uniform with the white apron with the red cross on the bib?"

She placed a hand on her chest where the red cross would be as Emyr nodded.

"That's the one. It's blue with a white collar, as I recall, and there's a sort of little cape that comes with it." He leaned forward, resting his hands on his knees. "But as nice as the uniform is, there's something even better. I've arranged for an incredible centrepiece for the exhibit." Penny and Victoria edged forward a little on the bench to be closer to him.

"I was the treasurer of the committee that raised the funds for the restoration of the bardic chair of Hedd Wyn, and the committee has granted permission for it to stop off at the Hall for a couple of days on its return journey to Yr Ysgwrn. So it was actually the opportunity of having the chair at the Hall that gave me the idea to hold the dinner party to mark the end of the First World War."

"That's amazing!" exclaimed Penny. "Mrs. Lloyd was just telling me about the Black Chair this morning, and its sad story." She looked excitedly from Victoria to Emyr and back again. "Isn't it strange how coincidences like that happen?"

"I'm tempted to say that nothing is ever a coincidence where Mrs. Lloyd is concerned," said Emyr, "but in this case, it would seem like one. But its restoration has been in the news lately, so it may be on people's minds."

"What chair?" asked Victoria. After Emyr filled her in on the history of the Black Chair, she asked, "And will the chair be on public view here in Llanelen, as well? In the museum, maybe, so everyone will have a chance to see it?"

"Unfortunately not. There wouldn't be time to arrange something like that. It's just going to be a brief, private stop at the Hall. Maybe even for just the one night. Details still to be arranged."

"But if you're up at the Hall for the dinner, presumably you'll get to see it," Penny remarked to Victoria. "Lucky old you."

Victoria grinned. "Yes, lucky old me."

"I hope you'll get to see it as well, Penny," said Emyr. She raised her eyebrows. "It's a lot to ask, I know, but I wondered if you'd help organize the dinner party. There's so much to do, and I couldn't possibly pull together an event like that on my own." He gave her a winsome, slightly pleading smile. "As you've just seen. I can't even get the date right. And you're really good with that sort of thing. You did a fabulous job of organizing everything that time we hosted the television antiques show at the Hall."

Penny dove right in. "Let me think," she said. "We can ask Florence to organize the dinner itself—the meal, that is. She'll have some great menu suggestions. She'll definitely need help with food preparation, though, but we can bring in staff from the hotel for that, and waitstaff, too, probably, and hopefully Gwennie will be available to clean and prepare the dining room—oh, and the library."

"And Heather Hughes for the flowers, of course," Victoria chimed in.

"Oh, and maybe we could involve Lane Hardwick with the coffee service," said Penny. "He loves coffee and he'd really enjoy having that responsibility. And besides, the experience would be good for him."

She'd met young Lane Hardwick a few months ago when she'd been painting a set of watercolours at the ruins of a local castle and he'd been part of a volunteer team clearing away nearly a century's worth of overgrowth from what had once been magnificent formal gardens. He'd been struggling to find his place in the world, but Penny had heard that since Emyr had hired him to work in the Ty Brith Hall gardens, Lane had been flourishing.

"I'll take that as a yes, then," laughed Emyr. "And by the way, it's all a bit hush-hush, so please keep this under your bonnets for now. But knowing this place, I'm sure word will get around soon enough."

Chapter Two

"You'll never guess!" exclaimed a slightly out-of-breath Mrs. Lloyd a few days later. She set down two bags of shopping on the work top of the sunny kitchen of the two-storey grey stone house on Rosemary Lane that she shared with Florence Semble. Florence peered into one of the bags.

"No, I probably won't guess," Florence said, although she suspected what was coming. "So you'd better tell me."

"Emyr Gruffydd is giving a dinner party!" Mrs. Lloyd announced with a hint of triumph in her voice. "It must be, oh, nine or ten years since there's been a dinner party up at the Hall. Of course he's not around nearly as much as he used to be, but still." She rubbed her hands together with glee. "A dinner party! It'll be the good old days all over again."

"Oh, good, you remembered the lemon." Florence pulled a lemon out of the shopping bag, rubbed her hand along its dimpled skin, and then set it aside. "I'll need that later for my shortbread." She returned her attention to the contents of the bag, then casually asked, "How do you know about the dinner party?"

"I hear things."

"Of course you do. But where did you hear about the dinner party?"

"Someone behind me in the queue at the Co-op mentioned it. Apparently she works at the Red Dragon Hotel, and she said some of the staff had been asked if they wanted to earn a bit of extra money by working at a fancy do that's going to be held up at Ty Brith Hall on the Remembrance Day weekend. And then the person ahead of me finished up and it was my turn to be served, so I didn't get to hear any more."

When Florence did not reply, Mrs. Lloyd gave her a piercing look. "You're very quiet, Florence. Did you already know about this dinner party?"

"I might have done."

"Well, why on earth didn't you tell me? Really, that's almost like a betrayal of our friendship. Now stop fussing with the shopping and sit down and tell me everything you know."

Florence sighed. The minute Penny had approached her about taking charge of the cooking for the dinner party, she'd known Mrs. Lloyd would be a handful. She'd insist on knowing every detail, and even worse, seeing herself as she did as the centre of what passes for high society in Llanelen, she would expect an invitation. And if she didn't get one, well, she'd be bitterly disappointed, things might get a bit tense in the charcoal-grey house on Rosemary Lane, and it was Florence who had to live with her.

The two women had met several years ago, and Mrs. Lloyd had invited Florence to come and live with her as her companion. Florence, who was eking out a grim retirement on a small pension in Liverpool at the time, had leapt at the chance to live in a tastefully decorated home with a spacious, well-equipped kitchen where she could indulge in her great love of cooking and baking. Florence adapted quickly to town life in Llanelen, making friends and teaching an old-fashioned cookery class to young mothers. She had been quietly appalled that many of them, raised on crisps and ready meals, barely recognized a vegetable, never mind knowing how to peel a potato or slice a carrot. But she was touched by their eagerness to learn how to prepare healthy, nutritious meals on a tight budget so they could do better for their own children than their mothers had done for them.

Florence poured hot water into the teapot to warm it, gave it a gentle swish, then tipped the water into the sink. She dropped two tea bags into the pot, poured hot water over it, replaced the lid, and set the pot on the table along with two cups on matching saucers and a plate of her homemade biscuits. As the minutes passed while they waited for the tea to steep, she ignored Mrs. Lloyd's watching her through slightly narrowed eyes. A heavy silence hung over them until Florence finally gave the tea a brisk stir, removed the tea bags, and then poured it. Mrs. Lloyd added a splash of milk to her cup, then settled back in her chair and crossed her arms.

"Well, Florence, I'm waiting. Let's hear it."

"I knew you'd want to know every last detail, Evelyn, but

I was asked not to mention the dinner, and I do respect confidences."

"But surely they didn't mean you weren't to tell me!" *That's exactly who they meant I wasn't to tell*, thought Florence, smiling to herself. "And exactly who asked you not to mention the dinner party? And why were you told about it in the first place?" She emphasized the word *you*. "Well?" demanded Mrs. Lloyd. She unfolded her arms, laced her fingers together, and rested them on the table. "Well?" she repeated.

"Apparently Emyr's giving this dinner party, and Penny asked me if I'd look after the food part of it. I'll create the menu and cook some of it, with help from the hotel kitchen staff. For the preparation and plating and so on."

"And what's Penny got to do with it, I'd like to know."

"Well, she's planning it."

"Penny's planning a dinner party up at the Hall? Go on, pull the other one!"

"Well, yes, apparently she is. Emyr asked her if she'd organize the dinner party."

"Well, look, Florence, we can do this the hard way or the easy way. You might as well go ahead and tell me everything you know."

"Well, you're going to hear all about it sooner or later," admitted Florence. "Word will get out."

"This is Llanelen, Florence," said Mrs. Lloyd with an exasperated sigh. "The word is always out."

And who helps it get out, I'd like to know, thought Florence. But she let that pass, and merely said, "I don't know all that much about it myself, mind. I only know what I've been told."

"Well, go on then. Tell me what you do know. I'm all ears. And don't leave anything out." Mrs. Lloyd leaned forward eagerly, hoping Florence knew more than she thought she did.

"Well, it sounds to me like they're planning one of those fancy evenings at a country house like you see on telly. There's meant to be an exhibit of World War 1 artefacts, including a special chair, and Victoria's going to give a performance on her harp, and of course, there's the dinner. But the menu hasn't even been approved yet, and besides that, there's really not much more I can tell you."

"But you haven't told me the most important thing!" Mrs. Lloyd exclaimed.

"What's that?"

"Who's invited?"

"Well, I don't know, do I? I haven't been told how many guests will be invited, so even if the menu had been approved and I knew what type of food to order, I wouldn't know how much. The invitations will go out sometime in October, and after that, when the RSVPs come in and we know how many are coming, we'll finalize the dinner details. I've been thinking they'll want both beef and lamb, and probably a fish course. Or maybe not. They don't do big, lavish dinners like they used to. How those Edwardian women managed to eat all that food and fit into those dresses with the tiny waists, I have no idea." Her teacup made a little chinking sound as she replaced it in its saucer. "And now that you know as much as

I do, I'd like to make a start on my baking, if that's all right with you."

"If you're sure you've told me everything, then yes, by all means." Mrs. Lloyd picked up her teacup and took a thoughtful sip. "I would say, though, Florence, that Emyr won't have to worry too much about the RSVPs. Anyone lucky enough to be invited will most certainly be there. This dinner is going to be the highlight of the Llanelen social calendar, and everyone will want an invitation."

Especially you, thought Florence.

* * *

By early October, Mrs. Lloyd was eagerly awaiting the arrival of each day's post. At the sound of the letter slot in the front door snapping shut, she called out, "I'll go," and bustled to the hall to scoop up the envelopes scattered across the carpet. She riffled through them, *tsk*ing at the sight of an advertisement or a bill and setting them aside to deal with later.

"Something must have happened to my invitation," she moaned to Florence after a few days of this morning ritual. "I know they've gone out, because I asked Bronwen and she told me that she and Thomas have received theirs. Could mine be lost in the post, do you think? Things do go missing in the post, you know. Every now and then you read in the newspaper about a letter posted from Margate or someplace like that in 1976 that finally got delivered. Lord only knows where it's been all this time." She peered anxiously at her friend. "Do you suppose that's what happened to my invitation? That it somehow got lost in the post?"

"I'm sorry, Evelyn, but I really don't know. I wouldn't think so, though. The post office is very reliable these days, what with postal codes and automatic sorting machines and the like." Florence hoped her response was tactful and kind without raising false hopes.

"I can think of one person who might know something about the invitations." Mrs. Lloyd gave Florence a look involving a deeply furrowed forehead that came across as sly and pleading at the same time. "Do you suppose you could ask Penny, the next time you see her, if she knows whether I've been invited?"

"I'm not sure if Penny has anything to do with the actual sending out of the invitations," Florence replied. "Someone in the estate office probably took care of that. And I very much doubt Penny has any say on the guest list. That would have been down to Emyr himself."

Mrs. Lloyd sighed, and over the next few days her response to the arrival of the post slowed down, until finally she stopped checking altogether and it was left to Florence to once again collect the envelopes from the hall carpet.

Chapter Three

"I won't be home for lunch today," Florence announced a week later. "I've left some cold ham and salad in the fridge for you, and there's a bit of leftover rice pudding if you want that." Mrs. Lloyd looked up from her magazine and acknowledged she had heard Florence with a brief nod. "After we finish up at the Hall, I'm going to the library to change my books," Florence continued, "so expect me home about teatime."

"How are you getting to the Hall?" Mrs. Lloyd asked.

"Victoria's driving us."

Without waiting for a reply, Florence retreated into the hall and left the house, locking the front door behind her.

The private road leading to Ty Brith Hall wound its way up the hillside for about three kilometres. At first narrow and flanked by a thick cover of rugged evergreens interspersed with deciduous trees just beginning to proudly display their bright autumn colours, the road widened as it got closer to the house and became a broad, approach avenue lined with beech trees, their golden-bronze leaves in beautiful contrast to their black branches.

"I've never been here before," Florence remarked as she caught her first glimpse of Ty Brith Hall. "What a lovely house. Very grand. Exactly what you'd want a country house to look like."

"It is grand," agreed Penny. "But not too grand. Emyr once told me that 'it doesn't try to be what it is not.' When we get inside, you'll see what he means."

Although not built on the scale of a castle or stately home, Ty Brith Hall's pleasing proportions somehow managed to make it imposing yet welcoming. Built of smooth grey granite in the mid-nineteenth century as the country home of a wealthy Victorian merchant from Liverpool, the three-storey house featured an asymmetrical facade, with an entrance tower and, along the roofline, a forest of gables and chimneys. The house had been perfectly situated to command magnificent views over the valley.

"Car park round the back?" Victoria asked.

Penny nodded. "That's where I told Heather to meet us."

Victoria brought the car to a stop near the back entrance beside a white delivery van with its doors open. When they had all piled out of the vehicle, Penny pointed to a red brick wall glowing in the late morning sunshine and remarked to Florence, "Over there is the old kitchen garden. It's rather overgrown now, though."

"I'd love to see it sometime," replied Florence. "There's nothing more magical than a walled garden."

"I agree," came a woman's voice from the interior of the white van. A moment later Heather Hughes, who had agreed to design the flower arrangements for the dinner, stepped out and joined them. She used to wear her dark hair scraped back in a tight ponytail but, at Victoria's suggestion, had recently had her hair restyled at the Spa, and it now provided a soft, flattering frame for her heart-shaped face. She held a spiral-bound notepad in one hand and grasped her phone in the other. Because Heather was such a dedicated gardener, her hands were often dry and cracked, with dirt embedded deep under her nails. She came to Penny regularly for nail care.

After introducing Heather to Florence, Penny took her notebook and phone away, handed them to Victoria, and examined the backs of Heather's hands and then turned them over.

"Your hands would do so much better if you wore gloves, but they're healing nicely. They're looking better. I can tell you've been using our hand cream."

"Thanks, Penny. You were right to insist that I use it. They don't hurt as much as they did in the summer."

"Your nails are a bit brittle, though. You're due for a treatment. Come and see me soon."

As Victoria handed Heather back her notebook and phone, a young man in his early twenties pushing a wheelbarrow filled with small branches emerged from the walled garden. He wore a dark-green apron over a pair of jeans and sturdy work boots. Seeing Penny, he set down the wheelbarrow and gave her an enthusiastic wave.

"Morning, Lane," Penny called out as she gave a cheery return wave in response to his greeting.

"That's Lane Hardwick," she said to the others. "He's got a mild learning disability, but since he's been working up here in the Ty Brith gardens, I hear he's absolutely blooming."

"Nothing is better for your sense of well-being than working in a garden," agreed Heather. "No one knows that better than I do. Being outside in the fresh air, seeing your hard, dirty work come to fruition—literally." She tipped her head in the direction of the walled garden. "The espaliered fruit trees growing in there are beautiful."

After watching Lane continue on his way, the women continued on theirs, crunching across the gravelled car park to the back door of the Hall. Penny lifted the knocker in the shape of a silver dolphin and tapped it a couple of times against its strike plate. A moment later a small woman wearing a lavender-coloured day uniform dress and a pristine, bibbed white apron opened the door.

"Come in," said Gwennie, taking a step to one side to allow them to enter.

"Go on through. You know the way, Penny." They followed Penny down the backstairs corridor with its grey slate floor into a spacious kitchen. Florence's mouth opened slightly as she took it all in.

Light poured in through a large set of windows that overlooked the garden. The glass-fronted cupboards, filled with crockery of every description, were painted a pale turquoise.

A bouquet of red and pink roses in a clear glass vase sat in the centre of a large work island, and the focal point of the room was a cream-coloured Aga with four ovens. Beside it was an empty dog bed.

"Trixxi not with you this morning?" Penny asked, referring to Emyr's black Labrador.

"Out with him," Gwennie said. "He said he'd try to be back before you left. I'm to show you around—a walk-through, Mr. Emyr called it—and then we'll go over the details of the dinner whilst we have a cup of coffee." Gwennie had worked for the Gruffydd family since she was a girl, and because Emyr often spent weeks at a stretch overseeing his Cornwall property, she also worked for Penny and Victoria at the Spa, cleaning, doing laundry, and just generally ensuring everything was spotless and in its place.

"I understand you're in charge of the food service," she said to Florence.

"I hope you don't mind," Florence replied. "I would hate to put you out of your own kitchen."

"No, I certainly do not mind." Gwennie offered a rare smile. "I've got all the house preparations for the weekend to see to, and that means airing out rooms that haven't been used in ages. I just wouldn't have the time or the energy to do all that and cooking, too, so I'm very glad to leave you to it." She gestured toward a door on the opposite side of the room. "Right. Well, where would you like to start? Shall we take a look at the dining room?" The others murmured agreement, and with Gwennie in the lead, they made their way along a wide hallway painted a rich, dark green, hung with paintings of pastoral scenes and still lifes in heavy, ornate frames. After passing several dark-brown wooden doors, they reached their destination. Gwennie threw back the door and they entered. "Not much to see here today," she said. The dining room had an unused, almost desolate air about it. A feathered mahogany table occupied the centre of the room, and heavy oak sideboards with a long serving table between them took up one wall. A diffused light filtered in through mullioned windows, one set overlooking the gravelled forecourt at the front of the house and the other offering views over the valley.

"I keep the dining room closed off because it's rarely used," said Gwennie. "We haven't had a proper luncheon or dinner in this room for, oh, I can't think how long it's been. Donkey's years. But you needn't worry. It'll be all right on the night."

"Oh, I'm sure it will," agreed Florence. "Now let me see." She examined the furniture. "We'll be having formal dining service, so we'll need . . ."

Gwennie moved to one of the oak sideboards and opened a door beside it covered with the same rich, red damask wallpaper as the walls. "This is the servery. You'll find everything you need in here," she said. "Go on, take a look."

Florence entered a room about the same size as her kitchen at home containing a sink, work top, warming oven, tables, and storage cupboards.

"We generally put the finishing touches on the plates here, just before serving. And if there's any delay, we can hold them here in the warming oven," Gwennie explained. "I can take over this part of service, if you like. Once the plates leave the kitchen, I'll make sure they're finished here for table presentation."

"That would be wonderful," said Florence, who then turned her attention to the cupboards. At an encouraging nod from Gwennie, she opened a couple of doors, revealing a massive selection of dishes.

"Oh, we have every piece of crockery and glassware you could possibly need, from soup tureens to brandy snifters," Gwennie assured her. "There's no need to hire anything. We've done much larger dinners than this one we're planning now. There's a complete dinner service here—the modern one that's used more often—and the older set is stored in the old butler's pantry off the kitchen. If you let me know what you need by way of serving dishes, I'll see they're washed and ready to use. We'll set the table the day before the dinner."

"And that door?" asked Florence, pointing to a door at the opposite end of the servery.

"That door opens onto another passageway that leads directly to the kitchen. It goes right past the butler's pantry. During dinner service the waitstaff will carry the dishes from the kitchen along that passageway and in through the servery door, while this door"—she gestured to the door they had just come through that opened onto the dining room—"is closed, and then, when everything's ready, the waitstaff open the door to the dining room and serve. The table will be cleared in reverse. There's even a red and green light signalling system you can use to let the kitchen know when you're ready for waiters to bring the next course. Service should happen seamlessly, without the diners being aware of the comings and goings behind the scenes. And certainly they shouldn't hear dishes rattling, orders being given, or any of that. Nothing to interrupt the conversation at the table or the guests' quiet enjoyment of their meal."

"Oh, I see," said Penny. "Keeps everything discreet."

"That's right. The passageway means that kitchen staff or waitstaff aren't seen in the main downstairs corridor that leads to the library and sitting room."

"I'd just like a closer look at the dining table," said Heather, edging back toward the dining room. "Do you know what kind of flowers Emyr has in mind?" She flipped open her notebook and asked Gwennie a few questions about the length of the dining table when extended, whether the table would have a cloth cover or place mats, and if taller floral arrangements were wanted for the sideboard.

"Well, I don't really know," Gwennie replied. "I can tell you how it was done in the old days, but whether Mr. Emyr wants to continue doing things that way, I don't know. That's to be discussed. And she may have her own ideas about the flowers."

At the word "she," Penny and Victoria exchanged a quick, puzzled look, but before either could say anything, Gwennie focused her attention completely on Heather as they measured the length and width of the table and Heather took several photographs of the room from various angles. She closed her notebook and announced she'd seen all she needed to, and the little group prepared to move on.

"Now just down here, on the other side of the corridor, is the library, where the special exhibit will be set up," said Gwennie.

She opened the library door and stood aside to allow the others to enter. Three walls were lined with dark, built-in shelving filled with books, and the fourth wall, facing the door, was painted a soft, sophisticated shade of sage green with a hint of grey. It featured a fireplace with an ornately carved mantelpiece and surround situated between two large windows overlooking green fields dotted with grazing sheep. Comfortable-looking chairs and a sofa upholstered in a muted grey-coloured fabric positioned on a worn, patterned burgundy carpet invited visitors to sit and thumb through the selection of magazines on a coffee table or choose a book. "Those are the original shelves," Gwennie pointed out. "They were fitted when the house was built."

One unit of floor-to-ceiling shelves was filled with old books with leather binding in brown, navy blue, and red, their titles printed in gold on the spines, but most of the books were newer—colourful hardbacks and paperbacks. The books looked read and the room looked formal and felt cozy at the same time, with just the right hint of old-book smell.

"What a beautiful room," exclaimed Penny.

"It is that," said Gwennie, "except when it's time for spring cleaning and every book has to be taken down and dusted."

She pointed to a grouping of furniture in the centre of the

room. "That will all be cleared, and that's where the exhibit will go, including the Black Chair."

"I was wondering about that chair," said Florence. "You'll have to excuse my ignorance, but I'm English and I'm sorry to say I'm not familiar with it. Penny told me a bit about the background story, and my friend at the library ordered in a book for me, but it hasn't come in yet. While it's wonderful that a poet would be given a chair, isn't that rather an unusual prize? Wouldn't, say, a plaque or trophy of some kind be more usual? Why a chair? What is the significance of that?"

"Well, I don't really know," said Gwennie. "I'm sure there's a reason, but it's just the way things have always been done, I guess. Tradition, you might call it."

The sound of approaching voices in the hall, accompanied by the unmistakable sound of the clicking of canine toenails on hardwood, signalled the arrival of Trixxi and Emyr. Penny grinned as a black Labrador bounded into the room and, tail thumping, made straight for her. Emyr followed a moment later, accompanied by a tall blonde woman who appeared to be in her late thirties. Both had removed their outdoor footwear; Emyr wore sturdy grey woollen socks, and the woman was barefoot. He greeted the visitors and then introduced his companion as Jennifer Sayles. Penny wondered if this was the "she" referred to earlier when Gwennie had said "she might have her own ideas." After answering a few questions about preferences for the dinner party flowers, Emyr and Jennifer disappeared upstairs, and Gwennie led everyone, including Trixxi, back to the kitchen.

"I wish I could stay for coffee with you," said Heather, "but I'm afraid I have to run along. I've got an order of fresh herbs in the van to deliver to the hotel in Betws, so I'd best be off. But I've got all the measurements and photos I need, so I'll leave you to it."

"I'll show you out," said Gwennie.

While they waited for Gwennie to return, Victoria checked her phone and Penny, seated at the table, sifted through a stack of documents in an orange file folder. Florence wandered around the kitchen, hands clasped behind her back, examining everything but touching nothing.

Soon after Gwennie returned, the whirring, rattling sound of the coffee grinder filled the kitchen, and while Florence put the kettle on, Gwennie arranged ginger biscuits she'd baked that morning on a white plate. When the kettle came to a boil, she poured hot water over the freshly ground beans in the French press, set it on a tray with cups and spoons, and then carried the tray to the table. Florence followed with the biscuits.

As they sipped their coffee and discussed arrangements for the dinner party, Penny scribbled notes on a lined pad. Although service at a formal dinner would normally involve waiters circling the table with platters of food and guests helping themselves, Gwennie suggested that it would be easier to serve the courses from the kitchen already plated, banquet style. When they reached the point where they thought they'd covered just about everything, Florence wrapped her hands around her cup and leaned forward.

"Penny, I've been wanting to ask you something," she said.

"I hope you don't mind, but it's about the invitations to the dinner. Are you looking after them?"

Penny winced. "Oh, I think I know where this is going. No, I didn't have anything to do with the invitations. Emyr, of course, drew up the guest list—it's his party, after all—and the estate office had them printed and sent them out."

"It's just that Evelyn's so upset that she didn't receive an invitation."

"Yes, when I saw that Mrs. Lloyd's name wasn't on the guest list, I knew how disappointed she'd be."

"You know what she's like. She's so confident of her standing in Llanelen society, and she places such a high value on events like this dinner party. She was so sure she'd be invited. For a few days she ran to collect the post each morning as soon as it arrived, but now she's given up. It's quite sad, actually, although it doesn't seem to have affected her appetite." Penny couldn't resist a little smile. "I was going to mention this to you earlier," Florence continued, "but then I thought it would be best to wait and see what happened, but now it looks as if she isn't going to be invited."

Penny pinched her lips together but didn't reply.

"I thought so," Florence said. "That look tells me everything." She hesitated, pushed her coffee cup away, and then said, "I do hate to ask, but I wonder if there's any way that Evelyn could get an invitation. Could you possibly pull some strings? Perhaps if you asked Emyr yourself, as a favour. I'm sure you can imagine how much it would mean to her to be invited. She's so desperate to go."

Penny opened her file and shuffled through a few papers until she found the one she was looking for.

"I know she is, but unfortunately, there are just so many places at the table, and everyone who was invited has let us know they're coming." As Florence's face fell, Penny continued, "But I've been giving this some thought, and there might be a way. Emyr has kindly invited me to the dinner; he meant it as a thank-you, but to be honest, I'll be too busy seeing to everything to sit down, so let me have a word with him and see what I can do."

"You would do that?" Florence exclaimed. "You would give up your place at the table for Evelyn?"

"Really, I don't mind," said Penny. "I'd just as soon eat with Victoria and you and Gwennie afterwards anyway."

"We'll be too tired to eat," said Gwennie, "and besides, we just want to get on with the clearing up. We usually just send leftovers home with anybody who wants them and leave it at that."

* * *

Three days later, Mrs. Lloyd passed through the front hall on her way to the sitting room, ignoring the square-shaped envelope lying on the hall carpet.

"Aren't you going to pick up the post?" Florence asked, drying her hands as she stood in the doorway to the kitchen. Mrs. Lloyd sighed, did as Florence suggested, and a moment later rushed toward her, triumphantly waving the cream-coloured envelope.

"It's come from the Hall, Florence! It must be my invitation! What did I tell you? Got held up in the post, just as I thought." She tore open the envelope, withdrew a stiff card, scanned it, and then read out loud: "'The honour of your presence is requested . . .'" She paused to savour the moment, and then, eyes shining, she continued, "'Champagne and hors d'oeuvres: 7 P.M. Dinner to follow. Saturday, November 10. Ty Brith Hall, Llanelen, North Wales.'" Her eyes swept over the card one more time; then she hugged it and its envelope to her ample bosom. "Champagne!" she sighed. "Now I have to think about what I'm going to wear! Do you think my burgundy dinner suit with the gold thread would be all right? Or perhaps I should treat myself to something new. Oh, Florence, I can't remember when I've been this excited about a dinner party. Everybody's going to be there and I just know this is going to be a night to remember."

Chapter Four

It'll be all right on the night, Gwennie had assured Penny, Victoria, and Heather when she showed them the dining room on their site visit a few weeks earlier. The old British theatre expression, often said during a period of difficult rehearsals when everything seemed to be going wrong to remind the company that no matter how hopeless it all seemed now, it would come together on opening night, had proved apt. It's much better than just all right, thought Penny as she, Victoria, and Gwennie surveyed the dining room to make sure everything was ready for the evening ahead.

The room had been transformed, magnificently. Gone was its earlier closed-up air of dusty disuse, and it now looked fresh, alive, and eager to receive and welcome guests. The table was set with twenty-five covers: gleaming white bone china plates with a gold band around the rim, sparkling crystal water glasses and stemware, and sterling silver cutlery featuring a classic floral pattern. Three silver candelabra, polished until they gleamed, each held six white tapers, waiting to be lit. The room smelled faintly of beeswax furniture polish and strongly of flowers, from the elaborate centrepieces of red roses along the table that were just the right height and the taller, more extravagant arrangements gracing the sideboards.

"I'm sure Emyr will be really pleased. Everything looks lovely, Gwennie," said Victoria, resting her hand lightly on the back of a chair. Although it looked as if everything had happened by magic, Penny and Victoria knew how hard Gwennie had worked to prepare the dining room.

Uncomfortable with praise and compliments for doing what she considered simply her job, Gwennie replied, "It'll look even nicer when the overhead lights are dimmed and the candles are lit." Reaching into her apron pocket, she pulled out two small boxes of wooden matches and offered them to Penny. "As you'll be front of house and I'll be busy in the kitchen, if you wouldn't mind lighting the candles just before the guests move into the dining room? Because there are so many, you might want to ask someone to give you a hand. You can throw the spent matches in the fireplace in the library or just put them back in the box." Penny took the matchboxes and slipped them into the pocket of her black trousers. "And now, if you'll excuse me, I'd best see if I can make myself useful in the kitchen. Florence has got her hands full." Gwennie checked her watch. "The guests will start to arrive in about half an hour and this is always the busiest time. You can't assemble the canapés too far ahead else you end up with soggy bottoms. So if you've a mind to, this would be a good opportunity for the both of you to slip into the library for a look at that Black Chair before the guests start to arrive and things get really busy."

They left the dining room by the door that led into the main corridor, and as they reached the library, Penny asked Gwennie if everything was in order for the evening.

"Yes, everything's under control. Why do you ask?"

"It's just that I saw the wine merchant's van in the car park when we arrived, and I hoped there wasn't some kind of last-minute mix-up with the order. All the deliveries were to have been completed by yesterday."

"They were," said Gwennie. "The wine people were just dropping off six complimentary bottles of champagne."

"That was nice of them," said Victoria.

"It was a thank-you gesture for all our custom over the years, and goodness knows we've certainly put enough business their way. Although maybe not so much lately."

"When I first saw the white van, I thought it might be Heather here to put the finishing touches on the flower arrangements," said Penny. "She's far too organized to leave everything to the last minute, but sometimes things happen. Her supplier might have let her down, say."

"Heather?" Gwennie frowned. "No, she's long gone. She had everything arranged just as you saw by late morning. And in the sitting room, and library, too."

"Oh, right, well, as long as everything's okay, I'll see you in a few minutes. You've done so much to get ready for this dinner. Sure you don't mind helping out in the kitchen?"

"Not at all. And as a matter of fact, I'm happy to. I've

enjoyed watching Florence work. She's brilliant at organization. There won't be any letdown there, I can assure you."

"Good to hear," said Penny. "Although I'm not surprised. And let's hope there won't be any more surprises."

Victoria raised an eyebrow. "Surprises?"

"Gwennie told me this morning that Jennifer Sayles hired a butler for the evening. Mr. Carter, he's called."

"A butler!" exclaimed Victoria. "Oh, well, hopefully Mr. Carter knows what he's doing and that'll take a bit of the load off the rest of you. Or at the very least, he won't get in the way."

"That's the last thing we need," said Penny. "Him getting in the way. We've already assigned tasks, so I hope his being here doesn't mean everybody gets confused about who's doing what and we end up in a terrible disorganized mess."

"Oh, I don't think that will happen," said Gwennie. "He's really just here to answer the door, announce the guests, usher them into the dining room, that sort of thing. More for show, really. I've already briefed the servers on their duties and shown them around, so they know where everything is and where they're supposed to be and what they're meant to do. And they've all got experience from working in the hotel, where service can get very hectic, so this should be a doddle for them. Although"—she paused for effect—"I had to remind them to put their phones away. There's one young lad who barely looks up at you, his attention is so focused on his phone. He was texting, or whatever it is they do. Texting while I was giving them their marching orders, if you can believe it. I soon put him right, I can tell you. And if I see anyone on their phones again while they're on duty, I'll confiscate them and they can collect them when they're ready to leave."

"And quite right, too," said Victoria. "Well, I suppose a butler will add a proper touch of class to the event. And Mrs. Lloyd will love him. She'd love to have a butler of her own, I'm sure, polishing up the silver and decanting the claret on Rosemary Lane."

Gwennie allowed herself a tight smile, then continued on her way to the kitchen as Penny and Victoria opened the door to the library. A screened-in fire, crackling merrily in the fireplace's inner hearth, cast flickering tongues of light across the carpet and combined with soft lamplight to create the perfect warm, welcoming ambiance on a cold, rainy autumn evening.

Several chairs and a sofa had been repositioned against the walls to make space for the exhibit featuring items and artefacts related to World War I. Arranged on a wooden dressmaking form was the ankle-length nursing uniform made of sturdy blue cloth, with a white apron and red mess cape, that had been worn by Emyr's great-grandmother. A black-and-white photograph in a silver frame on a nearby table showed a photo of the lady herself in the uniform, surrounded by soldiers and other nurses. Also displayed were a brass Princess Mary gift box that had been distributed to Allied troops at Christmas, 1914; a packet of letters tied up with a faded blue ribbon; and a man's battered gold pocket watch.

They turned their attention to the centrepiece of the

exhibit. Shrouded in a crushed black velvet cloth, just as it had been on that long-ago September day at the 1917 Birkenhead Eisteddfod when it had been placed in front of the assembly to be awarded to Hedd Wyn, the winning poet, was the bardic chair. Wordlessly, reverently almost, Penny and Victoria approached it and carefully lifted the corners of the black cloth, and bringing the corners together in a graceful, fluid motion, they folded it. Penny tucked it under her arm as she took her first look at one of the most iconic pieces of furniture in Wales.

Considered a superb example of early-twentieth-century furniture making, the wooden chair was of classic design with a high, straight back that rose to a peak, armrests, and a plain seat without upholstery or cushioning. Positioned on a plinth to signify the stature and importance of the person who sat in it, the Black Chair vaguely reminded Penny of the Coronation Chair in Westminster Abbey, without the canopy. But if the style of the bardic chair seemed plain, the richly elaborate carving that decorated it was not.

"Wow," said Victoria. "Look at the detail. I've never seen anything like it. It's magnificent."

A Celtic cross divided the chair back into four quadrants. At the top, just under the peak, the words GWIR YN ERBYN Y BYD—Truth Against the World—had been carved in a circle supported by two mythical beasts. Below that, and above an intricate pattern of Celtic knots and patterns that filled the rest of the chair back, were carved the words AWDL, the style of long-form poem in strict meter in which Hedd Wyn had written his winning entry, and in quotation marks, "YR ARWR"—"The Hero"—the name of his winning poem.

Greek key and chevron patterns provided borders and embellished the sides and rails of the chair. Other carved elements included Christian symbols, such as fish, dragons, two-headed serpents, flowers, and even a small horse.

"It's stunning," agreed Penny leaning in for a better look, "and the closer you look, the more you find. It's amazing, almost like carved lace, it's so intricate." She hesitated, wanting to run a hand over the varnished brown wood that had darkened to a burnished patina over time, but did not touch it. "But for some reason, because of its name, I thought the chair itself would be black."

"I guess the black comes from the cloth it was draped in," said Victoria. "Or maybe black as a mourning colour."

Penny picked up a piece of paper on the seat. "Emyr's speaking notes," she said. "For when he reveals the chair after dinner." She examined the document. "Let's see. It says here that the chair was carved in the Birkenhead workshop of Eugene Van Fleteren, a Belgian refugee, and is considered his masterpiece. It's believed to be made of oak taken from ancient roofing timbers salvaged from a monastery that was closed and burned down in the time of Henry the Eighth."

"Wow," said Victoria again.

Penny continued reading. "Awarding the national poet a chair dates back to the middle ages. Wales has a long tradition of honouring poets. Oh, and this is interesting. Remember Florence asked why poets were given chairs?" She glanced at

Victoria and smiled. "Because the chair symbolizes that the poet has a place at the table of princes." She scanned the rest of the text. "And finally, it says that for the Welsh people, this chair represents all the empty chairs in front of the hearth that the lads and men of World War I never came home to."

She replaced the sheet of paper on the seat of the chair. "A place at the table of princes," she repeated. "I really like that."

"That is good," agreed Victoria. "Well, it's a beautiful chair, there's no doubt about that. Even without its historical meaning, it would be something special. I especially like the way the dragons hold up the arms, and the Celtic cross on the back is stunning."

"It's such a great shame that the poet himself never knew he'd won it, and never got to see it," said Penny. But before Victoria could reply, the sound of the front door knocker signalled that the evening was about to begin.

"Oh, I guess I'd better get that," said Penny, handing the black cloth to Victoria. "Here, cover up the chair."

Just then a man wearing a black tailcoat and grey striped trousers, his white-gloved hands by his side, glided past the open library door.

"No, you don't have to answer the door now, remember? That's the butler's job, and that must be Mr. Carter himself," said Victoria.

"Oh, right. I forgot about him."

"He certainly looks rather smart, but do you find strange no one introduced him to us?"

"I do, actually. He made himself scarce all afternoon.

Anyway, everything's about to kick off, so we'd better hurry. Let's get this chair covered up."

Victoria shook out the black velvet cloth, and each woman taking two corners, they quickly redraped the chair. When they'd finished, Penny stepped back, examining the chair to make sure the cloth was centred. "It needs to move over to the left about two inches," she said with a little hand gesture, and when Victoria had made the adjustment, Penny nodded. "That's better. Both sides are even now."

"Oh, not too early, I hope," said a familiar voice in the hallway. "Am I the first to arrive?"

"Mrs. Lloyd," Victoria mouthed as a grin spread across Penny's face.

"You are indeed the first to arrive, madam," intoned the butler. "The cloakroom is just through there if you'd like me to hang up your coat, and then I'd be delighted to show you to the sitting room. Your hosts will be with you shortly."

Taking that as their cue to leave the library, Penny and Victoria headed to the kitchen to see what remained to be done and to offer their help if needed.

"Oh, thank goodness you're here," said Florence, wiping her hands on the striped blue-and-white kitchen towel hanging from the waist tie on her white apron. "You can stand by to start pouring the champagne when Gwennie gives the word. It's almost time. What's happening out there?"

"Mrs. Lloyd's just arrived, and Emyr and Jennifer Sayles should be downstairs in a minute or two," said Penny. "Does Mrs. Lloyd know about her, by the way? Jennifer Sayles?"

"Do you know, I don't think she does," said Florence with a twinkle in her eye. "That'll give her something to talk about."

Penny turned her attention to the young man hovering beside Florence, looking so earnest, so eager to please in a black suit that hung loosely on his thin frame. Lane Hardwick, hired to work in the gardens, had leapt at the chance to help with this evening's dinner, and being something of a coffee aficionado, or at least appreciative of a smooth latte, he was taking his role as beverage service manager seriously.

"Now then, Lane, I've got a really important task for you, besides serving the coffee. We're going to start the predinner champagne service in a minute, so when the glasses are full, you'll take a tray into the sitting room and walk round offering everyone a glass. You up for that?" He nodded eagerly, and she continued, speaking slowly and clearly. "Good. And then, after the guests have had their champagne and canapés, they'll go to the dining room for dinner, and you'll collect all the empty champagne glasses and plates and napkins from the sitting room and tidy everything up so the room looks nice for the concert. And then we'll set up the after-dinner service. That'll be your coffee station and dessert." She gave him a smile and reassuring pat on the shoulder. "That's a lot for you to do. Very important tasks. Think you can manage all that?"

Lane Hardwick returned her smile.

"But if you need any help, or you aren't sure what to do next, I'm here and you just come and ask me, okay?" Lane nodded. "Now I see that you're not wearing a poppy," Penny continued. "I've left a tray of them over there on that shelf"—she gestured behind her—"just as you come in the kitchen, so be sure to pin one on before you enter the sitting room to serve the drinks. And if you see any of the waitstaff without one, you can remind them that everyone is expected to wear a poppy, and you can show them where they are."

"I see you're not wearing a poppy. Let me get one for you."

"That's exactly right. That's exactly what you should say."

"No," said Lane, pointing at Penny's shoulder. "I see you're not wearing a poppy. I'll get you one." With that, he dashed over to the tray of poppies and returned a moment later holding one out for Penny. She accepted it with a broad grin and pinned it on her white shirt.

"Well done, Lane!"

"About the drinks, Penny. I'll be fine. Don't worry. I've been practising carrying drinks at home with a tray Mum gave me."

"Excellent!" Gwennie and Mr. Carter appeared in the doorway and Gwennie gave Florence a wave, signalling it was time for the champagne and canapés service to start. Mr. Carter hesitated, seemingly taking a moment to work out what was happening in the kitchen, then joined Penny and Lane.

"I'll help with that champagne, if you like," said Mr. Carter. "If you remove the foil and hand the bottle to me," he said to Lane, "I'll remove the cork and the young lady here can pour."

Although she found being called a "young lady" when she was in her fifties patronizing and ridiculous, Penny said nothing.

Lane did as he was told, and Mr. Carter, still wearing his spotless white gloves, deftly unwound the wire cage that kept the cork in place, then covered the cork with a white napkin and expertly turned the bottle while he pushed up with his thumbs and eased the cork out. Lane grinned at the sound of its soft, smooth pop. Mr. Carter handed the bottle to Penny, who poured it into the six glasses lined up on a tray. By the time she'd finished pouring, another bottle was open and ready for the next tray.

Lane and Gwennie disappeared down the hall, Lane balancing a tray of champagne flutes as if he were carrying a bomb and the experienced Gwennie following with a tray of canapés in one hand and a stack of snowy-white cloth napkins in the other. Mr. Carter beckoned the waiters hired for the evening to step forward, and as soon as the glasses on each tray were filled, they set off with them. Gwennie returned with an empty plate, picked up a full one, and disappeared again.

When the last of the champagne and canapés had left the kitchen, Penny finally had a chance to introduce herself to the butler. She estimated him to be in his early to mid-sixties. His thinning hair, which he wore swept over the top of his head from a deep side part, had been dyed a deep chestnut brown with a slightly reddish tinge. Rather than giving him a more youthful appearance, the unnatural hair colour served to deepen and emphasize the natural lines on his face. He peered at Penny over the top of dark-brown glasses in a round shape that had recently come back into fashion but gave him a curiously owlish look.

"Well, now, I guess we have a bit of breathing space until dinner is served," he said.

"I have to light the candles just before the guests enter the dining room," said Penny as the waiters appeared back in the kitchen after delivering the last of the champagne and canapés. "Do you have any idea how much longer that will be?"

Mr. Carter checked his watch. "Another five or six minutes. I'll give you a minute or two head start, and then I'll announce that dinner is ready."

A few minutes later he motioned to Penny that it was time for her to leave for the dining room. She approached the kitchen table where the waiters were seated and asked the one closest to her if he'd help her light the candles in the dining room. They didn't speak on the short walk, and when they arrived, she handed him a box of matches and they began to light the candles in the silver candelabra at each end of the table. The waiter finished first and moved to the third candelabra in the centre of the table. Penny joined him there a moment later. His hand was shaking so badly he had trouble holding the match to the wick.

"It's all right," said Penny. "I'll finish it. Give me your used matches and go back to the kitchen now. You'll be needed in a minute for the starter course."

* * *

Just after eight, Mr. Carter sidled into the sitting room. As the guests noted his presence, the din of conversation stopped, and in his clipped, precise accent he announced that dinner was served. Emyr and the mayor's wife, followed by Jennifer Sayles and the mayor, led the relaxed, chattering guests into the dining room just as Penny stepped back from the table after lighting the last of the candles. Holding the spent matches in her hand, she retreated to the far wall, dimmed the overhead lighting, and watched the arrival of the dinner guests.

Name cards created by the local craft group had been set at each place, and the diners found their places quickly. Emyr was seated at the far end of the table and Jennifer Sayles, as the official hostess, was seated at the other, nearest the door. She looked stunning. A simple knee-length, cobalt-blue woollen dress with three-quarter-length sleeves provided the perfect backdrop for the diamonds at her ears and wrist. Like everyone else at the table, she wore a red poppy pinned to her dress. Her blonde hair was tied back in the messy-bun style made popular by the newest bride to join the royal family, and she casually tucked a trailing wisp of blonde hair behind her ear as she engaged in a lively conversation with the mayor.

When all the guests were seated, Rev. Thomas Evans rose and said a brief grace. As soon as he had taken his seat, Mr. Carter closed the door to the hall and opened the door to the servery, and waiters entered the dining room carrying wine bottles wrapped in white napkins and the starter course, smoked salmon with prawns, horseradish cream, and a lime vinaigrette. After exchanging a quick glance with Emyr, who seemed happy that everything was under control, Penny ducked into the hall, closing the dining room door behind her, just as Lane entered the empty sitting room carrying a large tray. She poked her head round the door and watched as he collected the used plates and glasses as he'd been instructed, stacking everything neatly on the tray. Penny responded with an encouraging nod when he asked if he could take a moment to look at Victoria's harp, which had been set up in the corner of the room, and then she left him to it, taking the servants' corridor route to the servery.

* * *

Penny peered through the spy hole in the servery door that opened to the dining room.

"The first course is going well," she said over her shoulder to Gwennie. "The guests seem to be really enjoying the starter."

"That's good," said Gwennie. "How much longer does it look like they'll be?"

Penny put her eye once again to the peephole. "Another ten, maybe fifteen minutes. They're about halfway through. Everyone looks relaxed and happy. Lots of chatter going on." Penny stepped back from the door. "Do you want me to let the kitchen know?"

Gwennie lowered herself onto a stool in the corner. "Yes, that would be helpful to Florence. Timing is everything, so the guests don't wait too long and nothing gets cold."

As Penny opened the servery door that led to the hall, she was met by the clatter of a metal tray hitting the wooden floor, immediately followed by the unmistakable sound of shattering glass and breaking dishes. Oh no, she thought. I hope the diners didn't hear that.

She stepped into the hall and, because she couldn't tell which direction the sound had come from, glanced both ways. To her left, just past the library entrance, Lane lay sprawled on the floor, one arm outstretched above his head, the other at his side. Stepping over and around the shards of glass and jagged bits of crockery, she hurried to him. "Lane," she said as she knelt beside him and rested a gentle hand on his shoulder. "Are you all right? Do you want to try to get up? Can I help you up?" He didn't respond, but murmured something she couldn't make out because his face was turned away from her.

"What on earth's happened here?" asked Gwennie in a low voice as she joined them. "Good heavens! Is he hurt?"

"I don't know," said Penny, keeping her eyes on Lane. "I hope not. But I'm not sure what just happened. He fell with the tray."

"Perhaps he tripped on something," said Gwennie, "but I can't think what. It's just a bare floor. There's no loose bit of carpet he could have got caught up in." She tipped her head in the direction of the dining room. "The waiters will be here in a minute to clear away for the main course, and I've got to supervise them."

"What about Mr. Carter? Why can't he help you with that?"

"Because that's not what a butler does. His job is to stand with his back to the wall looking important and maybe top up a wine glass. Or at least, that's what he thinks his job is."

"Well, look Gwennie," said Penny. "If you can take care of the table service, I'll see to Lane. We don't want any fuss, and we certainly don't want to interrupt the dinner if we can help it. Do you think they heard anything in the dining room?"

"No, I don't think so. The dining room doors were closed. I heard because the servery door was open." As Gwennie returned to supervising the dinner service, Penny scrambled to work out what to do about Lane.

"Lane," she said. "I need you to talk to me. Do you think you can get up now? If not, do we need to call an ambulance?"

"No," said Lane, struggling to sit up. "I'm okay. Everything just went blank there for a minute."

"Did you say black?"

"That too, but I think I said blank. Everything just went blank."

"Maybe you hit your head when you went down. Can you remember what happened?'

Lane raised a hand to his head. "No. I cleared up in the sitting room, and then I looked at Victoria's harp for a few minutes to see how the strings were fastened on, but I didn't touch it, and then I was coming down the hall with my tray, and the next thing I know I was on the floor and you were there." He looked at the contents of the tray, in pieces strewn across the floor. "Oh, please don't be cross with me. I didn't mean to drop the tray. I don't know how that happened."

"Of course you didn't mean to, and no one will think for one moment that you did, and I'm not cross with you and nobody else will be, either. Now, the best thing would be if you were to rest for a few minutes in a quiet spot until we know you're all right."

"No, I'm fine, and I want to help with clearing up this mess. What should I do?"

"Well, if you're sure you're all right, you could make a start picking up the pieces of glass and plates while I go to the kitchen and find something to put the broken pieces in. We might need to wash down the floor if any champagne spilled on it, but we'll sort out that bit in a minute. I'll be right back." As Lane got to his knees, she added, "And be careful not to cut yourself."

Chapter Five

Penny was on her knees picking up the last of the shattered glasses and plates and dropping them into a grey plastic tub while Lane wiped the floor with a damp mop when Gwennie rejoined them.

"Well, at least the main course is on the table now," sighed Gwennie. "We lost a waiter right in the middle of the dinner, would you believe."

Penny gave her a sharp look. "You what? How could you lose a waiter?"

"He didn't come back. He served the starter, apparently went to the kitchen with the rest of the servers to wait for the second course to be ready to bring out, and then he must have just up and left. Nobody's seen him. Disappeared. It's true what they say about not being able to get good help these days."

"So you were one waiter short for the main course?" asked Penny.

"That's right. We managed, but thank goodness the

dessert and tea and coffee will be buffet style in the sitting room so we don't have to worry about any more table service. There's still the matter of clearing away the dining room table, though. We'll be one short for that. Never mind. We'll get through this. We always do." She stepped out of the way as Lane approached with his mop. "And I'm sure the guests will really enjoy Victoria's harp playing before they go into the library to see the exhibit. They'll all get a really good look at that famous Black Chair, and what a delightful way to end the evening. I'm sure they'll talk of nothing else all the way home."

"Oh, they might also be talking about Florence's delicious dinner, too," said Penny. "She's outdoing herself tonight with that beef Wellington. I hope there's enough left over for me to take some home."

Lane stopped his work and stood with both hands clutching the top of the mop handle. "I'm done now. You can't really tell in this light, but I don't think there are even any streaks."

"Thank you, Lane," said Penny. "You've been a wonderful help, and if you're sure you're up for it, it's time to set up the after-dinner beverage service. We'll get the waiters to help you, and once that's done, you can take a break and maybe have a quick bite to eat, and then be back here in half an hour at your coffee station."

* * *

After one last check of the sitting room to make sure the desserts, coffee, tea, and liqueurs were set up properly, Penny wished Victoria good luck with her after-dinner harp performance and exchanged a few final words with Gwennie and Mr. Carter, who were ready to oversee the dessert and beverage service. She was concerned because Lane had not arrived at his coffee station.

"This is not like him," Penny said. "I hope he didn't have a delayed reaction to the fall and he's collapsed somewhere. I'll have a wander round to see if I can find him."

"He must be somewhere," said Gwennie. "He may yet turn up. Late is better than not at all."

Florence looked up as Penny entered the kitchen, then returned to her task of dividing up the remains of the cheesecake. She placed neat slices into plastic takeaway containers, dropped a few raspberries on each one, and stacked them to one side. "You and Victoria can each take one of these home with you. I've also set aside servings of the main course for you. You just have to heat it up."

Penny nodded her thanks as she looked around the empty kitchen and then, cupping her hands around her eyes, peered out a darkened window. With the light from the room behind her, all she could see were droplets of water running down the glass.

Turning back to Florence, she asked, "What's happened to the waitstaff? Where are they?"

"I expect they're outside smoking and checking their phones."

"Smoking? In that rain? It's bucketing down."

Florence shrugged. "They'll be back in a few minutes to clear the dining room, get their pay, and then they'll be off, or so Gwennie said. There are just three of them now because the one fellow left in the middle of service. Gwennie wasn't best pleased about that."

"And it's not just the waiter who went missing," said Penny. "Lane was supposed to set up and help with the coffee and dessert and he's nowhere to be found. Have you seen him? Could he be outside with the waiters, I wonder?"

"Well, he could be, I suppose. I couldn't say. I haven't taken any notice of his comings and goings, or anyone else, for that matter. I've been that busy with the cooking, and had my back to the room for most of the time."

She leaned against the work top and removed her glasses, closed her eyes, and gently massaged her forehead.

"Oh, Florence," said Penny. "Of course you have. You've been on your feet, working nonstop for hours, and you must be exhausted. It's almost over and the clearing up can wait. Why don't you sit down and put your feet up for a few minutes? Can I get you anything?"

"I am suddenly very tired, but I must say I loved every minute of this. I've never had the opportunity to cook for such a group before, and I really enjoyed it. And with the help of a sous chef from the hotel, it wasn't that much work. But I did find the time management a bit stressful. Making sure everything was ready when it was supposed to be."

Penny nodded sympathetically as she cast an anxious glance in the direction of the door that led to the back passageway.

"I don't think you need to worry that he's not there," Florence said. "Lane, I mean. Gwennie and Mr. Carter can manage perfectly well overseeing the guests while they help themselves to dessert and coffee. There's really not much they need to do. It's not that difficult."

"Yes, you're absolutely right," said Penny. "Of course they can manage. It's not so much the service I'm worried about; it's Lane himself. He was really looking forward to working his own coffee station, so it's puzzling that he's not there. Wherever he is, I hope he's all right."

As Florence sank gratefully into a chair, Penny poured white wine into two small glasses and carried them to the table.

After a friendly chinking of glasses, Penny took a grateful sip. "Oh," she moaned, "if I'd known how demanding this event was going to turn out to be, I'm not sure I'd have volunteered to help with it."

"You didn't have to. So why did you?"

"I knew it would be a lot of work, but at the same time, I thought it would be rather fun being part of a country house dinner party. And it was, sort of. I enjoy organizing events. And as a thank you, Emyr's giving our local Stretch and Sketch Club enough money for several of us to have a little painting holiday on Anglesey next summer, so you could say I'm doing it for them." She shrugged. "And besides, he's a friend, and sometimes, as you know from living with Mrs. Lloyd, it can be hard saying no to a friend."

"Well, that's true."

"And what about you, Florence? Why did you agree to do it?"

"Well, like I said earlier, I've always wanted to try my

hand at cooking for a large dinner party—catering, as it were—and since no one sent their plate back to the kitchen, I reckon they enjoyed their meal. So that's rewarding for me. And like you, Emyr's making a donation to something that's important to me—the cooking class I run for new mothers. Now I can get our group a lovely set of new pots and pans, so seeing the looks on their faces will have made all this worthwhile." She waved at the remains of the dinner on the work top and then stood up. "I'd best get back to it."

"Me, too," said Penny.

Chapter Six

Victoria's concert had ended, and the guests, who had finished their desserts and coffee, were anxious to see the pièce de résistance of the evening—the Black Chair awarded at the 1917 Eisteddfod to the great Welsh poet Hedd Wyn.

When everyone had gathered round the black-draped chair in the library, Emyr took his place close to it. Penny, standing beside Victoria near the table that featured the exhibit of letters and photos, allowed her eyes to wander around the beautiful room. Jennifer Sayles stood near the door, her hands clasped in front of her, head held high. Beside her stood Mr. Carter, his hands similarly crossed in front of him, an inscrutable expression on his face. Several mobile phones went up, including Mrs. Lloyd's, taking photos before the unveiling.

As Penny turned her attention to Emyr, something caught her eye: a space of about two inches between the hem of the black cloth and the carpet. When she and Victoria had redraped the chair before the dinner, the hem of the cloth had skimmed the floor neatly and evenly on both sides. As her eyes moved up the chair, she realised the chair's profile was wrong. The Black Chair had a distinctive high back and a thronelike shape. Whatever that black cloth concealed was squatter and wider.

As her mouth went dry and her heart began to race, dreading what was about to happen, she placed the fingertips of one hand over her lips and touched Victoria's arm with the other, and as Emyr reached for the black drape, she closed her eyes. At the sound of a few titters of surprise, accompanied by gasps of disbelief, she opened them. Emyr, holding the black cloth in one hand, had revealed a chair from his own library, with the speaking notes on its grey, upholstered seat. He looked around the room in puzzled disbelief, as if hoping to discover that the Black Chair had magically materialized somewhere else—in the corner by the writing desk, perhaps, as a result of someone playing a monstrous practical joke. He exchanged an anxious glance with Jennifer Sayles, then took a few steps in Penny's direction. "Do you know anything about this?" he asked in a low voice, his head turned away from his dinner guests.

She shook her head, waiting for the surge of adrenaline to recede and her fluttering heart to return to normal. "I have no idea what's happened. Victoria and I examined the Black Chair just before the first dinner guest arrived, and it was right here. Honestly, I'm as shocked as you are." Emyr glanced at his guests, who had moved from stunned silence to whispering to the person beside them.

"We have to ring the police," Penny said.

Emyr rubbed his hand across his chin. "The police. I'm not sure. I hate to disrupt the dinner party and upset the guests, but on the other hand . . ."

"The chair is a valuable artefact," Penny reminded him. "Priceless. A precious part of the nation's heritage. If it has been stolen, the sooner the police know, the better. If it were my decision, I know what I'd do."

She was on the verge of reminding Emyr that he was responsible for the chair's safekeeping when he said, "Yes, of course, you're right. But I don't see how anything could have happened to it. There's bound to be a simple explanation and we don't want to overreact."

"Don't worry about overreacting," said Penny. "The police would far rather be called out now and it turns out be nothing than we wait and by the time we call them the trail's run cold. And you don't need to worry about upsetting the dinner guests, either," she added. "They've all seen the chair isn't here, and this excitement will have added enormously to their evening." Mrs. Lloyd will be dining out on this for weeks, she thought.

"Right, well, find out if Gwennie knows anything about the chair, and if she doesn't, then because you have contacts in the police, you'd better be the one to ring them. I'll see the guests out and leave the rest of it up to you."

"You can't do that," protested Penny. "You mustn't allow the guests to leave. The police are going to want to talk to everybody who was here this evening. I suggest you ask them to return to the sitting room, and if they'd like more coffee or tea, we can arrange that."

"They won't know any more about this than I do," Emyr said. "How could they? They've been with me in the sitting room and then the dining room all evening."

He turned to speak to his guests, and Penny, with Victoria right behind, darted down the hallway.

After the confusion and intensity of the past few minutes, she was momentarily taken aback by the kitchen's warmth, the lingering delicious smells and its apparent normalcy. Gwennie, who was stacking cooking utensils in bus trays to be taken to the dishwashers in the scullery, glanced at her, then paused and looked closer.

"Whatever is it now?" she asked. "You look terrible."

"It's the Black Chair," Penny said in a voice made louder by panic. "It's not in the library. You don't know where it is, do you? Did you arrange to have it moved for some reason?"

Gwennie's eyes widened. "Me? No, of course I didn't have the chair moved. Why on earth would I? Haven't I had enough to do all evening without moving the chair? The last I knew, it was set up, cloth and all, just where Emyr wanted it for the after-dinner viewing." Florence, who had been tidying up on the other side of the kitchen, stopped what she was doing and approached Gwennie and Penny.

"What's going on?" she asked. "Something's wrong. What is it?"

Penny explained to Florence that the Black Chair was missing.

"Emyr wants us to keep everything as normal as we can, without upsetting the guests," Penny said. "But if there's no simple explanation and the chair wasn't moved somewhere else for some reason, obviously I have to ring the police."

She looked at Gwennie, who nodded. "Of course you do."

"Right. My phone. Where's my handbag?" She looked around the kitchen. "I can't remember where I left it."

"I put all your coats and handbags in the butler's pantry for safekeeping," said Gwennie. "But there's a telephone just over there." She gestured to a small desk tucked away in the corner of the kitchen. "I use it for ordering supplies. Use that one, if you like." As Penny turned toward the desk, Gwennie spoke again. "Oh, and I'm sorry about this. As if we don't have enough to worry about, still no sign of Lane. And he was supposed to clear away the sitting room after the guests had finished their coffees and desserts, and take the glasses and dishes to the scullery, and that hasn't been done."

"Oh, God," said Penny, smacking her hand to her forehead. "I forgot all about him." Then she addressed Victoria. "Would you mind ringing Bethan to tell her the chair's missing?"

"Of course not."

Penny gave her a distracted smile of thanks, and Victoria dashed for the phone.

"I haven't seen Lane," said Florence. "Penny's already asked me about him. I can't remember the last time I saw him. I've been that busy with the meal and then the cleanup. This is only the second time the kitchen's been quiet all evening. Until now it's been filled with all sorts of people coming and going, and I had no idea who they were or what they were doing. Of course, I had my back to it. I've been in front of the Aga for most of the evening."

"Well, he seemed all right after that fall he took, but perhaps he needed to go somewhere for a lie-down," said Penny. "I hope he's okay. I'm sorry you had to do the dessert service on your own, but I'm sure you managed. With Mr. Carter's help, of course."

"The guests helped themselves," said Gwennie. "It was no big deal. Although he was a little damp, Mr. Carter, having been out in the rain. I expect he's dried off a bit by now. But the sitting room hasn't been cleared yet."

"Emyr's taking the guests back there now," said Penny. "They can't stay in the library. It's a possible crime scene."

"Well, I'm not happy that the guests are back in the sitting room before we had a chance to clear it. I don't like the idea of them sat there with all the used dishes piled around them," said Gwennie.

"And what about the waiters?" asked Penny. "Where have they got to?"

"They're clearing up in the dining room, and I told them they can start on the sitting room when they've finished."

"Argh," said Penny, raising her hands, fingers spread apart, to the sides of her head. "Lane. The chair. Clearing the sitting room. My brain's so overloaded it's about to explode. I could use a cup of coffee. I have to sit down for a moment and try to think things through."

"That's not a bad idea," said Florence. "Let's get the kettle on."

"They're on their way," Victoria announced as she rejoined them. "The police. They said no one's to leave."

Just as Florence was about to pour the coffee, the waiters returned, carrying trays laden with dishes, glasses, and cutlery.

Gwennie directed them to set the trays down on the work top and then turned to Penny. "I'd already told them to clear the sitting room. Is it okay if they go ahead and do that?"

Penny thought for a moment. "Have you got any food service gloves? It would probably be okay if they wore those and if we keep the dishes from the dining room and sitting room separate. It may be just an overabundance of caution, but you never know what the police are going to want."

Gwennie opened a drawer and removed what looked like a tissue box. She held it out to the waiters and they each put on a pair of disposable sanitary gloves, and then, carrying another set of trays, empty this time, they left the room.

"They'll be wanting to be paid before they go. Their pay packets are in the butler's pantry. I'll get them now," Gwennie said.

"No, you sit down," said Penny. "I'll get them."

"They're just on the table," said Gwennie. "You'll see them as soon as you walk in."

Adjacent to the kitchen and behind the servery was the butler's pantry. High, deep cupboards, holding china tableware in an old-fashioned floral pattern and silver tea sets, candlesticks, serving dishes in all shapes and sizes with matching lids, and trays, lined one wall. Another wall featured open shelving for mixing bowls, measuring jugs, pudding basins, and food storage containers. Below the shelves, large wooden boxes that had once contained flour and sugar, and wicker baskets and picnic hampers sat on the floor. A small round table in one corner would have held the wine journals and other records of the day-to-day operation of a well-run Victorian household. At the long rectangular table that almost filled the centre of the room, staff in days gone by would have cleaned the family silver and decanted wine.

The overhead light in the pantry was switched off, but in the shaft of light from the passageway, Penny could just make out the table. The wide oak floorboards creaked softly under her weight as she stepped into the room. The pay packets were on the table, just where Gwennie had said they would be, so she gathered them up and left the room.

Across the hall, a band of light showed at the bottom of the closed door to the scullery. That's odd, she thought. Penny knew from observing Gwennie at the Spa that she was passionate about not leaving lights on in empty rooms. She never did it herself, and if she noticed a staff member leave a room without switching off the light, she spoke to them about it and ensured the light was then switched off. But perhaps someone else had been in the scullery, Penny thought, or is in there now? She approached the scullery door, leaned against it, and listened. Silence. She pushed the door open and was greeted by a blast of cold, damp air. On the far wall was a deep stone double sink, flanked on one side by shelving and on the other by a commercial dishwasher. Another dishwasher, smaller and used exclusively for glassware, sat on the work top. A raised, slatted wooden mat, like a pallet, was positioned on the slate floor in front of the sinks.

Although updated with modern plumbing fixtures and appliances, the room served the same purpose it had a century ago. Then, the scullery maid, usually a girl of about fourteen or fifteen, probably from a nearby farm, would have spent long days in this room peeling and chopping vegetables and hand washing the family's fine glassware and dishes, and then the rougher crockery and cutlery used in the servants' hall. Finally, late at night and at the point of exhaustion, she would have had to tackle a mountain of heavy copper pots and pans, and all the while under the demanding eye of a scolding cook.

Neither dishwasher was in operation, and the soiled dish breakdown cart pushed against the wall to her right, where dishes, glasses and silver were held before being loaded into the machines, was empty. So was the table, where clean, dry dishes could be stacked or sorted before being returned to storage.

The door that led to the back garden was wide open, letting in the frosty November night air. Penny hugged her arms to her chest as she crossed the room and was just about to reach out and close the door when something told her not to touch it. Her arms dropped to her side. She hesitated for a moment, then stood on the threshold peering out into the looming darkness. The moon had not yet risen, and the only light came from a wrought iron lamp above the back door some distance away, bathing part of the short path to the car park in a misty, muted yellow halo.

With the scullery door open, she thought it possible that Lane had slipped out that way and could be somewhere in the garden or car park.

She stepped onto the gravel path that ran alongside the house and moved through the velvety blackness toward the light. The rain that had been falling heavily earlier had slowed to a soft drizzle.

"Lane," she called. "Are you out here? It's Penny. Are you all right?" When there was no response, she tried again. "You're not in any trouble, Lane. We just want to know you're all right."

She paused, straining to hear something to let her know that Lane was nearby, but there was no movement, no response, only muffled and indistinct voices coming from the car park. And then came the chirping of car door openers, followed by the sound of doors being opened and closed and engines starting up.

Oh, no, she thought. Emyr's let the guests go home. Why would he do that?

Dressed only in a pair of black trousers and a white shirt, to fit into the background with the waitstaff, and shivering in the freezing night, Penny realised it would be faster to continue on toward the back door rather than retrace her steps to the scullery. Hugging her arms to her chest again for warmth, she darted forward in the darkness, but lost her balance as she stumbled over something on the path. Struggling to stay upright, she instinctively reached out to the only support available to her, the side of the house. She clutched the wet, cold granite trying to steady herself. She managed to stay upright but scraped her palms against the roughness of the stone. When she felt her feet safely beneath her, she lifted her stinging hands away from the house and lowered herself to find out what had caused her to stumble.

She stretched out her hand, expecting to touch something natural and organic, like a rough wooden tree branch brought down by the heavy rain that had fallen earlier that evening. Instead, she felt soft, wet fabric. Sliding her fingers along it, she reached the end of the cloth and touched the cold, bare skin of someone's hand. Its fingers curled weakly around hers and held on.

Chapter Seven

"Hang in there," she said, squeezing the person's hand. "I'm going for help. I'm so sorry I'm not wearing a coat . . . I don't have anything to cover you with. I'll be back as soon as I can."

She raced to the back door and tried the handle. Locked. She lifted the knocker and banged it three times, then stepped back and bouncing lightly on her toes, waited for someone to open the door. "Come on, come on," she muttered. When she thought she couldn't wait one more second and was about to run back the way she'd come, to the scullery entrance, the door opened.

"Penny! What are you doing out there? You look half frozen," Gwennie exclaimed, as Penny brushed past her into the hallway, desperate for the warmth of the house. "Where have you been? We waited ages for you to bring those pay packets—I finally went looking for you."

"Oh! The envelopes," said Penny, holding up her empty hands. "I don't know. I might have left them in the scullery."

She shivered. "But never mind that now. There's someone out there, and he's hurt. Badly, I think." She hurried down the passageway that led to the kitchen as Gwennie trotted along beside her. "Please tell me Bethan's arrived. Has she?"

"Yes, she has. She's talking to Emyr now. But the hotel staff are still waiting for their pay packets, so we need to . . ."

Penny interrupted her. "Sorry, Gwennie, there's no time for that now. Please call an ambulance. Someone's injured outside the back door. And he's really cold. We need blankets." By now they had reached the kitchen, where Mrs. Lloyd, who had been speaking to Florence, broke off and turned to Penny.

"I was just asking Florence how much longer she's likely to be. Thomas and Bronwyn offered to drive us home, but I told them to go on and we'd get a ride home with you and Victoria. I hope that's all right."

"That's fine, Mrs. Lloyd, I guess. Sorry, don't mean to be rude, but I've got to speak to Bethan right away," she said over her shoulder as she flew by. She hurried through the kitchen, past the three tired, bored waiters and a startled Victoria, and down the main corridor to the sitting room where Emyr and his girlfriend, Jennifer Sayles, were talking to a professional-looking woman in navy blue trousers with a matching jacket. A uniformed police officer sat at the side of the room, his legs crossed and a notepad balanced on his knee.

"Oh, Bethan!" exclaimed Penny. "I'm so relieved you're here. Look, I'm sorry to interrupt, but there's someone lying on the path near the back door. He's still breathing, but just barely. He's badly injured." She waved an arm wildly in the direction of the kitchen. "I told Gwennie to call an ambulance. I don't know who it is. It's so dark out there I couldn't see properly, but his clothes are soaked and he may have been out there for some time. We need blankets."

Inspector Bethan Morgan of the North Wales Police and the uniformed officer with her sprang to their feet. "It's dark out there," Penny repeated. "You'll need a torch."

"Have you got one?" Bethan asked Emyr. "Would be faster than going back to my car to get ours."

"Yes, there should be one or two in the butler's pantry. Or somewhere," he replied. "Gwennie'll know. She'll get one for you."

As he and Jennifer seemed poised to follow her, Bethan motioned to them to remain where they were, and then beckoned to the uniformed officer. "Jones, you're with me. Let's go."

Penny sat on the pale-green sofa while Emyr and Jennifer walked to the window and, with their backs to her, exchanged a few quiet words. As Penny contemplated them, Victoria and Mrs. Lloyd entered the room.

"Bethan told us we're to wait in here with you," Victoria said, "and the waitstaff are to remain in the kitchen." She sat beside Penny on the sofa, and Mrs. Lloyd, her face a mask of eager confusion, sank into a chair beside an occasional table covered with family photos in silver frames.

"Will someone please tell me what's going on?" she said. "Everybody's rushing about, but nobody's really telling me anything."

"Someone's been injured," said Penny. "I found him outside. Gwennie called an ambulance."

"Oh, dear," said Mrs. Lloyd. "That doesn't sound good. Do we know who it is?"

Penny shook her head, and after that, a mantle of silence settled over the room until Bethan returned, with Florence and Gwennie behind her. All eyes turned toward her, but the look on her face answered their unspoken question.

"I'm sorry," she said. "He was beyond help."

"Oh, no. That's terrible," said Mrs. Lloyd. "The disappearance of the Black Chair was bad enough, but now a man's been found dead? What on earth happened?"

"We don't know yet, Mrs. Lloyd."

"The person," said Penny. "Is it . . ." She had difficulty saying the name. "Is it Lane Hardwick?"

"No," said Bethan.

Penny let out a sigh of relief. "Oh, thank goodness." Bethan gave her a sharp look. "Oh, I'm sorry. I didn't mean for that to sound so callous. It's just that Lane, well, you remember him," Bethan nodded. "Of course you do. That's how you know it's not him." Bethan had interviewed Lane earlier that year in connection with an incident at the castle where he had been working as a volunteer gardener.

"Anyway, Lane was helping out at the dinner and then disappeared, so when I stumbled across the person out there, I was afraid it might be him, but it was so dark, I couldn't tell. In fact, that's what I was doing out there. When I found the door of the scullery open, I stepped out to see if Lane might have gone out that way and was lurking about somewhere in the garden.

"So while I'm terribly sorry for whoever's out there, part of me's glad it isn't Lane. And that's all I really meant."

"Well, I can tell you that it's not Lane, but I don't know yet who it is." Bethan held up one of the white pay envelopes Penny had retrieved from the butler's pantry and then left in the scullery before she went outside.

"This was left over when Gwennie distributed the pay packets amongst the waitstaff and might provide a lead to the person's identity. Apparently one of the waiters disappeared during the dinner, and this envelope is intended for him, so there's a chance this missing waiter is the person out there. He was dressed in a black suit, like the other waiters."

"Can you who tell us whose name is on the pay packet?" asked Penny.

"Rhodri Phillips." Bethan looked from one face to the next. "Name mean anything to anyone?" As everyone exchanged blank looks, Penny asked, "How old would you say he was?"

"Hard to be precise, but I'd say late teens, early twenties."

"It's just that our receptionist is called Rhian Phillips, but I don't think she has a son."

"No," agreed Victoria. "She has a daughter, a bit older than that."

"Of course a lot of people around here share the same surname without being related," said Bethan. "Just think how many folks are called Jones. Or my name, even. Morgan's a really common surname."

Recently promoted from sergeant, Inspector Bethan Morgan had known Penny and Victoria for several years and turned to them when she needed extra insight or felt she'd exhausted all official lines of inquiry and was running out of ideas. In her late thirties, with copper-coloured curls and blue eyes that could sometimes appear cold and steely and other times warm and sympathetic, Bethan's approach to her work was methodical and measured. She was ambitious, and Penny believed she had a great future in policing ahead of her.

"So who hired the waitstaff?" Bethan asked.

"I did," said Penny. "At least, I asked Mrs. Geraint at the Red Dragon Hotel if she could send over some staff for the evening, and she sent the ones who worked here tonight."

"But you didn't actually recruit them? That is, take applications, do interviews, take up references, and so on?"

Penny shook her head. "No. Mrs. Geraint assured me they were all good workers and were on her books, so that was good enough for us." She glanced at Emyr, then turned back to Bethan. "Why? What are you thinking?"

"Oh, it's way too early in the investigation for me to be thinking anything," she replied smoothly. "It's early days. Very early days. And anyway, you should know by now I'm not one to speculate. I go in the direction the evidence leads me."

"Do you think the theft of the chair and the murder are related?" Victoria asked.

Bethan lowered her head, gazed at Victoria through narrowed eyes, and frowned, but in a tolerant, almost amused sort of way. "What did I just say? But the two may very well be connected. We'll see what the investigation turns up. But until we know more, we treat this as a suspicious death."

She directed her next words to Emyr. "That means you're in for the full forensics, I'm afraid. The team is on its way to seal off the area where the body was found, and the pathologist has been notified. And although we'll try not to disturb you, there will be big, bright lights overnight. We'll be starting as soon as we can."

"But why?" asked Emyr. "Can it not wait until morning?"

"No," said Bethan. "It cannot. We don't want to lose any bits of forensic evidence that might be out there, and the rain we had earlier isn't helping. Oh, and we didn't see any CCTV installations. You don't have that as part of your security arrangements?"

Emyr grimaced and made a little noise of dismay. "Erm, well, we don't really have any security measures like that in place," he said. "We never thought we needed them. Times have changed, I guess."

"CCTV would have been incredibly helpful. I recommend you get that seen to," Bethan advised, with droll understatement. "And while you're at it, get some better lighting out there. Motion detection sensors, the lot. Burglars love back doors with poor lighting. Or in your case, almost no lighting, which suits intruders even better."

Mrs. Lloyd, who had been following all this with her mouth slightly open, reached down one side of her chair and then the other. "My handbag," she exclaimed. "I must have left it in the kitchen." She stood up and hurried out of the room.

"Now then," Bethan continued, "the constable's with the waitstaff and we're making arrangements to drive them to the station. It's late and they're tired, so we may not get much out of them, but we have to separate them and talk to them as soon as we can while their recollections are fresh. And that's the only staff? Just the three waiters?"

"Well," said Penny, "depends who you call staff. I'm assuming you don't consider Gwennie and Florence staff. There was a sous chef helping Florence in the kitchen with preparation, but he left before dinner service started, and a butler was hired for the evening." Her eyes sought out Victoria's. "Gosh, I can't remember the last time I saw him. There's been so much going on."

"He was in the library for the unveiling of the chair, and I think that's the last time I saw him," said Victoria.

"Anybody?" said Bethan, gazing around the room. When there was no response, she cleared her throat before giving Emyr a meaningful glare. "It's a shame the guests and apparently this butler fellow were allowed to leave. We would have liked to talk to everyone tonight. You're going to have to give me everyone's names and contact details."

"Yes, I can certainly do that," said Emyr, "but as I said to Penny earlier, no one left the dining room during dinner."

"That doesn't matter," said Bethan. "They might have seen something at any time that could be relevant. They all need to be interviewed, so you'll have to provide all their names."

"I'm sorry," said Emyr. "I wasn't thinking clearly. Bronwyn

was anxious to get home to Robbie—that's her dog—and when she decided to leave, everyone else did, too. I asked them to stay, but, well, I couldn't very well hold them all here against their will, could I?"

"I'm surprised they left," said Penny, when Bethan did not reply to Emyr's explanation. "You'd think they'd want to stick around to see what happens. I know I would have." Her words evaporated into silence.

Finally, Emyr spoke. "Look," he said, "I'm terribly sorry about the person who's been found outside, this Rhodri Phillips, if that's indeed who it is, but I'm desperately worried about the Black Chair. This is rather embarrassing, but it was on loan to me for a couple of nights, en route from the restorer back to its home at Yr Ysgwrn. Naturally, I assured the restoration committee that it would be perfectly safe here; I had no reason to think otherwise. Nothing like this has ever happened before." He paused as his brows knitted together. "Although in hindsight, that kind of thinking seems foolish. It seems that I was a bit naïve."

"More than a bit, if you don't mind me saying," commented Bethan.

Mrs. Lloyd, her handbag draped over her forearm, slid back into the room and returned to her chair.

"The thing is," Emyr continued, "we've got to get that chair back. The Prince of Wales himself is coming to open the newly restored farmhouse, and it's got to be in place for that."

"And when is this due to take place?" Bethan asked. "The opening?'

"Three weeks."

"Three weeks? In that case, we'd better get our skates on, hadn't we? Well, now that I've seen what there is to see in the library, as I said before, forensics will be here to process everything. The library will be sealed tonight. So don't go in there. Don't touch the chair that was substituted for the stolen chair, and keep it under the black cloth. Unless the thieves are total idiots, which I doubt, given what happened here tonight, they were wearing gloves. And of course, people have been in and out of that room since the chair was taken, so I don't think forensics will get much, but we might get lucky. You never know. Just leave everything as it is until we've finished up, inside and out, and we'll let you know when that is."

Her constable poked his head in the door and gave her a questioning look. She gave him a quick nod of acknowledgement and then turned her attention back to the people in the room. "Right, well, if nobody has anything else to tell me, we'll be off. Got a long night ahead of us. We'll be interviewing each of you over the next few days."

"I'll show you out," said Emyr. He returned to the sitting room a few minutes later and said, "I'm afraid the police are going to focus on the death of that young man and the theft of the chair will take a back seat to that investigation. You hear all the time about the police having such limited resources. I mean, I can understand that someone's death is more important than a chair, but still . . ."

"And those aren't the only problems we've got," said Penny.

Emyr groaned. "We've got a death and the theft of the Black Chair. Isn't that enough?

"Lane," said Penny. "Lane Hardwick's gone missing."

"Maybe he was upset because he dropped that tray in the hall earlier," mused Gwennie. "He's a very sensitive boy. You have to be very careful how you talk to him because he takes everything to heart so."

"No, I think there's more to it than that," said Penny. "I know Lane. He didn't run away because he dropped the tray. I'm pretty sure he ran away because he's frightened. I've seen him do this before. He handles a bad or threatening situation the only way he knows how, by trying to escape it."

"I hope he's okay," said Victoria, stifling a yawn. "But to be honest, I think we'd better call it a night. I'm sure we're all exhausted and it's time we were on our way. Since Bethan said to leave everything as it is, I'm just going to leave the harp there for now, and I'll be back in the next day or two to collect it."

"You can leave it here as long as you like," said Jennifer. "It looks beautiful. It really suits this room, or maybe the room really suits it. Not sure which way round."

The group stood up. "You'll need to go out the back way," said Gwennie, "so you can get your wraps."

They trooped into the hall, and as they passed the library door, now sealed off with blue-and-white police tape, Penny paused.

"I can't stop thinking about Lane. I'm sure he saw something tonight, or he knows something. And if the people responsible for this"—she gestured at the library door, meaning the space behind it where the Black Chair had stood—"if those people find him, he could be in real danger."

Chapter Eight

The cheerful jingling of Penny's mobile the next morning woke her, and through a sleepy haze she picked it up off her nightstand and checked the time. 7:08.

"Hello?" she said, battling her way into full awareness.

"Oh, sorry, did I wake you?" said the woman's voice in her ear.

"No, no, it's all right. I was awake. Just lying here, thinking about getting up." Penny winced, wondering why people bothered with that little exchange, when it should be obvious to the caller that they *had* woken up someone, and it should be just as obvious to the person who had just been woken up that the caller could tell from their voice that they'd been roused from a deep sleep. Still, the just-wakened person insists he or she wasn't asleep. And then the real conversation begins.

Penny listened and a moment later, startled, sat up on one elbow, brushed the hair from the side of her face, and rubbed her left eye.

"Oh, no," she said. "Oh, Victoria, that's terrible. Yes, I'll get dressed right away. Right. See you when you get here. Coffee. Yes, of course. Front door will be open. Just come in."

After brushing her teeth, Penny pulled on a pair of jeans and a cozy sweater and hurried downstairs. She unlocked the front door on her way to the kitchen, then filled the kettle and switched it on. She popped a couple of frozen croissants on the work top to thaw and waited.

At the sound of a car pulling up, she finished arranging the coffee tray, then carried it into the sitting room just as Victoria opened the door. Penny set down the tray and gestured to a chair. She poured two cups of coffee and handed one to Victoria.

"So tell me," said Penny. "Tell me everything."

"Rhian phoned me about seven, just before I phoned you. The police called round to her sister's late last night, and it's really bad news. The worst possible. That body you found at the Hall last night is Rhodri Phillips. And it turns out that he was our Rhian's nephew. The whole family is devastated."

"I'm sure they are," said Penny. "It's unimaginable."

"Anyway, Rhian was ringing to say that she won't be in to work for a few days. She's not sure when she'll be back, but I told her to take as long as she needs, and of course she was concerned about how the Spa would manage without her."

"Well, we'll manage somehow. We always do. You and I can take turns covering the reception desk, and we can always count on Eirlys to help out. She's really good at greeting the customers and keeping everything organized."

"True. Anyway, Rhian rang me because I look after staffing

issues at the Spa, but what she really wanted was to ask for your help. She said it would make a big difference to the family if they knew you were looking into the death of her nephew. Along with the police, of course. The family's still in shock and not really processing anything, but they want to know that everything possible is being done."

"Absolutely. I was awake for the longest time last night going over everything in my mind. How did the thieves get in without being seen? And is the theft of the chair related to the death of Rhodri Phillips? And if so, how? And which came first? The theft or the murder? If it was a murder, of course, but I think we can assume that it was. And then, of course, there's Lane. I still think he saw or heard something, and the fact that he's gone missing tells me that he knows something important and he's frightened. At least, I hope that's the case. I hope whoever took the chair didn't take Lane as well. I probably should have mentioned this to Bethan last night."

"That could all be true," agreed Victoria. "But where do we start?"

"We start with Lane, because if I'm right, he could be in danger. Poor Rhodri is beyond help, and although the chair is valuable—priceless, even—in the end, it's just a . . ."

"A beautiful piece of furniture with historical significance." Victoria finished the sentence.

"Exactly. So we need to find Lane. And when we do, he might know something that can then help us find out who murdered Rhodri, and when we know that, with a bit of luck, that will lead us to the chair. Of course, it could work the other way, too. When we find the chair, it could lead us to discover who killed Rhodri Phillips. But either way, let's start with Lane."

"Okay," said Victoria. "But remember, as long as Rhian is away, we're not going to be able to take time away from the Spa to go sleuthing."

"That goes without saying. So let's make the most of today. The first thing to do is ring Lane's mother. For all we know, he may even be home by now. While I'm doing that, why don't you get the croissants in the oven? They'll just take a few minutes to warm through."

Lane had gone missing a few months ago and, after spending an uncomfortable, wet night on the grounds of a ruined castle, had made his way back to Llanelen, where Penny had found him, hungry and tired, trudging along the riverbank, in the company of Dilys, an elderly naturalist who wandered the lanes and fields foraging for plants and herbs.

Penny had taken him to the café on the town square, called his mother to let her know her son was safe and then given him a hearty fry-up while they waited for his mother to collect him. Penny now thumbed through the calls list on her phone, looking for his mother's number. When she found it, she pressed the green button and took a sip of coffee while she waited for Shelagh Hardwick to answer. When she did, Penny introduced herself, explaining she'd been at the Hall last night and was calling to ask if Lane had made it home safely. While she listened, Victoria returned carrying two plates, a croissant and a dollop of marmalade on each one. As she set the plates on the coffee table, Penny raised her eyes to meet Victoria's, and shook her head gently.

"All right then, Mrs. Hardwick, can you think of anyplace he might have gone? Anyplace that's familiar and comforting to him?" Penny asked. A moment later she smiled, and continued, "We'll keep our eyes open for him, and if we hear anything or see him, we'll be in touch right away. Oh, and have you spoken to the police?" She gave a little start and held the phone a little way away from her ear. "I see. Yes, well, still, I'd give them a call if I were you and let them know he's not with you."

When she'd wrapped up the call, Victoria asked, "What did she say that was so funny?"

"It wasn't funny, exactly, but when I asked her if she knew of a place that was safe and comforting for Lane, she said, 'Yes, I do. His own bed.'"

"I thought you might have mentioned something to her about Lane possibly being in danger."

"I almost did, but then I thought I'd have to tell her too much, and besides, I didn't want to alarm her. There's nothing she can do about what happened, and I'm sure it would just add to her stress. She's anxious to get him home."

Victoria helped herself to a warm croissant, broke a piece off, and spread a little marmalade on it. "I don't think he'd go back to Gwrych Castle, do you? It's pretty far for him, and the weather last night wasn't good. And he travels by bus, so that doesn't seem like a good possibility."

"No," said Penny. "And I don't know that he has any friends he'd be staying with." She mulled that over for a moment. "Unless . . . No, that's just too crazy."

"What is? Tell me what you're thinking."

"Dilys. Again."

Chapter Nine

"Dilys," Victoria repeated. She pronounced the name, drawing out the *s* in a slightly contemplative hiss as she leaned her head against the back of the sofa.

"Well, she was with him that other time he went missing and I found the two of them together on the riverbank. She'd helped him find his way home on the bus, I believe."

Victoria sat up and spread a bit more marmalade on a bit more croissant. "But then, of course, the problem is finding her. You know what she's like, rambling and roaming all over the place. She could be anywhere. And besides, we don't even know where she lives. At least, I don't. Do you?"

Penny gave a slight shake of her head. "No, not really. But Dilys and her brother used to live in one of the tied cottages on the Ty Brith Hall estate, and she's been known to stop there when she's in the area, so if Lane had ever been to that cottage to see her, it would make sense that he would go there last night."

"That's true. And if she is stopping at her brother's old

cottage, Lane could have easily walked there from the Hall. Do you think he could have found his way to it in the dark?"

"It's possible. And if he did go to Dilys's cottage, he could have spent the night there, even if Dilys wasn't there and it was empty. I think it's worth taking a look to see if he's there."

* * *

"Maybe we should let Emyr know we're looking for Dilys," Victoria said as they drove toward Ty Brith Hall. "If he sees us wandering about on his property, he'll wonder what we're doing."

In response, Penny picked her phone out of her bag and rang him. After speaking for a few minutes, she glanced at Victoria. "He said, 'Be my guest.' He didn't sound in a very good mood. The police forensics team is all over the place, and I don't think he has the time or inclination to think about Lane or Dilys."

"About the cottages. Wasn't there a plan a while ago for them to be done up as holiday lets? If that's the case, Dilys would hardly be living in one. It would be much too grand for the likes of her."

"I heard that Emyr got the planning permission, but as far as I know, he hasn't moved forward with the project."

"So if they're still empty, this could be promising."

"And if Dilys is living in one, I wonder if Emyr even knows. You know what she's like, the way she comes and goes. One minute she's there, and the next, she's vanished, like a plume of smoke. She could be camped out in one of his cottages, right under his nose, and he'd be none the wiser, because she'd be gone the next day."

Victoria laughed. "Dilys is such a wild creature. She's going to do what she wants to do."

A few minutes later they arrived at Ty Brith Hall, left their vehicle in the car park behind the house, and set off down the path that led to the terrace of workers' cottages.

"Are you all right?" Victoria asked. "Sure you want to do this?"

"Yes, of course I am. Why wouldn't I be?"

"Because you haven't been back here since the night of that terrible fire."

A light breeze ruffled their hair. The ground, littered with frost-crisped leaves, was firm beneath their feet, but the silent, brown landscape was beginning to soak up the morning warmth and the earthen path would soon soften. The path led them through a small stand of bare trees to the empty, silent stable yard, with its cobbled stones that had once rung with the rhythmic clip-clop of horses being led back to their stalls after their morning runs. Penny paused in front of the disused stables built of the same granite as the Hall. The blackened stones, charred, glassless window frames, and missing roof stirred memories of a fire that had broken out here several years earlier. She raised her right hand to her ear, as if to block out the roaring, whooshing sounds of the inferno and the shouts of the firefighters as they struggled to contain it. But most of all she remembered the acrid smell of the smoke and how its lingering stench had clung to her, permeating every pore of her body for what seemed like weeks. She'd got rid of all the clothes she'd been wearing, and after several sympathetic treatments by Alberto, the Spa hairdresser, he'd finally said there was nothing more he could do, and she'd realised that the smell was no longer in her hair or on her body but in her mind. She had not been back here since that night, and uneasy with the memories the stables evoked and the feelings rising within her, she stuffed her hands in the pockets of her jacket, gave Victoria a resolute smile, and the two walked on. Leaving the stables behind, they skirted a derelict barn and lambing shed, and beyond these outbuildings lay the terrace of workers' cottages. Several decades ago, when the estate had included a self-sufficient, productive, and well-staffed home farm with flower and vegetable gardens, a working dairy, and cattle and sheep husbandry, a few of the more fortunate workers and their families had been provided with tied housing in the cottages. Now the stone buildings sat forlorn and empty, waiting to be given the new life that had been promised them as desirable holiday lets.

Penny and Victoria continued on until they reached the end cottage. This had been the home of Pawl Hughes, former head gardener of Ty Brith Hall. Under his stewardship the flower gardens had been spectacular in every season: dancing daffodils under the trees to welcome spring, peony beds for fresh-cut, feminine flowers in early summer, fragrant roses in every hue throughout July and August and lasting well into the autumn, and clusters of mid-winter fire to provide flames of colour throughout the darkest days of winter. When Pawl's health had declined, Dilys had materialized to care for her brother, until the night his life came to a terrible end in the fire that haunted Penny.

After a quick glance at Victoria for reassurance, Penny curled her fingers into a fist and rapped on the wooden door.

"I wonder if she'll answer," Penny said. "Even if she's in there, she might not come to the door. Dilys is just so unpredictable. You never know what she's going to do."

"No, you don't, but we're about to find out."

Just as they were about to give up, there came a shuffling on the other side of the door. It was opened a few inches to allow a dark eye to peer at them and then opened a little more, revealing a woman with pinched, thin lips and grey hair parted in the centre under a shapeless brown felt hat. Her all-weather coat, faded into an indeterminate colour somewhere between dark green and grey, hung just below the knees of a pair of grey trousers Penny thought might once have belonged to her brother. Her feet were encased in sturdy, well-worn brown walking boots, fastened with one brown lace and one black.

"Oh, it's you," said Dilys. "I was just getting ready to go out. You've not come at a convenient time."

"Yes, well, sorry about that," said Penny. "But I've got something important to ask you. Victoria's with me. May we come in for a moment? We won't keep you."

"You've always got something important to ask Dilys," the woman replied. "The only time you want to talk to me is when you need my help with something. Yes, all right, you may come in, but be quick about it. What is it you want?"

She opened the door as wide as it would go and turned

away from them, revealing a straggly ponytail tied back with a piece of raffia.

Penny and Victoria stepped across the threshold. The ground floor of the cottage consisted of one room that served as a basic kitchen and sitting room. Every inch of rough, whitewashed wall and surface was covered with something. Musty books and bottles made of green, brown, and purple glass and seashells jostled for space on thick wooden shelves and tables. Bunches of lavender plants and a variety of herbs in various stages of the drying process hung upside down from the low ceiling beams. The room smelled of the passing of time. The dust on the deep-set windowsills, deeper now than it had been five or six years ago when Penny was last here, mixed with the papery aroma of faded photographs, candle wax, and seasoned wood. A narrow wooden staircase at the rear of the room led upstairs to two tiny bedrooms and a bathroom, all with sloping ceilings and small windows. A brown teapot, accompanied by a half-full teacup with a chip out of the rim, sat on a table covered with bits of bark and stems of bright red-and-yellow berries.

"There's a boy gone missing," Penny said, "and we wondered if you've seen him."

"What boy?" Dilys asked. "Dilys doesn't know any boys." Dilys's habit of often referring to herself in the third person sometimes irritated Penny, sometimes amused her, but today she took no notice of it.

"Yes, you do. A young man, then. Lane Hardwick. You know him. You were kind enough to help him once before, so

I wondered if you're helping him again. We think he may be in trouble and that he might have come to you."

Dilys frowned. "Oh, that boy."

"Yes, that boy."

"What's he done?"

"He hasn't done anything, but he went missing last night in the middle of a party at Ty Brith Hall. He didn't help set up the coffee like he was supposed to. Which was surprising, because he loves coffee and had really been looking forward to organizing and offering his own coffee service." Penny raised her voice as she lifted her face to address the low-beamed ceiling. "He's not in any trouble. We want to talk to him, that's all."

"Are you sure he's not in any trouble?" Dilys asked.

"No," said Penny, "he's not in any trouble." She placed a tentative hand on the side of the classic Brown Betty tea pot and then lifted the lid and peered at the contents. The lid clinked into place with a sturdy ringing sound as she replaced it. "He's not in trouble," she repeated, emphasizing the word *trouble*. "But he might be in danger."

"Why do you think that?" The tone in Dilys's voice had changed to one of suspicion, and her hazel eyes, with glints of green, narrowed.

"Because a young man, probably the same age as Lane or not much older, died up at the Hall last night in unexplained circumstances, and we think Lane might have seen or heard something. So, tell me, do you know where he is? Have you seen him? This could be important."

"Maybe I have, and maybe I haven't," said Dilys.

"I think you have," said Penny. With anyone else she would have found the drawn-out conversation exasperating, but experience had taught her this was exactly the sort of thing to expect from Dilys. "The teapot's still warm and there's more than enough tea in there for two cups." She lifted the lid again and raised the teapot to her nose. "What on earth is it, by the way?"

"I'll thank you to leave my teapot alone, if you don't mind. But since you ask, it's my own special herbal blend that I make for myself. I don't like those awful store-bought tea bags you use." She made a little *pfft* of disgust.

"I know you don't. That's why I don't invite you round for a cup of tea very often." Penny exchanged a quick glance with Victoria, and realizing she'd got as much information as the conversation was likely to yield, Penny gave up. "Well, look, Dilys, let's leave it like this. If you see Lane on your travels, tell him that his mother's worried about him—just like she was the last time he went missing, I might add—and so am I. Be sure to tell him he's not in any trouble, if that's what he's worried about. And tell him I'd like to talk to him."

"You'd like to ask him questions, more like," said Dilys. "The way you do."

"Well, yes, that too. He might know something important about what happened up at the Hall last night, and may not even be aware that he knows it. And if does know something, I'm sure he'd like to help us. But most of all, we want to make sure that he's safe. For now, that's the most important thing. There are some bad people out there." She lowered her voice so that Lane, if he was upstairs listening as she thought he might be, couldn't hear. "Look, Dilys, he could be in danger. If you see him, bring him to me. We can look after him. We can make sure he's safe." Dilys pinched her lips together as her gaze shifted to a wildly overgrown plant with sword-shaped leaves in the dimmest corner of the room. "Right, well, we'll leave you to get on with your day," said Penny.

* * *

"What was all that hush-hush whispering business at the end all about?" Victoria asked as they retraced their steps along the path that would take them back to the car park. Ahead of them, the peaked outline of the Ty Brith Hall roof was silhouetted above black, skeletal tree branches against a bright-blue sky. Smoke curled out of the chimneys and then, caught by the breeze, drifted up and away over the valley until it disappeared.

"I didn't want to alarm or frighten Lane. I'm pretty sure he was hiding in an upstairs bedroom, listening to every word. The floorboards in those old cottages have wide gaps in them so you can easily hear what's being said on the next floor."

"What makes you think he was upstairs?"

"She'd made enough tea for two and it was still warm, so someone had been drinking tea with her this morning. My money says it was Lane. And then he scurried upstairs when we arrived, taking his cup with him. That's why Dilys took so long to open the door. As you suggested earlier, I think it's quite likely that he spent the night there."

"Well, if he is with her, then at least he's safe."

"For the time being, anyway."

Chapter Ten

They crunched across the gravelled car park, and when they reached Victoria's car, Penny scanned the ground floor windows of the Hall while she waited for the metallic click that indicated Victoria had unlocked the passenger door. As she heard the click and reached for the door handle, she raised her eyes to the first floor, where a figure stood at a window, hand resting on the edge of the curtain, gazing down at her. She waved gently at the figure, but the person did not respond, just stepped back into the room and disappeared from view. It was all over in seconds, and Penny climbed into the car and settled into the passenger seat for the short drive back to town.

"So what's next?" Victoria asked. The bright, crisp November morning had warmed up nicely. Penny gazed over the hilltops, covered in low-lying, wispy clouds, before replying.

"It's Remembrance Day Sunday, so I'd like to attend the service at the cenotaph." She checked her watch. "We've got plenty of time to get there. And after that, it would be a nice gesture if we dropped off some flowers at Rhian's house, don't you think? To let her know we're thinking of her."

"That's a good idea. We'll pick up some flowers after the service."

Victoria parked in her usual spot at the rear of the Spa, and drawn by the sound of the local brass band's enthusiastic—if occasionally off-key—version of *It's a Long Way to Tipperary*, they walked the short distance to the granite cenotaph graced with bronze plaques bearing the names of men who had given their lives in several wars. About a hundred people of all ages, talking quietly amongst themselves and most dressed warmly in casual clothes of jeans, jackets, and wooly hats, each with a red poppy pinned on the collars or chests of their coats, had gathered at the monument. At fifteen minutes to eleven, as the band segued into *Pack Up Your Troubles in Your Old Kit Bag*, Rev. Thomas Evans, his white surplice flapping gently in the light breeze, appeared at the head of a small group of veterans, cadets, serving members of the three branches of the armed forces, and local dignitaries. They were accompanied by flag bearers who marched proudly, banners held high, and when the party reached the cenotaph, they lined up smartly. Two elderly veterans in wheelchairs, gloved hands folded and resting lightly on the dark-green plaid rugs covering their laps, were greeted with enthusiastic applause.

When everyone was in position, the music stopped, and Rev. Evans began to speak.

"We gather here today, on the one hundredth anniversary of the Armistice that ended the First World War, to remember those who made the ultimate sacrifice . . ." As Penny listened, her eyes wandered over the assembled townsfolk. There, at the edge of the crowd, her cairn terrier Robbie on a lead and watching the proceedings with his bright, brown eyes, was Bronwyn Evans, the rector's wife. Beside her stood Mrs. Lloyd and Florence, all three women better dressed than most in knee-length coats. Florence was bareheaded, but Mrs. Lloyd wore a black beret, tipped to one side, that complemented her smart red coat with a black velvet collar.

At the end of the row of dignitaries, holding the wreath that had been handed to him when he arrived, stood Emyr, dressed in the blue uniform of an officer in the Royal Auxiliary Air Force, and behind him and off to one side was Jennifer Sayles. Penny recognized her as the figure she had seen at the upstairs window of Ty Brith Hall that morning. At first they seemed like an ordinary couple attending a formal service, but as Penny looked closer, they had that unmistakable, constricted look about them of two people who had recently been arguing, perhaps in the car on the way here. Emyr's shoulders seemed filled with tension as he stared straight ahead, maintaining an emotional distance between himself and his companion, and Jennifer's red lips were pressed together in a tight line that drooped slightly at the corners of her mouth. If she knew how aging that was, she wouldn't let herself do it, thought Penny. Something about her that Penny hadn't noticed before now struck her as familiar, although she couldn't place where she'd seen her.

At the stroke of eleven o'clock, the final notes of the "Last

Post" faded away and the townsfolk of Llanelen joined with millions across the nation and the Commonwealth to observe the two-minute silence. Penny bowed her head. She paid silent tribute to the members of her own faraway Canadian family who had served in both wars, and she thought of the servicemen and servicewomen, from all countries, symbolized by the poet Hedd Wyn, who had never made it home.

And then the atmosphere of dignified, respectful silence was broken by rowdy teenage boys on bicycles, jeering at the crowd and shouting profanities at one another as they rode by. Those honouring the memory of the war dead raised their heads, glared at the offenders, and then exchanged annoyed glances. But the damage was done, and a few moments later, when the bugler played "Reveille," indicating that the silence was over, the crowd rustled and stirred back to life. After the service concluded with wreath laying, a blessing, and finally the playing of the national anthem, the group exchanged parting words with their neighbours and, thinking about getting home to prepare lunch or meeting up with a friend at the pub, drifted away.

Mrs. Lloyd exchanged a few words with Emyr and then made a beeline for Penny.

"Oh, Penny. I just asked Emyr if there's any news after last night, and he was quite short with me. 'Of course not!' he said. How was I to know that?" She glanced at Victoria. "Anyway, you have to ask, don't you? He said he was in a bit of a rush. He's driving his young lady to the Junction railway station to catch the train back to London. Has to get back to her fancy job. Works in public relations, someone told me last night."

Penny watched as Emyr and Jennifer Sayles shook hands with the mayor and then left.

"She's taking the train to London," repeated Penny. And then she remembered where she'd seen Jennifer Sayles. She'd been one of Meg Wynne Thompson's bridesmaids, all those years ago, at Emyr's ill-fated wedding. Penny had done the bridal party's manicures, but naturally Jennifer had shown no sign of recognizing her. After all, who would remember a manicurist? Penny thought back to the day the bridesmaids, excited and chatty, had come to the little salon she'd operated in Station Road. So much time had passed and everyone had changed. She didn't even think of herself as a manicurist anymore; she thought of herself as the co-owner of a thriving business and a reasonably successful watercolour artist.

She turned her attention back to Mrs. Lloyd as she was saying, "Yes, yes, Florence, I'm coming,"

"I left that chicken in the oven roasting for our lunch," said Florence. "But now I've got to get home to baste it and put the potatoes on. If you want to dillydally here, that's fine, but I'm leaving now."

"I'm amazed that Florence would be cooking today," said Penny as Florence set off, with Mrs. Lloyd hesitating in her wake, torn between scurrying after her friend and wanting to talk to people. "If I'd worked as hard as she did yesterday preparing that incredible dinner, I'd be having leftovers or takeaway today."

Victoria laughed. "So would I! And I'm not sure I would have had the energy to turn up for this service, either. Right, then, shall we pick up some flowers and then make our way over to Rhian's?"

The local flower shop was closed on Sundays, so as they walked the short distance to the supermarket, Penny asked Victoria if she'd noticed the body language between Emyr and Jennifer Sayles.

"I did. Very frosty. Something was most definitely not right there," Victoria replied. "They looked like they were on the verge of breaking up. As if they didn't even like each other very much."

"They seemed happy enough last night, so it looks like they had a falling out either overnight or this morning. They'd certainly been arguing, wouldn't you say?"

"Yes, I would. I wonder what about."

As the automatic doors of the supermarket swished open, they entered and chose the best bouquet on offer, an all-white assortment of roses and carnations. With Victoria carrying the flowers, they made their way to a row of identical terraced, red-brick houses, each with a small garden and overhang above the door. Victoria's eyes swept over the houses, and she pointed halfway up the street. "I'm pretty sure that's it."

Penny rang the doorbell, and a few minutes later Rhian appeared.

"Oh," she exclaimed. "I wasn't expecting to see you! But do come in."

"We hope we're not intruding," said Penny, "but we

wanted to tell you in person how sorry we were to hear about your nephew."

Victoria held out the flowers. "And to let you know that if there's anything you need from us to please just let us know. And take all the time you need off work. We know you need to be with your family now."

"Oh, thank you," said Rhian, taking a step back and holding the door open with one hand. They found themselves in a dim, narrow hallway, with a kitchen at the far end and, on their right, a set of dark-brown stairs with a threadbare runner leading to the first floor. "Actually, you've come at a good time. My sister's been on the phone all morning, and my mother's terribly upset. She's still in shock, I think. Well, that's understandable. You don't expect to wake up of a Sunday morning and be told your grandson's dead." She gestured to a door on their left. "Go through."

Penny and Victoria entered a drab, cramped sitting room. A mud-coloured three-piece suite, with old-fashioned white crocheted arm covers, overpowered the room. A floor lamp with a tasseled shade, a small, cheap bookcase whose shelves bowed under the weight of romance novels, and a curio cupboard filled with figurines of Georgian and Victorian ladies dressed in sweeping skirts and flower-bedecked bonnets, waiting patiently for their suitors, fought for space with the sofa and chairs. And underneath it all was a rather tatty carpet featuring a swirly pattern of brown and yellow roses. The room's everyday ordinariness was relieved by the contrast of an unexpectedly modern painting hanging above an elderly electric fireplace. In a traditional, dated sitting room like this one, Penny would have expected to see a print of a rural scene, grazing sheep against a mountainous backdrop, perhaps. But to her artist's eye, this painting, vibrant, and confident in its use of strong colour choices and bold, broad brushstrokes, seemed remarkably out of place. Knowing Rhian, Penny thought the painting could not possibly reflect her tastes.

She directed her attention from the painting to the small woman with bright copper-coloured hair slumped in the armchair. She raised dull, red-veined eyes to take in the visitors.

"Mam, this is Penny and Victoria from the Spa," said Rhian. "You know, where I work." The woman gave them a curt nod and then turned her eyes to her daughter, as if seeking further explanation. "Mam, I'm just going to put these lovely flowers they brought us in some water. Do you want me to make you another cup of tea when I'm in the kitchen?"

Mrs. Phillips groaned. "One more cup of tea and my bladder'll be fit to burst."

"I'll take that as a no, then."

With a resigned gesture, Rhian directed Penny and Victoria to the sofa, and once they were seated, Victoria offered their condolences to the dead youth's grandmother. The woman acknowledged her words without replying but dabbed at her eyes with a balled-up tissue, which she then placed on the table beside her where it joined a sad little pile of others. A heavy silence settled over the room, broken only when Rhian returned, carrying the flowers in a glass vase. She set it on the table in front of the window and adjusted the white net curtains around it.

"There," she said. "They look lovely, don't they, Mam?" She sat down at the end of the sofa, knees together and her body turned toward Penny and Victoria. "It was good of you to call in, and bring us flowers," she said. "You can't image how terrible this morning has been. The police have been wonderful, though. They sent a female support officer round to stay with my sister and keep her informed."

"I'm glad," said Victoria. "The police seem to be so much better at that sort of thing than they used to be. They show more sympathy and understanding to grieving families."

"Would it help to talk about your nephew?" Penny asked. "Perhaps you'd tell us a bit about him. What kind of person he was, and so on."

"He wasn't like most lads his age from around here," Rhian said. "He knew what he wanted to do in life, and when he left high school he went off to the university in Bangor. He was the first in our family to go to uni. We were so proud of him, weren't we, Mam?" Her mother sniffled agreement as she gave her puffy eyes a halfhearted dab.

"We thought he was doing well, but he fell in with a wild crowd, Rhodri did, and started drinking and taking drugs, and ignoring his studies, so he never made it past first year. To be honest, my sister, being a single mum and all, had been strict with him growing up. Too strict, I guess, and sometimes kids just can't handle all the freedom when they leave home, and they go a bit wild and get into all kinds of trouble."

"Oh, I know how that can happen all too easily," said Penny. She'd been on a similar path during her first year at university in New Brunswick, and although she'd managed to squeak through the required courses and narrowly avoid the fate that had befallen Rhodri, a few of her friends, who'd spent too much time at the bridge table or in the local bars, hadn't. They had left at the end of the spring term, never to be seen again.

"Anyway, our Rhodri ended up having to move back in with his mother here in Llanelen, and he really struggled. His dreams were crashing down all around him and he didn't know what to do with himself. Had no direction, no purpose. But he kept up with his love of art. In fact, he painted that picture over the fireplace, didn't he, Mam?" Her mother sniffed again in agreement. "Rhodri's mother—that's my sister—she thinks there were more paintings, but they must have got left behind in Bangor when he moved out of his student digs. And he did them all in his own time, too. They weren't part of his coursework."

"He was very talented," Penny said. "But tell me. When did Rhodri move back to Llanelen?"

"Over the summer. He sat his exams in May, then when the results weren't what he'd hoped for, he didn't go back for the autumn term. I think he was planning to try to get into art school, Liverpool maybe, where it would be more hands-on and less academic. He took on some casual work at the hotel so he could have a bit of spending money and pay his mum for room and board, so we thought he was on the right track. I mean, sometimes it takes a while for young people to sort themselves out, doesn't it?"

Mrs. Phillips let out a little exclamation of agreement and spoke for the first time. "He was a good boy at heart, Rhodri was. He never meant anyone any harm."

"How old was he?" Victoria asked.

"He was just about to turn twenty." Rhian picked up a framed photo from the mantelpiece and handed it to Penny. "Here he is just finishing high school, so this was taken a year or so ago."

Penny tipped the photo to catch the light filtering through the net curtains and saw the face of the young man who had helped her light the candles just before the guests entered the dining room and whose hand she had briefly held as he lay dying on the wet walkway outside Ty Brith Hall. Now, knowing the family connection, she could see a hint of his aunt Rhian in his small dark eyes set in a rectangular face, but his nose was longer than hers, and his lips were full where hers were thin. "Have the police given you any indication of what might have happened?" Penny asked, handing the photo of Rhodri to Victoria.

"No. They said they wouldn't speculate and that they should know more after the . . ." She glanced at Mrs. Phillips. Penny, realizing that Rhian did not want to risk upsetting her mother any further by using the word "postmortem," gave her a quick nod of understanding. Since today was Sunday, the earliest the postmortem would be performed would be Monday.

"It was something to do with that bad crowd he got in with, I'm sure of it," Mrs. Phillips said. "And I'll tell that to the police and anyone else who cares to listen."

"What can you tell me about this bad crowd?" Penny asked.

"Oh, the lads he knew when he was in high school. The ones who left early and never got any qualifications while Rhodri completed his A levels. The troublemakers who live on the council estate. Just about every one of them is known to the police, I'm sure of that."

"We might have seen a few of the younger ones this morning during the Remembrance Day service at the cenotaph," said Victoria. "Rode by on bicycles, disturbing the two minutes of silence with their shouting and swearing."

"Sounds like them," replied Mrs. Phillips. "That's how they start out. No respect for person or property. And of course as they get older, they lose the bicycles and cause all kinds of problems in cars. Although how they can afford to run a car, I have no idea, since they're all work shy."

"And what did Rhodri study at university?" asked Victoria.

Rhian turned to face her mother. "History and art, was it, Mam?" When the older woman nodded, she added, "He loved both those subjects."

"He certainly was talented," Penny said again. "The loss of a young person is always a great shame, but it seems all the sadder, somehow, when a life showing promise is cut short." Rhian's mother let out a choking sob.

"There's something I'd like to ask you," said Penny. "I

don't know if you can help, but I'm sure you'd want to, if you can. You see, there's a lad gone missing. He's about the same age as your Rhodri, eighteen or nineteen, but I wondered if there's a connection, since both young men were at the Hall last night. Lane Hardwick, he's called." She looked from Mrs. Phillips to Rhian. "Does the name ring a bell? Did the two know each other?"

"Not that I know of," said Rhian. "But if you think it might be important, I could ask my sister."

"It might be worth looking into," said Penny. "At this stage, it's difficult to say what's important and what isn't, but I'm sure as the investigation continues, the police will find out what happened." She rested her hands on her knees, and after making eye contact with Victoria, the two rose.

"Before you go, Penny," said Rhian, "I just want to say if there's anything you can do to find out how Rhodri died, please do. I know the police will do their best, but you've helped out before in other cases, so if there's anything you can think of that would help us, we'd really appreciate that."

"Her?" said Mrs. Phillips. "What on earth could she possibly do that the police can't?"

"I know she doesn't look terribly clever," said Victoria with a winning smile, "but you'd be surprised. She's solved cases in the past, and sometimes the police turn to her for help."

"Oh, one of those clairvoyant types, is she?" sniffed Mrs. Phillips.

"No," said Victoria, managing to keep her voice on the polite side of a bristle. "She's a rather good amateur sleuth."

"Well, we mustn't take up any more of your time. It was nice to meet you, Mrs. Phillips, and again, I'm so sorry for your loss."

"I'll show you out," said Rhian. She closed the door between the sitting room and the hall behind them. "I apologize for the way she spoke to you just now," she said. "Mam's beside herself with grief, and the shock hasn't even worn off yet. She doesn't know what she's saying. But if you can help, we'd be so grateful."

After assuring Rhian that she'd do everything she could, Penny added, "I didn't want to mention this in front of your mother, in case it upset her, but it was me who found Rhodri outside. He was still alive, and I held his hand for a minute before I went for help. I'm just so sorry that I couldn't do anything for him, and even sorrier that we didn't find him sooner."

Rhian's eyes filled with tears. "Actually, it helps to know he wasn't alone, even if it was just for a moment or two. And I'm glad it was you who was with him."

The door closed behind them, and Penny and Victoria made their way through the quiet Sunday streets to the Spa.

"Do you want to come up for a bit of lunch?" Victoria asked. "I'm not sure what I've got in, but I could rustle us up something, as long as you're not too fussy."

"No, you're all right," said Penny. "I think I'll just have a coffee in the café to gather my thoughts before I go home."

"It feels like we've had a long morning, but I don't know that we accomplished much of anything."

"Oh, I think we did," replied Penny. "If Dilys knows

where Lane is, I'm quite sure she'll do her best to convince him that it would be best if he came out of hiding. And if he is with her, he can't stay there forever. In fact, she might just be the only one who could convince him to let us know he's safe. Which, of course, I hope he is."

They had reached the town square, and as Victoria continued on her way, Penny pushed open the door to the café and entered its fragrant warmth. She ordered and paid for a latte at the counter, then took a seat at a window table. Head resting in the palm of her hand, she gazed out at the town square, where an elderly couple waited for the light to change so they could cross the street and a young couple pushed a stroller containing a well-bundled-up toddler. The server set the latte in front of her, and Penny turned away from the window to smile her thanks.

As she dipped a spoon into the foam, she turned her attention again to the town square. The elderly couple had made it across the road, and the couple with the child in the pushchair had reached the other side of the square and were about to disappear down a street that led off it. As she continued to watch, the door of the pub across the way opened and a man emerged. After checking his phone, he pulled a pair of black gloves out of his pocket and put them on. Then he set off, with a pronounced limp, in the direction of the bank. Penny picked up a paper napkin off the table, wiped a circle in the condensation that clouded the window, and peered through the clear space she'd created. As the man turned to look back the way he had come, she instinctively shrank back from the window and wrapped her fingers around the latte glass as if seeking comfort and reassurance from its warmth.

Although she hadn't been able to see his face, the man's gait had given him away. She had no doubt who it was: the last person she had expected—or wanted—to see.

Chapter Eleven

Michael Quinn, with his irresistible Irish accent and seductively deep blue eyes.

As the churning in her stomach subsided and her thudding heart slowed and returned to normal, Penny finished her latte, and after deciding not to stop in at the Spa to tell Victoria who she had just spotted, she left the café and set off for home.

As always, walking provided the perfect accompaniment to thinking. And why, she thought, shouldn't Michael Quinn be in town? He lived in Bangor, a reasonable driving distance from here, and might have any number of good reasons for being in Llanelen today. She hoped the reason he was here had nothing to do with her.

She'd met Michael, an art historian, at the touring antiques appraisal show held at Ty Brith Hall she'd helped organize in the spring, and when he'd taken a special interest in her, she'd fallen hard for his good looks and Irish charm. She'd invested time and emotional energy in what she'd thought was a blossoming romance and had been embarrassed and crushed to learn that while she'd been falling for him, he'd conveniently forgotten to tell her that he was married, and still living with his wife.

Although Penny was grateful she'd learned the truth about his marital status before their relationship had progressed too far, she felt betrayed and angry. Angry with him for his deceit, and angry with herself for being so susceptible to the way he looked and talked. She hadn't seen him again until today, and she'd thought him well out of her memory range. She felt ambushed by the swirl of emotions that seeing him just now had awoken in her, although she wasn't sure why. She'd thought there was nothing left to feel for him, except perhaps residual loathing. But if that had been true, why had she had such a visceral reaction to seeing him again?

She unlocked her front door, recently painted a distinctive charcoal grey, and entered her cottage. After hanging her coat in the cupboard, she set her bag down at the bottom of the stairs and headed for the kitchen. She opened the refrigerator door, peered in, and took out the remains of a piece of cheddar cheese. She sliced it, set it on a plate with a few crackers and a handful of red grapes, and carried the plate through to her sitting room. She nibbled on the cheese as her mind whirled, remembering the pleasant days she'd spent with Michael Quinn. On one occasion, he'd taken her to see the bluebells in bloom; on another they'd had an outing that had started out light and fun but had taken a frightening turn when he'd been hit by a cyclist on a mountain bike, injuring his leg. Or was it his hip? In any event, he'd been unable to walk, and they'd been stranded in the forest overnight until she'd been able to summon help in the morning. She rested her head against the back of the sofa, trying to remember which leg Michael Quinn had injured, and conjured up the image of the man she'd just seen limping out of the pub. That man favoured his left leg. She cast her mind back to visiting Michael Quinn in hospital, his left leg propped up. Yes, it was his left leg that had been injured, and there had been concern for his hip as well.

She set the plate, empty except for a few grape stems, on the coffee table, and as a wave of tiredness washed over her, she reached for the light blanket folded over the arm of the sofa. Then, in a smooth, easy motion, she pulled it over herself as she stretched out. She turned on her side, tucked her hand under the green-and-yellow-striped cushion, and within minutes of closing her eyes, drifted off into a light sleep.

* * *

She awoke to the sound of knocking, not on the front door that a regular visitor would be expected to use but on the back door, which led from the kitchen to a secluded area bounded by a low stone wall.

Penny threw back the light blanket and padded to the back door. Since only one visitor had ever knocked on that door, she had a pretty good idea whom she was going to see. She turned the key in the lock and opened the door. The person she expected stood some way off, watching from the other side of the stone wall, and after seeing her charge safely delivered, she melted into a patch of trees.

Penny turned her attention to the person in front of her.

"So, Lane. Dilys brought you. Good. You'd better come in." She stood to one side to allow him to enter her kitchen. "Do you want a coffee or tea?"

"Have you got a latte?"

"No, sorry, just regular coffee. But it's pretty good."

"All right." And then, remembering his manners, he added, "Thank you."

Penny put the kettle on while Lane watched her, arms hanging loosely at his sides.

"Dilys brought me," he said. "I didn't know where you live. I couldn't have found my own way here. I've never been to your house before."

"No, Lane, you haven't," said Penny. "Now, then. Would you be more comfortable here in the kitchen"—she gestured to a small table with two chairs—"or would you prefer the sitting room?"

"I don't know," Lane replied. "I've never seen your sitting room, so how could I know where I want to sit?"

"I see your point. Why don't you take a look around and then decide where you'd be more comfortable?"

Lane peered into the sitting room, his eyes roving over its pastel shades and soft, plump furniture. He then pointed to the table. "I'd like to sit here. It's more like the café. Without the latte."

Penny handed him a clean towel and gestured to the sink.

"Maybe you'd like to wash your hands before you have your coffee." While he did that, she took a few chocolate digestives out of a biscuit tin and arranged them on a plate.

"Will that do you?" Penny asked, "Or would you like something more substantial? I could do you scrambled eggs and toast."

"A piece of toast would be grand, please. With jam. I like jam."

"I've only got marmalade. Will that do?"

"Suppose so."

Penny dropped a couple of slices of brown bread into the toaster, poured hot water on the coffee, and suggested Lane sit down. She brought everything to the table and waited until he'd smothered his toast with butter and Florence's homemade marmalade before she eased into the reason for his being there.

"So Dilys brought you?"

Lane nodded. "She said you wanted to talk to me."

"That's right. I do. And Bethan Morgan, the police officer you met before, she'll want to talk to you, too. Would it be all right with you if I rang her and let her know you're here with me so she can come round and talk to you?" Lane's eyes shifted toward the back door, as if he were reassuring himself an escape route was available to him, if he needed it. He cut his toast into four and looked at his fingers. Penny handed him a paper napkin. "And there's your mother," Penny continued. "We'd better let her know you're here, don't you think? She'll be worried about you."

"Yeah, could do," said Lane with a nonchalant shrug. "I'm not bothered." He frowned. "But as for the police lady. Couldn't you just ask me the questions? I don't want to talk to her right now."

"Maybe I could ask the questions and she could listen to your answers," said Penny, knowing that was highly unorthodox, but as long as Bethan got the answers she needed, and if it was the only way to get Lane to talk, she'd probably go along with it. But Lane shook his head.

"Okay," said Penny. "Well, what I really want to know is why you didn't serve the coffee at the dinner. We were all very surprised and disappointed when you weren't there. You love coffee, and you would have done such a great job setting up your very own coffee station and serving the guests."

Lane reacted to this praise with a broad, open grin.

"Maybe you'd like to pour the coffee now."

Lane picked up the *cafetière*, and when he'd finished filling their mugs, Penny continued, "So what happened? Why did you leave the dinner party?"

Lane did not reply, so Penny pressed him. "Did something happen, Lane? Did you see something? Or maybe you heard something that frightened you?" She added a splash of milk to her coffee and waited for him to reply. His eyes shifted again to the back door.

"I can't tell anyone," he said in a low voice. "They made me promise not to tell. They said if I told anyone, I could get hurt."

Penny's heart beat faster. "Promise not to tell what, Lane?" When he didn't reply, Penny took a sip of coffee, her mind racing, knowing that what she said next could determine whether Lane would open up to her or not. But she had to ask, and she had to phrase her questions delicately so she didn't alarm him, or put words in his mouth.

She relaxed her shoulders and gave him what she hoped was a reassuring smile. "No one's going to hurt you, Lane. You did the right thing coming to see me, and now that you're here, it would be really good if you could tell me what happened. When you say 'they,' who do mean? Who made you promise not to tell?"

Lane's eyes darted around the room.

"I don't know who they were. I'd never seen them before."

"Okay. And what did they make you promise not to tell? Was it something you saw? Is that it? You saw something?" Lane frowned while he thought this over, and then shook his head slightly.

"All right. I'll take that to mean you didn't see something. But maybe you saw someone? Maybe you saw someone in the hall who wasn't supposed to be there? Someone who surprised you? Someone who spoke to you?"

Lane scrubbed his eyes with balled fists but said nothing.

"So let's just for a moment say that's what happened. You saw someone. This person, was he a guest at the dinner party?"

Lane shrugged.

"You don't know. Well, was he dressed like the people at the party? Was he wearing good clothes? You know, like a nice suit?"

Lane's eyes narrowed, and Penny took that as a no. But

then, it was highly unlikely that a dinner guest would have been involved, as Emyr had said that none of the diners had left the room. One of the waitstaff, then. Rhodri, perhaps?

Lane drained the last of his coffee, set the mug down, and stood up.

"I'm tired and I want to go home now. My mother will probably be worried about me."

"Yes, she will. Look, I think it would be best if I ring her and let her know you're here, and she can come and pick you up." Now that she knew Lane was safe, Penny wanted to keep him that way. She didn't like the idea of his walking into town on his own. "The thing is, you've already had a long walk, all the way here from Dilys's. I know it doesn't seem far when you're in a car, but when you walk, well, it's quite a way. And I doubt Dilys's spare bed is very comfortable. You probably didn't get much sleep last night."

"I didn't."

"And then there's her awful tea."

Lane managed a sloppy grin.

"Right, well, I'll ring your mum and she'll be here in no time, and then you can go home and have a nice bath and sleep in your own bed tonight. What do you think of that?"

"That would be grand."

"But look, Lane, it would be really helpful if you could try to remember everything you saw and heard at the dinner party last night, and when you're ready, if you can tell me something, anything, it could be important, and that little bit of information you give us could be exactly what we need to help the police find out what happened to Rhodri Phillips." Lane's body stiffened as she said the word "police," so she corrected herself. "You might be able to help us find out what happened to Rhodri." When Lane sat back in his chair, she added, "Did you know that something very bad happened last night? One of the waiters died." He nodded slowly. "Maybe Dilys told you." His body shifted and his eyes drifted once more to the door. Penny realised he was coming to the end of what he could tolerate, but she ventured one last question. "Did you know Rhodri Phillips, by the way? He was a bit older than you, but your paths might have crossed."

"No, I haven't heard of him."

"Well, if you do want to talk about what happened last night, you come and see me, okay? Sometimes we remember things later."

"I did remember something. I didn't drop the tray."

"What do you mean?"

"The tray that spilled on the floor. I didn't drop it."

"Okay. Then how do you think it landed on the floor?"

"He knocked it out of my hands."

* * *

When Lane had left with his mother, Penny rang Inspector Bethan Morgan to let her know that he was safe and on his way home. When Bethan asked if he had said anything that might be useful in the investigation of either the theft of the Black Chair or the death of Rhodri Phillips, Penny hesitated before replying, "He wasn't very clear, but he saw someone or something and said they threatened to hurt him if he told anyone. He used the word 'they.' And then he said 'he' knocked the tray out of his hands, that he didn't drop it. But he wouldn't tell me who spoke to him and threatened him.

"He's scared," she added. "Give him a day or two, and he might be ready to open up, but I think it's really important that you talk to him soon."

When the call ended, Penny lowered her phone and remained standing, gazing out her front window at the black branches of the apple tree. She thought about the theft of the chair and the death of Rhodri Phillips. Were they connected? The simplest answer, which was always the best, was yes, they were.

Had Lane seen something? The chair being carried out of the library? Who had spoken to him? Was it the person who had organized the theft of the chair, or the person who had actually stolen it? And were they one and the same person, or two people?

The theft could have been planned by one person, she reasoned, but must have been carried out by at least two people, because more than one person would have been required to lift that chair. And it had been removed quickly and quietly, without attracting any attention, so other people would have been needed to act as lookouts and open doors. The thieves had used the bustle and confusion, the coming and going of the dinner party, as the perfect cover to move through the house. The guests were neatly out of the way—first in the sitting room and then the dining room—and the staff in the kitchen were so preoccupied with their work that they wouldn't have taken any notice of extra people in the house as long as they looked like they belonged to the group working on the dinner party. Waiters, maybe, or tradesmen, perhaps.

Tradesmen? She remembered the white van in the car park, and when she'd asked Gwennie if Heather was still at the Hall putting last-minute touches on the floral arrangements, Gwennie had replied that Heather was long gone and the van probably belonged to the wine merchants making a last-minute delivery. But what if it hadn't? What if it belonged to the thieves? What was it Gwennie had said? That the wine merchants had made an unexpected delivery of a complimentary case of champagne. Had they used that as a ruse to enter the house?

And the critical thing was, how had the thieves known where the chair would be? And then she realised that someone familiar with the layout of the house must have been involved in the planning.

She opened the dinner party file folder and pulled out the guest list. She went through the list of names, asking herself if each person could have been involved in the theft of the Black Chair.

Mrs. Lloyd? Don't make me laugh.

The Reverend Thomas Evans? Absolutely not.

His wife, Bronwyn Evans? No way.

The mayor? Never in a million years. He wants to get reelected!

The mayor's wife? Of course not. She loves that role.

Emyr Gruffydd? What possible reason could he have to steal from himself, as it were? If he wanted to steal the chair, he'd have found a much simpler way to do it.

After working her way through the rest of the names on the guest list, pausing to consider what she knew about each person, she couldn't imagine any of them being involved in some way with the theft of the chair. She was left with just one name that gave her pause: Jennifer Sayles, Emyr's new girlfriend. And it wasn't that she thought Jennifer might have had something to do with the theft; Penny just didn't know her well enough to exclude her as she had the others.

The whole evening—the guests, the staff, who was where and when—was becoming a big blur. I have to bring some order to this, she thought, and I can start by trying to work out when the theft of the chair occurred.

Chapter Twelve

She opened the downstairs cupboard and, rummaging past winter coats and boots, reached to the back and pulled out a whiteboard.

She propped it up on a chair in the sitting room, closed the curtains, and began to write.

She started at 6:30, when she and Victoria had entered the library and admired the Black Chair. Then, at 6:50, when Mrs. Lloyd had arrived about ten minutes early, she and Victoria had redraped the chair in its black shroud. And to the best of her knowledge, that was the last time anyone in the house had seen it—except, of course, the thieves. Two and a half hours later, about 9:30 or so, after the short concert in the sitting room while they'd had coffee and dessert, the guests had trooped into the library to view the chair. But when Emyr removed its protective cloth, the Black Chair had been replaced. So what had happened during the two and a half hours between when the chair was known to be there and the discovery that it was missing?

She scribbled some more, then stepped back to examine her timeline.

At approximately 7:45 P.M., the guests crossed the downstairs hall to progress from the sitting room to the dining room, and about five minutes after that, when they were seated, the door separating the dining room from the hall was closed. About ten minutes after that, Lane came down the corridor and entered the sitting room to clear away the remains of canapés and drinks. He took his time, stopping to examine Victoria's harp. About 8:10 or 8:15, he dropped the tray in the corridor. And that was when he met the person or persons who threatened him.

By 8:20, the starter course was over, and the dining room table was cleared. A few minutes later, just before service of the main course was about to begin, Gwennie realised that Rhodri was missing.

So the window of opportunity for the theft of the chair—assuming it was related to the death of Rhodri Phillips—must have been between, say, eight ten, when someone spoke to Lane in the corridor, and 8:30, when Rhodri was missing. Penny circled the times, then replaced the cap on the marker and set it in on its ledge. She went to the kitchen, poured herself a glass of wine, and returned to the sitting room, where she contemplated the whiteboard while she ran through all the events of the evening in her mind, picturing every situation and replaying conversations.

Chapter Thirteen

"What do you know about Jennifer Sayles?" Penny asked Victoria the next morning.

"Jennifer Sayles?" Victoria pushed the start button on the coffee brewer.

"Yes, Jennifer Sayles. Emyr's new girlfriend."

"I don't know anything about her. Is there something I should know about her?"

"I'm not sure. I was trying to place her, and then I remembered that she was a friend of Meg Wynn Thompson, Emyr's fiancée. One of her bridesmaids, in fact. Other than that, I don't know anything about her. I've been thinking about all the guests who were at the dinner, and we know the others so well, I can't imagine that any of them could have had any part in the robbery. I mean, Mrs. Lloyd? Thomas and Bronwyn? Hardly. And as for the rest, they're just honest, hardworking townsfolk, and Bethan will probably eliminate every one of them pretty quickly. They wouldn't have the resources, and I don't think they'd have the desire to pull off something like this."

"So are you saying Jennifer Sayles might have?"

"No, not saying that at all. It's just that we don't know enough about her to be certain she didn't."

Victoria picked up her plain white coffee mug, looked at it, and thought for a moment. "Didn't Mrs. Lloyd say she works in PR in London?" Penny nodded. "We might want to think about getting our own branded coffee mugs. And we've been talking about the need to create more awareness of the other services we offer, like massages and facials."

"Oh," said Penny, "you mean like we could have a PR campaign?"

"Exactly," said Victoria, taking a sip of her coffee and peering at Penny over the top of her mug. "A small campaign, of course, but it might be worth our while to invest a few thousand pounds into it."

"And don't forget the hand cream," said Penny. "It's amazing, and everyone who uses it loves it. We could do so much more to promote that."

"So why don't we see what Jennifer can come up with?" suggested Victoria. "Although I'm sure she's used to huge budgets and campaigns, so she might be way out of our league."

"We can ask," Penny replied. "I was going to Google her this morning, anyway. The only thing is, if she and Emyr have broken up, as we thought yesterday they might have, he probably wouldn't want her coming back to Llanelen to work with us."

"That's for her to decide," said Victoria. "If she doesn't want to, that's fine, and if there are problems, they can work it out between themselves. This is purely business."

"Of course it is," said Penny. "Purely business."

"Right," said Victoria. "Speaking of business, got your keys? We open in ten minutes, and you're on the front desk this morning. See you later. Good luck."

Penny brewed herself a cup of coffee and carried it back to her office. The cumbersome desktop computers that she, Victoria, and the receptionist had used for a couple of years had been replaced by sleek laptops. She opened hers, entered her password, and typed JENNIFER SAYLES in the search bar.

She scanned the list that came up and then chose a link to JSPR, a boutique PR company in London. She clicked on the link, and up came a photo of Jennifer Sayles in full hair and makeup, including bright-red lipstick, wearing a tailored black jacket over a crisp white shirt with the top buttons undone. Her hands rested on her hips in a confident, open stance. Penny reviewed the list of services offered and the client list, then turned to the biography of the owner of the firm, Jennifer Sayles. At the end of a long list of professional accomplishments and a brief description of her education (University of Manchester), Penny reached the end of the entry—a one-sentence note on her family: JESSICA SAYLES IS THE YOUNGER DAUGHTER OF SIR ANTHONY SAYLES AND HIS LATE WIFE, CYNTHIA (NEE RICHMOND). Penny clicked on the link that displayed the JSPR client list and noted an impressive list of lifestyle, food, and fashion brands. So the Llanelen Spa was in the right area, but hardly in that league, and Penny would have felt ridiculous asking Jennifer to consider taking them on as a client. So much for that idea.

She was about to Google Sir Anthony Sayles to see if she could learn more about Jennifer's background when she realised with a flash of panic that she'd been on the Internet too long. She checked her watch. It was past time to open. She should have been at the front desk five minutes ago. She closed her laptop, grabbed her keys, and dashed down the hall to the reception area. She unlocked the front door and had barely made it behind the reception desk when the door opened and in walked Mrs. Lloyd.

"Oh, Penny," she said, slightly out of breath. "I've just popped in hoping for a quick word." She glanced around the empty reception area. "I wondered if there's any news since yesterday."

"News?"

"About what happened on Saturday night at the Hall. My goodness, surely you can't have forgotten."

"No, no. Of course not. It's just that I wasn't with you for a moment there." Before Mrs. Lloyd could reply, the door opened again and the first client of the day entered.

"Oh, good morning," said Penny. "You're here for your appointment with . . ." She glanced at Rhian's computer, which she hadn't had time to switch on. Mrs. Lloyd, looking annoyed at having her conversation interrupted, stood slightly to one side as the client unbuttoned her coat and took off her scarf. Seeing her grey roots, Penny took a chance and asked, "Is it Alberto you're seeing? Getting your hair done, are you?"

The woman nodded. "Rhian not in today?"

Penny was about to shoot Mrs. Lloyd a look warning her

not to say anything but then thought that Mrs. Lloyd might not be aware yet that the waiter who had died Saturday night was Rhian's nephew. "No, she's taking a few days off," said Penny.

"Oh, she's not ill, I hope," said the customer.

"Oh, no, nothing like that." Penny switched on Rhian's laptop, and then remembered she didn't have the password to sign in. "She's just taking some personal time. Now, if you'd like to just go on down the hall to Alberto's salon, he'll be waiting for you." And then Penny realised she hadn't printed out the appointment lists for the day, so Alberto would have no idea whom to expect, and neither would Eirlys in the manicure studio or the skin care specialist or the masseuse. "On second thought," Penny said to the client, "I'll walk with you down to the hair studio and let Alberto know you're here." She turned to Mrs. Lloyd, who was hovering over the magazines. "I'll be back, but I may be a few minutes."

"No, you're all right, Penny," said Mrs. Lloyd. "This is your workplace, and I can see you're busy. I'm sure you'll be in touch if you hear anything. I'd best be on my way."

At that moment, the door opened and Eirlys entered, ready for her day's work in the manicure studio. She looked at the desk where Rhian should have been and raised an eyebrow.

"Just stay there, please, Eirlys, and if you can, start up Rhian's computer," Penny said. "I think you know her password. I'll be right back." Mrs. Lloyd listened to the exchange, looked from Penny to Eirlys, and then, her hand on the door, hesitated, as if changing her mind about leaving. But a moment later she pushed it open and disappeared into what promised to be a blustery day.

"I'm sorry we haven't had a chance to notify you," Penny said to Eirlys when she returned to the receptionist's desk after delivering Alberto's client. Eirlys looked up from the computer.

"I guess you haven't printed off the work lists for today," she said.

"No, I haven't. Would you mind doing that?"

"I'll just switch on the printer." She reached under the desk and then straightened up. "It takes a minute to warm up."

"Eirlys, look, something's happened. Rhian needs a few days off, so you'll be on the reception desk a bit more than usual. Victoria and I will be filling in as well."

"Or you could get a temp in," said Eirlys.

"Well, yes, if we have to, we will. But listen, just so you know . . ." Penny briefly explained the circumstances under which Rhian's nephew had died on Saturday night.

"Oh, not Rhodri," exclaimed Eirlys.

"It sounds as if you knew Rhodri. Was he a friend of yours?"

"I wouldn't call him a friend, exactly. He came here one evening a few months ago to drop something off for Rhian, and I was just leaving and she introduced us. We went out a couple of times. He was a nice enough bloke, but he just wasn't my type, if you know what I mean."

"No, I don't know what you mean." When Eirlys didn't reply, Penny prompted her. "Was he gay, or did you think he was?"

"No, it wasn't that. Definitely wasn't that." Eirlys let out a wheezy little laugh. "It was really more the people he hung out with. I didn't feel comfortable with them. In fact, I didn't like them at all."

"What were they like?"

"Rough."

"Rough?"

"His mates, they . . . it seemed to me they . . . I don't know, exactly, but it's almost like they had some kind of hold over him. He seemed a little afraid of them, to be honest. There was something about them that seemed . . ." She struggled to find the right word and then came up with "menacing." Penny leaned forward to encourage her to continue, but the door opened behind her, and as Eirlys peered around her to see who was coming in, Penny shifted to one side and turned her head to see who it was.

"Only me!" Mrs. Lloyd called out in a cheery voice. "Sorry to bother you again, but I seem to have misplaced my gloves. I realised I didn't have them when I was leaving the bank, so I wondered if I might have left them . . ." She scanned the reception area and spotting them on the magazine table, picked them up, arranged them palms together, and held them in her left hand. At this moment the printer chugged into action and spat out several sheets of paper.

"The appointment lists for today." Eirlys glanced at the documents before handing them to Penny. "Hair is full, but we're light in the manicure studio. Do you want me to take the appointments, or would you prefer that I stay here?"

"You stay there. Probably best if I do the manicures and you manage this desk. You're much better with booking appointments than I am. Sometimes I put people in for the wrong day and it causes all kinds of problems. And you're brilliant at greeting customers." She turned to Mrs. Lloyd. "Isn't she?"

"Yes," said Mrs. Lloyd, bestowing a warm smile on Eirlys. "She certainly is. You're very lucky to have her."

"I've got to get back to work, now, Mrs. Lloyd," Penny said, holding up the client lists. "We're short-staffed, as you know, with Rhian away, and opening today hasn't gone very well, but we'll be fine now that Eirlys is here. But before you go, there's something I need to tell you." Just then the telephone rang, and when Eirlys picked it up, Penny and Mrs. Lloyd stepped away from the desk.

"I hoped there might be," said Mrs. Lloyd eagerly, her blue eyes crinkling with anticipation.

"I'm not sure if the police have released the name of the victim yet, but his family has been informed, and you know it anyway from Saturday night, but what you might not know is that Rhodri Phillips was our Rhian's nephew."

"Oh, I see," said Mrs. Lloyd in a low voice. "That's why she's taking some time off. Yes, of course. That makes sense. But the thing is, do we know yet how he died?"

"No. But it's only Monday. The earliest the postmortem would likely have been scheduled is today, so we might know more soon. And I'm sure the police are working every line of inquiry, interviewing everybody, examining every avenue open to them."

"Oh, I've no doubt about that," replied Mrs. Lloyd. "They haven't contacted me yet, though, to interview me or take my statement. I assume they will. Right, well, you've got a busy day ahead of you, and I must get on with my errands, so I'll leave you to it."

But Penny's day wasn't particularly busy, giving her lots of time to mull over the events of Saturday night and Sunday. It would soon be forty-eight hours since the chair had been stolen, and she wondered if it was even still in the country.

When the last well-coiffed, manicured, and massaged clients had departed, followed by the staff, Victoria and Penny walked through the empty rooms, checking that the work stations were clean and tidy for the next morning.

"Feel like coming upstairs for a glass of wine?" Victoria asked.

"No, not tonight, thanks just the same. I'm going to see Jimmy. I haven't been for about a week and a half, and he'll want to hear all about the theft of the chair."

"He'll probably have some interesting thoughts on that," said Victoria.

"I'm counting on it."

Chapter Fourteen

Bundled up against the mid-November night with a cheerful red-and-black-checked scarf looped around her neck and her hands kept warm in the handmade black knitted mittens Victoria had given her for Christmas last year, Penny breathed in the fresh, cold air. She was happy to be on her way. Her short journey would take her along the bank of the River Conwy to the nursing home, where her friend Jimmy Hill had lived for several years.

The familiar smell of disinfectant and old age that greeted her as she entered the building no longer bothered her as it once had. Penny returned the receptionist's greeting and made her way to the residents' lounge at the rear of the building.

She found Jimmy in his wheelchair chatting with another resident. "This is Mrs. Lynch," Jimmy said. "She's a new girl. Only been here about a week or so." Mrs. Lynch's violet-blue eyes twinkled in a friendly, interested way, and her hair, framing her surprisingly unlined face in soft white waves, looked freshly washed and set. Penny's attention drifted momentarily while she wondered about Mrs. Lynch's skin care regime.

"Jimmy's been telling me all about you, so he has," Mrs. Lynch said in a soft Irish accent. "Thinks the world of you," she added. To Penny's ears, she pronounced "thinks" to sound like "tinks."

"Well, I'm very fond of him, too," Penny replied. "We've been pals for a long time."

"Well, Jimmy, I'm sure you'll be wanting some time alone with your visitor, so I'll be off now," said Mrs. Lynch.

"I'll join you for a cup of cocoa later, maybe," said Jimmy.

"Aye, that would be grand," she replied, beaming at him. And then grasping her stick and leaning on it, she rose heavily to her feet. "It doesn't get any easier," she said, "this old age thing. My legs feel like they're made of lead today. I can barely lift them." And then, with a final nod at Jimmy, she plodded across the room, one slow step at a time, her beige stockings pooling around her ankles, in the direction of a small group of women clustered together on the other side of the room. Rather than joining them, however, she sat a little way off by herself and took out her phone.

Jimmy turned a pair of faded, watery blue eyes to Penny and held out his hand. "She's always on that phone," he remarked. "I don't see what's so smart about it. You can't have a decent conversation with her. Always being interrupted by that phone beeping."

"Grandchildren, perhaps," said Penny.

"Maybe," said Jimmy, "Anyway, what's the craic, as Mrs. Lynch would say?"

"I wondered if you'd heard," said Penny. "Theft up at the Hall on Saturday night." Jimmy's eyebrows shot up. He'd had a long career as a petty thief in the North Wales area, with occasional forays as far as Liverpool. A slow smile spread across his face as he took off his glasses, gave them a wipe on his shirt, and settled into his chair.

"No, I haven't heard. Tell me about it. Every last detail. Don't leave anything out."

"I'll start by saying the robbery was clever and seemed well planned. And the timing was no coincidence."

"At the Hall, you said. So, posh. Jewellery, was it? I remember that time Lady What's-Her-Name's tiara was stolen from a country house. It was a sensation. Front-page news for days. The tiara was never seen again, of course. Would have been taken to London or Amsterdam within a day or two and broken up and the diamonds sold. The police were so desperate to recover it, they even put the word out appealing to folks in my line of work to let them know if we heard anything. Of course we never did, and if we had, whether we'd have shared that information with the rozzers, who never did much for us, is another story."

"Well, at least the artefact stolen from the Hall won't be broken up. At least I don't think it would be. I certainly hope not."

"What are we talking about? What was taken?"

"The Black Chair."

"I'm not with you." Because Jimmy was English, not Welsh, he did not know the history of the Black Chair. When Penny finished describing how the chair had been awarded posthumously to the poet Hedd Wyn at the 1917 Birkenhead Eisteddfod, the cultural significance of the chair to the Welsh people, and how it had come to be at the Hall on its way back from refurbishment, he let out a long, low groan, mixed with a resigned sigh.

"Oh, no," said Penny. "That doesn't sound good."

"No," said Jimmy. "It isn't. It could have been taken to be held for ransom, or even to raise money for terrorists, but I think it was most likely stolen to order for a private collector."

"Why do you think that?"

"You could never sell something like that, even on the black market. Way too hot. And the market for it, just as a chair, would be small. Not worth the effort on that account. No, its value lies in its history, its association. The story behind it, if you like. It's not like Lady What's-Her-Name's tiara."

In response to Penny's puzzled frown, he continued, "Well, they're diamonds, aren't they? They have value in their own right, just because they're, well, diamonds. And if there's a historical association with them, all the better."

"So what do you think is happening to the chair right now?"

"Every antiques expert in the country will have been made aware of the theft and asked to be on the lookout for it. There could even be a global watch on it. Art and antiquities is the third-most profitable criminal enterprise in the world, behind drugs and arms dealing. Very unsavoury people, let me tell you. And here's what the black market in looted antiquities looks like. They disappear, smuggled out of the source country, and then, eventually, miraculously reappear, sometimes many years later, in the market country. By then, of course, they've acquired a bunch of phony papers designed to make it look like they've got a legitimate provenance. And they pass through a lot of hands before they reach their new owners, who are willing to pay a lot of money for them. And these new owners aren't fussy about how the antiquities were obtained or how much they cost. But that won't be the case for something as well known and documented as this chair.

"No, I'd wager that this particular chair was stolen to order for a private collector."

"But if that's the case, it may turn up eventually," said Penny. "That's happened with art plundered by the Nazis, which is gradually being recovered, and some is even being returned to its rightful owners, the families that owned it before the war."

"True. But that's taken over seventy years."

"We can't wait that long. We've got to get it back, because it's part of an exhibit that the Prince of Wales is coming to open in about three weeks." They sat for a moment in a defeated silence, and then Penny said, "How do you think the thieves pulled it off? Will the next words I hear be 'inside job'?"

"Inside job."

"How inside are we talking?"

"Deep inside. First, someone had to know the chair was going to be at the Hall. Then, they had to know exactly whereabouts in the Hall it was going to be. You can't have thieves wandering around asking staff, 'Excuse me, we're here to nick the Black Chair; can you tell us where we might find it?' and third, there's the access issue. In the event the back door was locked, you need someone to open it, or better yet, to make for easier timing, make sure it will be left unlocked. And in this case, because the item being stolen is substantial in size—unlike, say, Lady What's-Her-Name's tiara—there has to be enough people actually inside the building to carry it out quietly, and without damaging it. This is important. Someone was willing to pay a lot of money to have a lot of people go to a lot of trouble, and they wouldn't have coughed up all that money unless they were sure they were going to get what they were after, and in perfect condition. They wouldn't settle for damaged goods."

Penny clasped her hands together and leaned forward. "Okay. That's a lot of information for me to process. Let's take all this one step at a time. You said someone had to know the chair was going to be at the Hall. Who had to know? Who is that someone?"

"It could be one of two people. Either the person who wanted the chair knew it would be there and arranged to have it stolen, or that person asked someone else to arrange for it to be stolen. Are you with me? Or the theft started at the other end, with the person who arranged for it to be stolen knowing it would be there, and he had a buyer, or figured he could find someone who would want to buy it once he had it in his possession, so the theft started with him. Lots of ways it could happen."

"Let's come back to the second person, the person who knew it was going to be there and thought he could find a buyer after he'd stolen it. Now, as far as I know, there was nothing in the papers or any publicity about the chair going to be there."

"I should hope not."

"So let's think about who might have known that the chair would be at Ty Brith Hall that night."

"Did the people at the dinner party know they were going to see it?"

"Yes," said Penny, starting to understand what Jimmy was getting at. "I'm afraid they did."

"Well, that's all it would take. Remember during the war there were those posters 'Loose lips sink ships'? A guest could have mentioned to a friend that the Black Chair was going to be there, and that friend told another friend, and so on. Word gets around, and really quickly, too."

Penny's heart sank. Mrs. Lloyd. From the moment she heard the Black Chair was going to be on view, she would have told anyone and everyone about the dinner. "And knowing which room in the Hall where the chair was?"

"Easy. Someone on the inside just has to find out where it is and then text someone in the gang, preferably well before the event to make planning easier, but if needs be, even while the gang is waiting outside to go in and get it."

"So a waiter, maybe?"

Jimmy nodded. "Someone like that. A waiter would be good cover." Penny remembered Gwennie having to tell a waiter to switch off his phone. Of course, he could have been texting anyone, letting his girlfriend know what time he expected to finish, say, but still . . .

"Let's talk about what kind of collector would be interested in an artefact like the Black Chair," said Penny. "Someone with a keen interest in the First World War, or twentieth-century Welsh literature, maybe."

"Someone with deep pockets. Operations like this don't come cheap."

"And do you think the Black Chair is still in the country?"

Jimmy inhaled sharply. "Hard to say. No, make that impossible to say. But it could be. There's a chance that it is, because of its size. It would be difficult to smuggle across a border because of its size, unless it could be taken apart. And it would need extensive paperwork that it may not have. I hope it is still in the country, because the chance of recovering it is much greater if it's still here in the U.K."

After a moment, he added, "But there is something else that might happen to it. The worst-case scenario."

"Oh, no."

"Yes. It could be destroyed."

"Destroyed?"

"You see, while the collectors place a high value on the work and are desperate to own it, the people who are hired to steal artwork or artefacts, they don't actually give a toss about it. They don't care about beauty, or cultural or historical value.

They aren't bothered about whether or not it's exposed to the wrong temperatures or high humidity. To them, it's just an object and the only value it has is what they can get for it. And if things get too hot, if the police are getting close, for example, before they can deliver it to the new owner, they have no problem getting rid of it so they don't get caught with it."

"Getting rid of it. You mean . . ."

"Your chair could end up at the bottom of a lake. Or cut up for firewood."

Penny groaned. "Oh, God, I hope not. I can't bear to think of something awful like that happening to it."

"I know you're always interested in crime, but you seem to be taking a special interest in this. Why is that?"

"Two reasons. First, because I was the one looking after the dinner party. Emyr asked me to organize it."

"So you feel you're somehow responsible for this, because it happened on your watch?"

Penny lowered her eyes and mumbled, "Something like that."

"Well, let me disabuse of you that notion, my dear. This heist was weeks in the planning, and there's nothing you or anyone else could have done to prevent it. The house would have been thoroughly checked out in advance. They would have been familiar with the routine of everyone in the house, and known the location of every motion-sensitive light, every security camera . . ."

"There weren't any," said Penny.

"You must be joking," said Jimmy. "In this day and age?

I'm really shocked. So making off with that chair was taking candy from a baby. Well, there you go. Once the thieves knew there was no security, there would have been no deterrent, no reason for them not to go ahead. So as for you thinking you could have done something to prevent the theft, I rest my case."

"Emyr's having security lights and cameras installed this week, or so I understand."

"Horse. Barn door," scoffed Jimmy. "You'd think he would have known better, a beautiful house like that. But nevertheless, the police will be doing everything they can to recover it. They'll pull out all the stops for a national treasure."

"Well, the thing is, there's more to the story. I haven't got to the worst bit yet. A young man who was working as a waiter at the event died, but I don't have all the details yet." Penny described how she had found Rhodri Phillips, barely clinging to life, behind the house. "Sadly, he died even before they could get him to hospital, and it turned out that he's the nephew of our receptionist at the Spa. The family's terribly upset, as you can imagine."

"Oh, of course they would be. I'm so sorry to hear this."

"So you see, the two crimes seem to be connected—the robbery, and the death of Rhodri Phillips. At least they happened at the same place, at the same time. I'm convinced that finding the chair will lead us to the murderer. But Emyr's afraid that the murder will get more attention from the police. You know how they're always going on about how limited their resources are."

Jimmy smiled. "I wish they'd been a bit more limited in my day. The police always seemed to have plenty of time and all the resources they needed back then, at least as far as me and my mates were concerned."

"Look at you now. As respectable as they come. And they say leopards don't change their spots." She stirred in her chair. "It's getting late and I haven't had my dinner yet, and I need to get home to feed Harrison. He doesn't like when I'm late. Doesn't speak to me for the rest of the evening."

She reached over and kissed Jimmy on his papery cheek. As her lips grazed his skin, he reached up and clung to her arm.

"Come and see me again soon," he said. "Keep me informed. Let me know if there's anything I can do to help."

"I'm surprised the police haven't been round to talk to you."

"The police? Talk to me? Why would the police want to talk to me? They know what they're doing. They don't need any help from an old codger like me. What use am I to anyone stuck in here? I didn't see anything. I don't know anything."

"Oh, yes, you do. You're a wonderful local resource. I've learned a lot, and the police might, too, if they took the time to talk to you. And I'm sure you'd love helping the police with their enquiries."

Jimmy grinned.

"And yes, I will come and see you soon. As soon as I learn more." She buttoned up her coat and wrapped the scarf around her neck. "Well, enjoy your cocoa with Mrs. Lynch. It seems you've got a new lady friend every time I come to see you."

"That's because there's a high turnover in here, Penny. No one stays very long."

Penny had stayed longer at the nursing home than she'd planned to, and the reception desk was unattended when she left. She paused at the visitors' book to sign out but discovered she'd forgotten to sign in, so she completed both entries. As she was about to set off for home, she realised how hungry she was. She thought about what she had at home to eat, and knowing her fridge was practically empty, and since the Co-op wasn't much out of her way, she decided to pop in and pick up a few fruits and vegetables and perhaps a piece of salmon so she could prepare a decent dinner.

She entered the welcome warmth of the supermarket and strolled up and down the aisles, filling her basket, and was soon on her way. But instead of taking the usual way home, along the river, the detour to the supermarket meant she'd have to take the slightly longer route through the town. Carrying a reusable cloth tote bag in each hand, she set off at a brisk pace, passing darkened shops, some closed for the night and a few boarded up with TO LET signs. While she'd been in the supermarket, it had started to rain, and now, with both hands full, she'd have to set the bags down on the wet, dirty pavement to put up her hood. She chose to make the best of it, to just keep walking and get home as quickly as she could.

Although she was used to it by now, when she'd started living in Llanelen she'd been surprised by how quickly town turned into country. The houses just came to an abrupt stop and fields took over. There was the last house and beside it, a field. Soon the pavement below her feet disappeared, replaced by a well-trodden dirt path that ran along the roadside. Streetlights, spaced further apart here than they had been a few minutes earlier, were the only source of light. Droplets of rain slanted in their arcs of yellow light, making a light, swooshing sound. Black tree branches waving at the side of the road cast shadows, which Penny's active imagination saw as figures dancing.

She picked up the pace, hearing and seeing no one, until she reached the fields close to her home. Normally, they were empty except for grazing sheep that came and went with the seasons, and in late summer they were filled with the sights, sounds, and smells of the annual agricultural show. The fields had been empty when she'd passed by on her walk to work this morning, but now they were buzzing with activity.

In the jerry-rigged lighting that had been erected at the far end of the field, she could make out camper vans, trucks, cars, and caravans, some distance away from the road, filling the fields. Dogs barked, and men called out to each other.

She slowed down long enough to take it all in, then hurried the rest of the way home, and a few minutes later let herself into her cottage.

She set down the rain-soaked bags and took off her wet boots, leaving them to one side to dry. She shrugged out of her coat, glistening with rainwater, and ran her fingers over her damp hair to see if it was wet enough to need a toweling. Deciding it would dry quickly enough, she ducked into the sitting room, switched on a couple of lamps, and drew the curtains against the darkness outside. She leaned over to pat Harrison curled up on the end of the sofa and switched on the gas fire. The fire sprang to life, and with the closed curtains and the soft warmth of the lamps, the room became instantly cozy and comforting.

She picked up the shopping bags and carried them along with her wet coat into the kitchen. After draping the coat over the back of a chair to dry, she switched on the radio to listen to the news, set the oven to preheat, and began unpacking the shopping. As she placed the salmon and broccoli on the work top, a beep from her coat pocket signalled an incoming text.

LOCK YOUR DOORS.

Chapter Fifteen

A cold shudder ran through her as a surge of adrenaline propelled her across the kitchen floor to the back door. The key was in the lock, and it was in the right position, but she tried the door handle anyway. The door was locked. With a pounding heart, she checked the text again for the phone number, but it wasn't one she recognized. Was she being watched? Stalked?

Although she was quite sure she must have locked the front door behind her when she came in, she couldn't remember doing it, so she raced through the sitting room. Just as she placed her hand on the key, she was startled by a knock. She hadn't heard a car approach, but then she'd been rattling about in the kitchen and listening to the radio. She crept to the front window and gently pulled back the curtain. Through the sodden darkness, and with the glow from the lamps in the sitting room behind her, she could just make out the outline of a car she didn't recognize.

The knocking came again. She returned to the door, and

with her mouth so dry she could barely speak, she forced out two words. "Who's there?" she croaked.

"Gareth."

She flung the door open. "Bloody hell! What are you playing at?"

The former Det. Chief Inspector Gareth Davies, now retired, stood on her front step, rain pouring down behind him.

"I'm sorry I didn't ring to let you know I was coming over. I was going to, and then . . ."

"The text? Was it from you?"

"Yes."

"It frightened me half to death. What did you mean by it?"

"Look, would it be all right if I came in out of the rain for a moment, and I'll explain."

"Yes, of course," Penny said.

At one time it had looked like a fine romance was in the offing between her and DCI Davies, as he'd been then. But although he could claim her affection and respect, that essential spark needed if a relationship was to move to the next level just wasn't there for her, and he didn't have her heart. She'd kept him in the "friend zone," as she'd overheard a young customer say to Eirlys in the nail studio. And then Gareth had met Fiona Barton from Scotland, who had lured him out of Penny's friend zone and into her . . . well, Penny wasn't sure what her zone was, but she was sure it was a step up from the friend zone, and it was in Edinburgh. At the end of the summer Gareth had announced that he was selling his house in Llandudno and moving to Edinburgh to be with her.

"I wanted a quick word. Look, if I've come at a bad time, I'll just say what I've come to say, and then I'll be off." He gestured at the door.

"No, it's all right. Now that you're here, go on through." She reached for his coat and draped it over the newel post of the staircase.

"Good. Well, I won't stay long," Gareth said, easing himself into one of the comfortable wing chairs. I hope not, thought Penny.

"You mentioned that you wanted a quick word?" she prompted.

"Yes. I wanted to tell you, warn you maybe, that travellers have pitched up down the road from you in the fields where the agricultural show was held, and you need to be careful. I've often thought that your cottage, delightful as it may be, is a little too isolated, and that leaves you vulnerable. I know in the past you've been a little lax about locking your doors, so please make sure you do that. You don't want to take any chances with that lot on your doorstep."

He was right about the unlocked doors. There had been times over the years, especially in summer, when Penny had gone to work leaving the back door open so Harrison could come in from his garden wanderings or make his way outdoors after a nap. She cringed when she thought how lucky she'd been that she hadn't been burgled.

"You're right, of course," said Penny, "and you'll be happy to know I don't do that anymore. I always make sure the doors are locked, but I appreciate the warning. On my way home just now, I did see a group of people setting up what looked like a campsite in the field and wondered who they were and what they were up to."

"They're travellers," Gareth repeated. "And they won't have been given permission to be there. And since it's private land, the council can't do anything about moving them on."

A diverse group of people of Irish or Romany descent, some groups of travellers choose to live in permanent homes while others opt for the open road, moving from place to place. Travellers on the move almost always meet with animosity and resistance from authorities and civilians alike.

"I had quite a few dealings with travellers as a police officer, and although I always tried to be nonjudgemental, we did have to make arrests, mostly for theft. So I just wanted to warn you to be on your guard and remind you to keep your doors locked."

"I'll do that," said Penny. She thought about the two pieces of salmon sitting on the work top, and it flashed through her mind, but only for a second or two, to invite him to stay for dinner. That might be the polite thing to do, but surely if someone drops in unexpectedly while you're in the middle of preparing dinner, you're not obligated to invite them to join you. And besides, what if there'd been just one piece of salmon? The bottom line was that she simply didn't want to invite him to stay for dinner, so she didn't. She knew he never touched alcohol while was driving, so there was no point in offering him a glass of wine. And as for a cup of tea, which might be what he was hoping for, it just seemed like it would take too long to wait for the kettle to boil and fuss about with the tea things, dragging out the visit unnecessarily. And anyway, he'd dropped in unannounced, and given her such a fright. So she offered him nothing.

As she was mulling over all these possibilities, his eyes wandered around the room, taking everything in. "Looks just the same. As nice as ever." He then turned his attention to her. "And you. You're looking well."

His "you're looking well" remark struck an uneasy chord, so she decided to try to move things along. "I've left the oven on and I haven't fed Harrison yet, so if . . ."

He sprang to his feet. "Oh, of course. You've had a long day, and I'm sure you're anxious to get on with your evening."

"I am a bit tired," Penny admitted, "and hungry, too, if I'm honest. But if you're around for a few days, perhaps we can catch up over a cup of coffee."

"I'd like that. I'm not sure how long I'm staying. Just tying up a few loose ends to do with the sale of the house that had to be done in person."

"I'm sorry if I overreacted when you arrived," Penny said as they walked to her front door. "It's just that your text frightened me, and I didn't recognize the number. If I'd known it was from you, I wouldn't have been so alarmed."

"I've got a new phone and changed my number, so your phone wouldn't have recognized it."

When he was gone, she popped the salmon in the oven and set the timer. She poured herself a glass of wine, took it through to the sitting room, and called Victoria.

"Gareth's back," she began. "He was just here. No, I don't know how long for, and I didn't ask him about Scotland. He didn't let me know he was coming over, and I was tired and hungry, so I wasn't terribly hospitable. We might meet up for a coffee." They chatted for a few more minutes, and when the timer pinged, Penny returned to the kitchen to turn the salmon, put the broccoli on to steam, and microwave a packet of rice.

And now he was back. Penny's emotions were no longer mixed. She was happy he'd found the happiness he was looking for, and if she was honest with herself, just that tiny bit relieved he'd found it well away from Llanelen, leaving her to get on with her life as a fulfilled, independent woman.

She didn't know how long he'd been back in the area, but thought not long enough to have heard about the theft of the Black Chair and the as yet unexplained death of Rhodri Phillips. Surely if he had heard, he would have mentioned it.

Or maybe not. Perhaps all he wanted to do was warn her about the travellers, but she did wonder how he knew about them. After all, as he himself had said, her cottage was isolated, and very few people would drive down her road, past the encampment, on the way to somewhere else. Perhaps he had been coming to see her anyway, to let her know he was back, and used the travellers' camp as an excuse to call in.

She watched the evening news while she ate her meal, and

when she was finished, she carried her used dishes to the kitchen, washed them, and laid out a bowl and mug ready for her breakfast in the morning.

After checking that the doors and windows were locked, as she did every night but tonight a little more mindfully than usual, she went upstairs, and a few minutes later she was settled in bed with her library book. After reading the same paragraph several times, she closed the book, rested it on her knees, and gazed at the curtained window. As she mulled over the events of the past two days, something Lane had said danced around in the back of her mind, taunting her. She willed it to come forward, to show itself, but just as it got tantalizingly close, it danced away and receded into that hidden place in the mind where ideas wait to be discovered.

With a sigh, she switched off the light, adjusted her pillows, and slid down into the warmth of her bed. She closed her eyes, struggling one last time to capture what Lane had said, but eventually gave up and lay in the dark, Harrison cuddled up beside her, listening. When she was sure all she could hear was the sound of the rain pattering against her window, she allowed herself to drift off to sleep.

Chapter Sixteen

A police car with its distinctive blue-and-yellow markings was parked on the verge beside the travellers' campsite the next morning. In daylight, Penny could make out details that had been obscured by last night's rain and darkness. Old, rusted vans and cars and newer caravans had been parked all over the fields, tearing up the grass and leaving a muddy pit in the middle of them. Dogs tied on short chains barked loudly, and a few men, dressed in jeans and jackets, sat in a semicircle in front of a fire, smoking and ignoring the dogs. A heavily pregnant woman carrying a child on her hip emerged from one caravan and disappeared into another. Men's shirts pegged on a washing line that had been strung up between two vehicles hung motionless in the still air.

As Penny approached the police car, the engine started up and the passenger-side window slid smoothly down. "'Morning," Inspector Bethan Morgan called out to her, leaning over from the driver's seat. "If you'd like a lift into town, jump in.

I was beginning to think about leaving but thought I'd give it a few more minutes in case you happened by."

Penny climbed in. Bethan checked the rearview mirror and, with one last glance over her shoulder at the encampment, pulled away.

"Keeping an eye on the travellers?" Penny asked.

"That's exactly what I'm doing. I want to make it really obvious that we're keeping them under surveillance."

"But why you? That seems like something an ordinary police officer could do. Surely it doesn't need someone with a DI rank."

"Oh, I needed a little quiet thinking time on my own," said Bethan. "You know how it is. And sometimes I just like to see things for myself." She shifted gears. "How's everything with you?"

"I had an unexpected visitor last night. Gareth sent me a text and then dropped by to tell me to keep my doors locked," Penny said.

"Quite right, too," said Bethan. "As a police officer, I always recommend that people keep their doors locked. It would save us no end of bother if folks would take our advice. Seems strange, though, his coming all the way from Edinburgh to advise you to lock your doors." She cast a quick glance at Penny and grinned. "Hell, I could have told you that. I didn't know he was back. I wonder how long for."

"I don't know," said Penny. "He mentioned he had some personal business to take care of. He didn't stay very long. I'd had a long day, and I was hungry and tired and just wanted to get on with my dinner, to be honest. I didn't ask too many questions and he didn't volunteer much information."

"Still, it's a bit odd he drove over to yours to warn you about the travellers, because the encampment only went up last evening."

"That's what I thought," said Penny. "He had to have driven by to have seen them, to know that they're there. So it occurred to me that he must have been on his way over to my place anyway, and then the travellers became a convenient excuse to call in. If there was another reason, he never got around to it. But I'm interested in the travellers. Did you speak to them at all this morning?"

"No, I didn't. Why?'

"I wondered if they're Irish, that's all."

"Oh, I don't need to speak to them to know that they're Irish. They've been here before and are known to us. Why do you ask?"

"I'm not really sure. It just seems that there's a lot of Irish coincidences in my life right now. I'm pretty sure I spotted Michael Quinn in town on Sunday, coming out of the pub. I didn't see his face clearly, so it's possible, I suppose, that I'm mistaken, but the man that I saw certainly walked like him. He had that limp and I had a very strong sense that this person was none other than Michael Quinn."

"Michael Quinn? From the antiques show?"

"Yes."

"Well, he just lives in Bangor, so it wouldn't be too much

of a stretch for him to have come to Llanelen on a Sunday, I suppose. Maybe he was here to enjoy a Sunday lunch with friends. Was he with anyone?" Was he with his wife, you probably mean, thought Penny.

"No, he was by himself. Came out of the pub, crossed the square, and disappeared round behind the bank."

"Hmm. And when DCI Davies—sorry, old habit, Gareth—visited you, did you discuss what happened at the Hall on Saturday night?"

"No. As I said, I was that tired. I didn't have the energy or inclination to get into a conversation with him about Saturday night, or anything else, for that matter. It had been such a long day, and I was drained. I just wanted to be left alone to eat my dinner."

Bethan laughed. "Oh, poor you. I know that feeling so well. 'It's just not the right time. I'm so not into this right now.'"

"That's exactly what it was like." Penny then brought the conversation back to Saturday night. "But speaking of the events at the Hall, I wondered if you've got the postmortem results yet."

Bethan slowed down and flicked her turn signal. "We have. Rhodri Phillips died from a blow to the head, just about here." She raised her hand off the gear lever and tapped the left side of her head. "Probably with a stone or rock, something heavy and hard like that, of uneven shape. The pathologist couldn't be too specific. Possibly a brick, even. And then his head injury was complicated by the effects of hypothermia. He was out in the cold and rain for some time."

"Oh, no," groaned Penny. "Do you mean that if we'd found him sooner, he might have survived?"

"He might have," said Bethan. "But you mustn't blame yourself. You weren't to know."

"The head injury. It was slippery out there," said Penny. "In the dark, in the rain, could he have fallen and hit his head?"

"Not a chance," said Bethan.

"Because?"

"Because whatever made contact with his head wasn't there. If he'd fallen and hit his head, we'd have found the rock or whatever it was beside him, or at least nearby. We didn't find anything like that."

"Could he have been attacked elsewhere and then somehow ended up where I found him?" Penny asked.

"The forensics from inside the house hasn't shown anything to indicate the attack took place there, and there was nothing on his clothes or shoes to lead us to think he'd been attacked anywhere other than where he was found."

Penny thought that over. "So Rhodri was outside, in the rain, at the back of the house. Why? Had he just gone out for a smoke or to use his phone, interrupted the robbery in progress, and tried to stop it? Or had he been part of it . . . he'd let someone into the house and then gone outside with them? And then they got into an argument, then whoever it was hit him, Rhodri went down, and whoever it was disappeared with the rock or stone?"

"That's too much speculation at this point," said Bethan. "And as for the rock, or whatever it was that he was hit with, unfortunately it could be at the bottom of the river by now." She gave the River Conwy a fluttery little wave as they drove alongside it. "We may never find the rock or brick, but that wouldn't be unusual. We don't always find the murder weapons because we're not always on-scene that quickly."

They'd reached the town limits. "Have you had a chance to speak to Lane yet about the people who threatened him on Saturday night?" Penny asked. "I'm worried about him. It could be the same people who attacked Rhodri. At least, I'm assuming it was more than one person. Lane said 'they' told him he'd be in big trouble if he told anyone what happened."

Bethan did not reply and a few moments later slowed the vehicle and parked near the town square. She switched off the ignition and shifted sideways in her seat. Penny did the same so they were turned slightly toward each other.

"It could be the same people," Bethan said.

"So that's a real concern. And even if he's not in actual, real danger, if Lane imagines he is, goodness knows how he'll react or what he'll do. Something really frightened him, and that's why he ran off to hide with Dilys. He was still frightened when he talked to me on Sunday. He does know something, and I think he wants to tell us, but he's afraid to because of that threat hanging over him. I know it's hard to get information out of him, but I thought he might be ready to talk by now. It's really important to find out who spoke to him."

As soon as the words had escaped her lips, Penny hoped she hadn't come across as telling Bethan how to manage her case. Bethan's response was smooth and measured.

"I'll send someone to talk to him today, if I can. He's on our list, of course, as is everyone who was there that night, but with our limited resources, we can't get to everyone all at once. We've been interviewing the waiters and the guests and that's been very time-consuming. So far, the guests have turned up nothing. All pillars of the community, and nobody saw anything. Same with the waiters. They did what they were supposed to do and took remarkably little interest in anything else going on around them. And, of course, we've been looking into the life of our victim, Rhodri Phillips. Trying to piece together his last few days. What he did, who he was with."

Penny decided to chance it. "And?"

"And nothing. Yet. The problem at this point is not just that I don't have the rabbit; I don't even have a hat. But something'll turn up. You just have to have faith in the process. One piece of information, one observation, one answered question will give us a bit of traction, and when we get that break, everything will start to come together."

Penny gathered up her handbag and lunch. "I'd better get going. Like you, we're short-staffed. Rhian is needed at home with her family, so we're all doubling up on reception duty." She placed her hand on the car door. "Lane said something on Sunday that's bothering me, but for the life of me I can't remember what it was. It actually kept me awake last night trying to remember. I just feel if I can remember what he said, it might start us off in the right direction."

"Then I hope it comes to you," said Bethan. "There's always that one light bulb moment that, if it doesn't exactly crack the case wide open, at least shines enough light to pry it open a little. And if you think this thing that Lane said—whatever it is—could do that, if it's that important, then please think harder."

Penny waved Bethan off and waited until she had disappeared up Station Road in the direction of the police station before crossing the town square. She reached the Spa's black wrought iron gate, pushed it open, reminding herself for the thousandth time that they really must do something about its awful squeaking, and walked down the path that led to the Spa's front door. As she entered, Victoria looked up from the reception desk, looking much calmer and better organized than Penny had the day before when she'd tried to open the business for the day. They exchanged morning pleasantries and Victoria held out several weekly magazines. "The news agent just dropped these off. If you don't mind gathering up the magazines from reception and the quiet room," she said, "and putting out the new ones. I'll take last week's *Country Life*, and Eirlys takes *Woman's Weekly* home to her mother."

"How do the appointments look for this morning?" Penny asked as she reached out for the magazines.

"A few for you, Alberto's booked solid, and Eirlys will cover reception over the lunch hour. We're good."

Penny set off down the hall to the quiet room. A small

space reserved for private conversations or a reflective moment alone, it was decorated in soothing, sophisticated neutral colours of cream and taupe and featured two deep, squishy chairs upholstered in chocolate brown faux suede arranged to face each other and a low coffee table between them. On a small floating shelf mounted under a watercolour of the Spa building as it had been before its renovation, painted by Penny herself, a grouping of LED candles, there to provide a convincing atmosphere without the fire hazard, waited to be switched on. At Penny's touch they flickered into artificial life.

She then turned her attention to the magazines on the coffee table. Leaving the monthly ones, she scooped up the weeklies, swapping two current ones for last week's. She arranged the magazines neatly and took one last look around the room to make sure it was tidy. She was just about to leave when a cover line on *Country Life* caught her attention. ALSTON COURT, SUFFOLK: A VIVID INSIGHT INTO TUDOR LIVING ON THE GRAND SCALE.

She picked up the magazine and sank into a chair. With the publication resting on her knee, she ran her finger under the cover line, her finger pausing at the word "grand."

Grand! That's the word Lane had used that had been eluding her. What had he said? She'd asked him what he thought of something and he'd replied that it sounded like a grand idea, or words to that effect. It was such a strange word choice for him. He'd used the word "grand" in a decidedly Irish way, the way an Irish person would. Not grand in the sense of great or magnificent, but grand in the sense of fine.

He must have been talking to an Irish person, Penny thought, and picked up the word usage from them. Of course it didn't necessarily follow that he'd heard someone say the word "grand" on Saturday night, but then again, it was a possibility. She felt a vague stirring of excitement, the feeling that she might be on to something, or at the very least, that this was something worth pursuing. The big question remained: who had spoken to Lane at the Hall on Saturday night and put fear into him on such a grand scale?

Chapter Seventeen

Penny pondered that question all morning, and by the end of the day she'd come up with a vague plan. If Lane wouldn't tell her who had spoken to him, maybe that person would confirm that he was the one who had spoken to Lane. If, of course, that person was who she suspected it was. But to speak to him, she'd have to square some time off with Victoria, and she knew that was going to be a hard sell.

"Now Victoria," she began. "You're not to be annoyed with me, but I need a bit of personal time off tomorrow morning." Victoria looked up from the box of hand cream she was unpacking and arranging in a display of Spa-branded products.

"Oh, really. Must you?" she said. "You know we're short-staffed. I was counting on you to do reception cover tomorrow morning."

"I'll try to be back by lunchtime."

"Where are you going?"

"Bangor."

"Bangor? What's in Bangor?"

"Lane said someone threatened him on Saturday night. On Sunday, I saw Michael Quinn right here in Llanelen, coming out of the pub. At least I think it was him. I didn't actually get a good look. But he had a limp on his left side."

"Well, it sounds like something that awful Quinn would do, be in the pub. I'll give you that."

"Yes. And Lane won't tell me who threatened him, but on Sunday he used the word 'grand' in that almost cliched Irish way, and I think it could have been Michael Quinn who spoke to him."

"So let me see if I've got this straight. Someone threatened Lane on Saturday night during the dinner party at the Hall, causing him to drop a tray full of plates and glasses. Then, on Sunday, he used the word 'grand,' so your theory is he must have been threatened by an Irishman, and out of all the Irishmen in all the world, the Irishman who threatened him was Michael Quinn because you just happened to see a man, who may or may not be Quinn, limping out of the pub at Sunday lunchtime?"

Penny laughed. "Well, when you put it like that, it sounds even more ridiculous."

"I'm not finished yet. So now you want to go to Bangor tomorrow morning and confront Michael Quinn, and say what to him, exactly?"

"I'm not sure. I haven't worked that out yet."

"I give up. I can't even say something like, 'Well, I suppose you know what you're doing,' because clearly, you don't. But I hope it'll be worth it, and you owe me for this."

"Yes, I do."

* * *

The next morning, Penny caught the early bus to Llandudno. The little blue-and-white vehicle wended its way down the valley until about forty minutes later it reached the town of Conwy. Through narrow streets, passing under the grey stone arches that formed part of the medieval town walls, it went, until it reached the bus stop at the railway station, where she changed to the Number X5 headed for Bangor. The bus sped along the coast, past rugged hills and green fields dotted with sheep on her left, and the Irish Sea sparkling in the morning sunshine on her right. An hour or so later it pulled into Bangor. She got off at the main bus depot in the town centre and made her way to a well-kept, three-storey, pebble-dashed house within the shadow of Bangor University.

She'd been here once before, when Quinn had been laid up with his injured leg. The semidetached house was painted a light cream, with Wedgwood-blue window frames and door and a slate house sign that said RHOS-GOCH beside the doorbell. Faded red roses clung to trellises on each side of the door. As she walked slowly up the path that led to the front door, rehearsing what she would say if Michael Quinn's wife answered the bell, the door of the adjoining house opened and a woman carrying a couple of empty shopping bags emerged, obviously on her way to the shops. She locked her front door and pushed on the handle to make sure it was secure, and then, catching sight of Penny, said, "You look lost. Can I help?"

The woman's eyes had a sharp intensity about them, as if

nothing much got past her, and Penny found her presence inexplicably reassuring. "I was just about to knock on Michael Quinn's door."

The woman gave her a sympathetic, knowing smile. "Sorry, love, he's gone."

"Gone?"

"Hmm. Him and his wife broke up, oh, several months ago now, and first she moved out, leaving him here on his own, and then he left a few weeks ago."

"Oh, I see."

"The house has been rented. New people just moved in. A couple and two children. They seem like a nice family and he's something at the cathedral, I believe. But the street's always changing, and you never who you're going to get."

"No, you don't. Well, if Michael Quinn isn't here anymore, it looks like I've had a wasted journey."

"Sorry, love. And from your accent, you've come a very long way. American, are you?"

Penny smiled. "No, Canadian. But I haven't come that far. Just from Llanelen this morning. I live there now."

"Oh, I see. Well, I'm sorry you didn't get what you were after."

"It's all right," said Penny. "I can always do a bit of shopping now that I'm here." As they walked down the little asphalt path toward the street together, the woman said, "I'll walk with you." She gestured with her shopping bags. "I've got to pick up my prescription, and then I'm going to Marks. Want to get one of their Battenburg cakes for my tea."

As they fell into a comfortable walking rhythm, Penny asked, "Do you happen to know where Michael Quinn moved to? Is he still with the university?"

The woman shook her head. "Not this one here in Bangor. That fancy one in Dublin, maybe, the one with the library and the book everybody wants to see. I heard from her at number thirty-six on the other side that's where he moved to. Dublin. Well, it makes sense, I suppose. Him being Irish and all." The woman shifted her bags to her other hand. "But it's funny you should be here asking after him now, that Michael Quinn."

"Oh, why's that?"

"Because I heard nothing about his wife after she left—nobody came asking after her—and now here you are asking after Michael Quinn and you're the second one."

"Oh, really? That's very interesting. If you don't mind telling me, who was the other person asking after him?"

"Not a person. Three of them, there were. And that's the strange thing. I'd just watched a crime prevention program on the telly—you know the sort of thing, lock your doors and windows—presented by a lovely lady officer from the police, it was—and she said be on your guard because gangs of thieves are operating in the area, so when I saw these three lads out my lounge window, loitering about, I thought they were thieves. What's that American expression? Casing the place?"

"Casing the joint?"

"That's it. I thought they were thieves, casing the joint. By all accounts Michael Quinn had some nice artwork, so I thought they might be after that. I was only in their house a couple of times, see, and can't remember that much about how it was decorated, although they had it done up really nice, I do recall that."

I was only in it once, thought Penny, and I can remember every detail, from the sage-green sofa with the pretty lemon yellow–and–white pillows to the expensive-looking art books on the coffee table. And the woman was right. There had been original artworks, and prints, too. "So I decided to confront these lads, and out I come, even though I was only in my house slippers, and I said, 'May I help you?' like I said to you just now. And I thought they'd make some lame excuse and clear off. But they didn't. I was that surprised when they asked after Michael Quinn by name.

"So then, because they were young, I wondered if they might have been students of his from the university. Anyway, I told them he didn't live here anymore, like I told you just now, and they said thank you very much and left."

"And how long ago was this?" Penny asked. "When were they here?"

"Oh, not that long ago." She thought for a moment. "Two or three weeks, maybe?"

"And had you heard that he was planning to move out, or did it seem to happen in a hurry?"

"Now that I couldn't say. I wasn't close to them."

"And these lads . . . if you thought they were university students, they looked young, did they?" Penny asked.

"Well, youngish, I would say. Definitely not teenagers, early twenties, maybe. I'm not great at estimating people's ages. People from about twenty to forty all look the same to me. Young."

"Right, so early twenties, let's say. And they were dressed in what, jeans and trainers?"

"Jeans, yes, I think so. Don't know about trainers, but probably. It's just that look practically everyone has now. Everybody wants to be comfortable, nobody wants to look smart. These fellows, now, they just looked a bit rough, if you know what I mean. That's the only way I can think to describe them. Unshaven and not very clean."

"Well, they could have been just about anybody, I suppose," said Penny, her mind racing back to the young men Eirlys had described, friends of Rhodri Phillips, as "rough."

"Is there anything else you can remember about them?" Penny asked as they reached the shopping precinct.

"There was one thing that amused me," said the woman. "It was the way he said 'thank you.' He said it as 'Tank you.' Made me smile because my mother had an Irish charwoman when I was growing up who spoke like that."

"Oh," said Penny. "That's interesting. So you think they were Irish, do you?"

The woman nodded. "Well, it was lovely chatting with you." She frowned. "You asked a lot of questions. You're not from the police, are you? He hasn't done anything wrong, has he?"

Penny smiled. "No, I'm not from the police. If I were, I'd have said so right at the outset and shown you my warrant card."

A flicker of relief crossed the woman's face. "Well, that's all right then." She shifted her shopping bag to the other arm. "I hope you find him."

I do, too, thought Penny, as the woman walked away. Bangor railway station was so close, and it would be so easy to walk over there, buy a ticket to Holyhead, and from there catch the next ferry to Dublin. But the practical, responsible side prevailed, and she reached into her handbag and pulled out her bus day pass. She tucked it in her coat pocket, entered the Marks and Spencer food hall, and picked up a few treats and some good things for dinner before boarding the bus for home.

She gazed out the window, unseeing, as she sifted through the information the former neighbour of the Quinns had given her, trying to piece it together with what she already knew. And then two pieces clicked together, with such clarity and precision she started in her seat. Without thinking or hesitating, she pressed the button to indicate to the driver that a passenger wanted to get off. The bus slowed, then stopped near the entrance to Penrhyn Castle, but she had neither the time nor the inclination today to admire its elaborate stone walls. As she crossed the road, an idea came to her as to how she could make this work, and while she waited for the next bus that would take her back to Bangor, she pulled out her phone.

Chapter Eighteen

"Rhian? Hi, it's Penny. How are you doing?" Penny listened for a moment and then said, "Look, I might be on to something that could shed some light on how Rhodri died, but I need your help. Here's what I need you to do." After explaining that she needed Rhian to return to work tomorrow, Penny smiled when Rhian said she was more than ready to return to work, and that if Penny didn't mind, she'd like to come in that afternoon because she and her mam were getting on each other's nerves something awful. After letting Rhian know it would be more than all right for her to return to work immediately, Penny asked her to ring Victoria and let her know she'd be there soon.

"Oh, and Rhian, would you please text or e-mail me a photo of Rhodri? Soon as you can. Thanks."

A few minutes later, knowing that Victoria would be happy to have Rhian back on the reception desk that afternoon, Penny relaxed into her seat on the bus, and it wasn't long before she arrived back in Bangor. As the bus entered the city, she gazed up at her destination, the imposing late Gothic-style Main Arts building of Bangor University perched high on a hill overlooking the city.

Built in the early twentieth century of buff-coloured sandstone with a roof of Welsh slate, the building had weathered to a dull grey. It featured a cathedral-like central tower, stone chimney stacks, dormers, gables, and elegant windows, that radiated a spirit of robust Edwardian academic tradition and an undeniable sense of permanence.

After a short walk from the bus station, Penny darted across a busy street and walked up the long set of stairs to the Main Arts building. After pausing to take in the grandeur and elegance of the vaulted ceiling in the vestibule, she followed the signage to a bright, modern café with both table and sofa seating. She looked around for a table as she waited in the queue for a coffee. The tables were full, but one or two, meant for four, had empty seats.

Two young women seated at one of the tables broke off their animated conversation as Penny approached.

"I'm sorry," she said with a hopeful smile, "all the tables are occupied. Would you mind terribly if I sat here?"

"No, not at all," said one of the women, and after a moment or two, they resumed their conversation.

"Anyway, it's difficult to say who gets to decide what is beautiful," said the other woman. "And when. It depends on the time, doesn't it? I mean, no one really liked the work of the Impressionists when they were starting out. It was too modern! It broke the rules!"

"Exactly!" said her companion, who had been tracing little circles on the shiny black tabletop. "I wonder which starving artists today will be the must-have painters of tomorrow."

"That's a good question. Is it even possible? Does art occupy the same place in the world that it did even fifty years ago?"

Result! thought Penny. Art students. Now I just have to find a way into their conversation. She listened for a few more minutes, and then, starting to worry they might finish their lunches and leave, she said, "I couldn't help overhearing your conversation, and it brought me back to my own university days. I studied art history at Mount Allison University." Met with blank faces, she added, "In New Brunswick. Canada."

"Oh, cool," said one. "One of our courses included some Canadian painters. The Pacific Northwest. Emily Carr?"

Penny smiled at the way she said the name Emily Carr uncertainly, as a question.

"I hear the professors here are excellent," Penny said. "In fact, maybe you can help me. I'm looking for an old acquaintance of mine. Michael Quinn. He teaches here, I believe."

The two women exchanged an uncomfortable glance, and the one who had mentioned Emily Carr replied, "He used to teach here. But he didn't return this autumn. He's not on the faculty anymore."

"Oh, I see," said Penny. "Did he . . . ?" She let the sentence trail off.

"There were, ah, complaints," said the student. "From female students," she added, in case Penny didn't quite get the picture.

"Oh, I'm sorry to hear that. I worked with him on an antiques appraisal show, and I just happened to be in Bangor today, so I thought I'd look him up. I don't suppose you know where he is, do you?"

"I heard he'd gone to Dublin," said the student with the blonde ponytail.

"He sent a text to one of his students," said the other woman, "although she wasn't particularly happy to hear from him. Apparently he's working for an auction house in Dublin, doing fine art appraisals."

"That would make sense," said Penny. "He spotted right away that some sketches that a friend of mine had acquired in the 1960s were valuable. He definitely has an eye for quality work."

The two students exchanged a meaningful glance, and one said, with a slight smirk, "Quality work isn't all he has an eye for."

Penny's phone indicated an incoming text, and she glanced at it, then opened the photo of Rhodri that Rhian had just sent. "Do either of you know him?" she asked, holding out her phone to the woman seated beside her. "He was a student here."

The woman took the phone, looked at the photo, and then handed it to her friend, who glanced at it and returned it to Penny.

"Yes, that's Rhodri Phillips. He was in our year, but I heard he dropped out. I only knew him to see him, really," said the woman beside her.

The woman across the table from her frowned. "I know I'm asking a lot of questions," said Penny, "but it's just that something terrible happened to Rhodri, and his family has asked me to see if I can get some answers for them. If you haven't heard, I'm sorry to have to tell you he died on Saturday night under suspicious circumstances."

"That's terrible," said the woman across from Penny. "How did it happen?"

* * *

The three women chatted about Rhodri for a few more minutes until the students indicated they had to leave if they didn't want to be late for class, and after gathering up the remnants of their meal, they left Penny alone at the table. She got out her phone, Googled auction houses in Dublin, and settled on a couple as being likely places for Michael Quinn to be working.

As much as she wanted to walk directly to the Bangor railway station and depart immediately for Ireland, as she'd been tempted to do earlier, she realised this wasn't practical. As a Canadian, she needed a passport to enter Ireland, although a British citizen did not. So the journey would have to wait one more day, giving her time to go home, pick up her passport, book passage on the morning ferry, and pack an overnight bag. She walked back to the area where all the buses gathered and once again boarded the X5 for Llandudno. Maybe the necessity of deferring the journey to Dublin for one day was a good thing, she told herself. A twenty-four-hour cooling-off period to rethink this whole daft plan. You don't have to go to Dublin, she told herself. In fact, why are you going in search of Michael Quinn? What will you say if you find him? She couldn't answer that question, but by the time she reached Conwy and changed buses for Llanelen, she knew she was going and she'd work out what to say when she got there. Assuming she could find him, of course.

Chapter Nineteen

The approach by sea to any great port city starts off the same. An indistinct grey shape begins to emerge on the horizon out of the endless, unbroken expanse of water and sky, and passengers realise their destination is looming into view. A certain excitement ripples through the ship, and as the crew set about their duties in preparation for arrival, passengers go on deck and lean over the railings, watching the shoreline gradually become clearer. For some, it's their first glimpse of home after time away; for others, it's their introduction to a place they've never been where adventure awaits.

Penny did not join the passengers on deck but remained in the seat where she had spent the crossing of the Irish Sea until the call came for passengers to disembark. She answered an immigration officer's questions, and when he had stamped her passport and handed it back to her, she left the terminal building and boarded the bus that would take her to the city centre. As the docklands, with their gigantic stacks of red, green, and blue shipping containers and the massive orange cranes needed to move them, were left behind, she felt excited about being back in the Irish capital after so many years, but apprehensive about confronting Michael Quinn.

When the bus reached the city centre, she alighted and set off for the heart of Georgian Dublin. Under a grey sky filled with scudding clouds, she threaded her way through streets of grandly impressive four-storey brick houses all built before 1830, once the homes of the Protestant ruling class, now mostly divided up into modern flats or offices. She slowed to admire the distinctive doorways with many of their doors painted in bright colours: emerald green, turquoise, canary yellow, and of course, red, and above them the stylish arched fan lights for which they were famous. She continued until she reached Merrion Square, where most of the red-brick houses on three of its sides had been converted into offices, including the Dublin branch of an international auction house. She pulled a piece of paper from her pocket, checked the number of the building she wanted, and strolled around the square until she reached it. Holding the shiny black wrought iron railing, she climbed the steps, rang the doorbell, and waited. When a disembodied voice answered, asking the nature of her business, she replied, "I'm seeking information about an appraiser." The entry system buzzed, and grasping the round doorknob in the middle of the somber black door, she pushed it open and entered a cream-coloured reception area filled with natural light. The ornate plasterwork was breathtaking, and Penny paused to take it in. An impeccably groomed young woman dressed in an expensive-looking black suit over a white silk top looked up from her desk and raised an enquiring eyebrow. "I'm looking for Michael Quinn," said Penny. "I think he works here as an appraiser."

"He does work for us occasionally," the woman said, "but he does not work here full-time. Depends on what we get in. He doesn't have an office here."

"Oh, I see. Well, can you tell me where I might find him?"

The woman ran her tongue over her upper lip, as if that would help her make up her mind. "You might try the Celt, on Talbot Street. I've never been myself, but I hear they do a nice bacon and colcannon and it's popular with the lunchtime crowd. It's about a twenty-minute walk from here."

"Thank you very much," said Penny, understanding what the woman was telling her without actually telling her. "I appreciate the suggestion."

She checked her map and set off for the pub. She made her way through the streets, then crossed the three-span Talbot Memorial Bridge over the River Liffey, pausing halfway across to admire the magnificent Custom House, regarded by many as the most beautiful Georgian building in Dublin.

She started walking again, following the instructions on her phone, and soon arrived at the Celt pub, marked by orange, white and green balloons. Just inside the entrance, she paused to allow her eyes to adjust to the dim light. The beamed, low ceiling was a complete contrast to the high-ceilinged elegance of the building she had just left, but the whitewashed walls, covered with photographs and posters, had a traditional charm. As she absorbed the energy and atmosphere, she almost sensed him before she saw him, seated by himself at a table at the back of the room. Her heart pounding against her ribs at the sight of him, she hesitated, unsure whether to approach his table or get a drink first, and then decided it would be less awkward if she went to the bar, ordered a glass of wine, and waited to see if he noticed her.

"A glass of white wine, please." The barman poured a glass, slid it toward her, and took her money. She turned, surveyed several empty tables as if trying to make up her mind where to sit, and finally let her eyes come to rest on him. He glanced at her and she could feel him appraising her, and then a flicker of recognition passed across his face. He smiled a tentative, halting smile, as if unsure it would be returned. She took it as an invitation, and with pounding heart and dry mouth, carefully carrying her glass of wine, she crossed the room and reached his table.

"Hello, Michael." He stumbled to his feet and held out his hand.

"Hello, ah . . . Well, well. Fancy seeing you here. You're a long way from . . ."

"Llanelen. We met up at Ty Brith Hall in Llanelen when you were an appraiser on *Antiques Cymru*."

"Of course. Ty Brith Hall. Quite a few nice pieces showed up that day, as I recall. Good turnout. And the Hall was beautiful. I love those country houses. They all have that same *County Life* ambience. Muted colours, soft lamplight, books, patterned carpets, comfy furniture. And the owner of the property, our host for the day, what was his name? Sorry it escapes me. I'm not the best with names."

"Emyr Gruffydd."

"Emyr. That's right. Took a great interest in everything that was going on, as I recall. Even invited me in and gave me a fine single malt whisky in his library while he ran upstairs to fetch a painting he wanted my opinion on. But what am I like, rabbiting on? Forgive me. If you're on your own, would you like to sit down?" He gestured at an empty chair across from him. "Or perhaps you're meeting someone?"

Penny set her wine glass on the table and pulled out the chair. "No, I'm not meeting anyone, and I'd be happy to join you for a few minutes." His eyes travelled to the door. "But perhaps you're expecting someone?"

"No, no, you're all right. I'm just a bit surprised to see you here, that's all. How are you? Everything going well with you, is it, erm?"

He spoke quickly, stumbling over his words. Penny couldn't tell if that was because of how much he'd had to drink, his nervousness at seeing her, or something else. She took a sip of wine and then raised her eyes to him. He'd aged since the last time she'd seen him. His hair was greyer, the lines in his face had deepened, and a dullness in his eyes gave him a down-on-his-luck look.

"It's Penny. Penny Brannigan."

"Look," he said. "This is a bit awkward, so let's just get it over with. Of course I remember you, Penny, and I'm truly sorry for what happened. I should have been honest with you, but I was attracted to you, and I rather hoped that we might spend more time together, to see where things went."

"But you were still with your wife at the time," Penny said. "And you lied to me about her. You actually told me she was dead, and like an idiot, I believed you."

"That wasn't very nice of me, was it? But our marriage was effectively over even before I met you, and we broke up soon after you and I . . ."

His voice trailed off. After you and I . . . nothing, thought Penny. In the silence that followed, she took another sip of wine. "Well, that's all over now," Quinn continued. His eyes met Penny's, and he leaned forward slightly. "Coincidences do happen. I've ended up sitting beside someone in the theatre that I hadn't seen in years. What are the chances of that? That the two of us would decide to see the same play, on the same night, and out of all the seating assignments that must be possible, we end up next to each other. But I'm getting the feeling that you"—he gestured at Penny—"your being here isn't a coincidence. I heard from a student in Bangor that someone with an American or Canadian accent had been asking questions about me—oh, yes, word gets around—and I wondered if you might come to Dublin. I've been half expecting to see you."

"You're right," Penny said. "I did come looking for you. There's something I want to talk to you about."

"About old times? About the romance that never quite got off the ground?"

"No, not about that. Something else."

"Right, well, before we get to that, I'd like to know how you found me. Dublin's a big city, filled with pubs, and yet you walk into this one." Of all the gin joints in all the world, thought Penny.

"Actually, someone recommended this pub as a good place to have lunch, and I decided to give it a try."

"And you walk in, and just like that, here I am."

"And just like that, here you are."

"Aren't you the lucky one?"

"I guess I am."

"So you said you wanted to talk to me. What did you want to tell me? Or ask me?"

Penny wiped away at the condensation on her glass as she gathered her thoughts. "A lad—well, a young man—was killed in Llanelen on Saturday night. But maybe, with word getting around and all as you just said, you already knew that." Quinn did not react. And although she hadn't seen the face of the man who'd limped out of the pub on Sunday, she was so certain it had been Quinn that she decided to risk the old reporter's trick of stating something you believe to be true as a fact and then seeing how the other person responds. If he doesn't deny it, thought Penny, that will confirm it was him I saw. Here goes. Let's see what happens.

"And then on Sunday, I was having a coffee at the café on the town square and I saw you coming out of the Leek and Lily." She waited, and when Quinn did not contradict her or deny that he'd been there, she continued, "And you want to talk about coincidence? Here's one. It turns out that the young man who was killed was a former student of yours, so I wondered if you could tell me anything about him."

Quinn stroked the light stubble on his chin. "A student of mine? Who?"

"Rhodri Phillips. Do you remember him?'

Quinn took a sip of his Guinness and then thoughtfully examined the glass as if he'd never seen one quite like it.

"Rhodri Phillips." Quinn repeated the name, raising his eyes to the angle of the ceiling where it met two walls. He's tipped his hand, Penny thought. He knew Rhodri. People repeat a question or ask for clarification to buy time while they try furiously to think up a safe answer to a dangerous question. What he says next will be vague and evasive, Penny predicted.

"The thing is, you see, there've been so many students over the years, I couldn't possibly remember them all. Sometimes they come back to me years later, asking for a reference, and I have to find a way to politely decline, because the truth is I have no idea who they are or how they performed in my classroom. I could look up their grades, I suppose," he added with a shrug, "but really, what would be the point of that? If I don't remember them, it wouldn't be fair to say anything about them to a potential employer."

Penny pulled her phone out of her handbag and showed Quinn the photo of Rhodri that Rhian had sent her. "Maybe this will jog your memory," she said. "This is Rhodri."

Quinn maintained eye contact, and when he didn't look at her phone, she extended her arm a few inches closer to him.

His eyes slowly drifted downward, and he gave the phone a cursory glance before looking away.

"No, sorry." He shrugged as he tipped his glass to see how much of the dark liquid remained and then drained the last of it. "Not ringing any bells."

"Okay, well, I was just wondering why you were in Llanelen on Sunday." She gave him a second chance to deny that he'd been there.

Quinn's laugh was light and hollow. "Did you think I might be there to look you up?"

"No, that never entered my mind."

Quinn set his empty glass on the table. "How long are you planning to stop in Dublin?" he asked, without looking at her.

"I wasn't sure when I arrived, but now I think I'll go home on the evening sailing."

"A pity you won't be staying longer, but I suppose if there's nothing to keep you here . . ." He shrugged. "Still, if you've got nothing planned for this afternoon, I highly recommend the National Gallery. Some absolutely wonderful works there. It's easy to find. Just over the Liffey and a little way along from Trinity College, if you know where that is. It doesn't take long to get to the ferry terminal, so you'd have plenty of time. And there are some nice cafés in that area, if you want to get something to eat."

He gazed longingly at his glass, and Penny picked up on the cue. "Would you let me buy you a drink?" She pulled a ten-euro note out of her purse and set it on the table. "Shall I get the drinks in? I noticed you limped on Sunday and thought your injured leg must be playing up."

"It didn't heal as well as I'd hoped," Quinn said. "I'm supposed to exercise it, but that's painful, so I don't walk as much as I should. Anyway, since you're closer to the bar and I'm sat here against the wall, why don't you go? Barry knows what I'm having."

Penny gathered up the bank note along with the empty glasses and walked to the bar, feeling his eyes boring into her back every step of the way.

"Same again for him, and I'll have a tonic water with a slice of lemon this time," she said. As the bartender pulled the pint of Guinness, she asked, "How many is this for him?"

"His second. He's usually here right at opening time." He gestured at the glasses of Guinness and tonic water. "Can you manage, or would you like these on a tray?"

"Yes, a tray might be a good idea. Thanks." She picked up the tray and carried it to the table. Quinn, who had been leaning back in his chair against the wall, idly scanning the room, straightened up at her approach—not at the sight of her, she knew, but at the glass of his precious Guinness.

"Oh, that's grand," he said, reaching for it before she could place the tray on the table. "*Slainte.*" He tipped the glass slightly in her direction before taking an eager gulp and letting out an appreciative, "Ahhh. That really takes the edge off." He licked the cream-coloured foam from his top lip. "You have no idea how much an Irishman misses his Guinness when he's away. Oh, I know you can get it anywhere, but everything about it just tastes best here at home. It even looks better."

She remained standing at the edge of the table, still holding the tray. "Did you just say 'that's grand'?"

Quinn frowned. "I don't know. I might have. Why? So what if I did? It's just an expression."

Penny set her glass of tonic water on the table. "I've got to return the tray. I'll be back in a minute." Quinn shrugged and turned his full attention to his Guinness.

"You all right, miss?" the bartender asked, twirling a wine glass as he polished its base with a clean white towel. "You look a bit peaky."

"Yes, I'm fine, thanks." Penny slid the tray across the polished surface of the bar.

"You sure? If he said something to upset you or you're not feeling safe, I can help. I can call you a taxi, and it'll take you wherever you need to go."

"No, it's not that. Barry, is it? I just need a minute to think." He put a menu in front of her. "Here. Pretend you're looking at that and deciding what you're going to have for lunch."

"Is he looking at me?"

The bartender's eyes flickered in Quinn's direction. "No, he's talking on his phone. Look, are you sure everything's all right?"

"Yes. Fine. But thanks. I appreciate your concern."

"Well, if you need me, you know where I am." The bartender shifted along to the other end of the bar to serve a customer and Penny remained where she was, her mind whirling. It was him, she thought. Jimmy had said whoever organized the theft of the Black Chair must have had an accomplice with inside knowledge, and Michael Quinn had that. He'd been inside the Hall on the morning of the antiques show, and he'd just told her he'd been in the library. He knew the layout of the house. He'd been in Llanelen the day after the chair was stolen. And with his use of the word "grand," Penny was positive Quinn was the one who had spoken to Lane and threatened him. So somehow Quinn had managed to get inside the house. But he couldn't have carried the chair out of the house with his injured leg, so his role must have been to provide information. Could he also have planned the theft? She told herself she needed to be careful now, to get as much information as she could without giving anything away. And above all, she mustn't let him know what she suspected. She rolled her shoulders, relaxed her facial muscles, put on the best smile she could muster, and returned to the table.

"So," she said. "You were just about to tell me what you were doing in Llanelen on Sunday."

"Was I? Well, you know. It's a pretty little town. I like to visit every now and then. I find the scenery so relaxing. And the pub is grand and they do B&B, so sometimes I stop over."

"There's a group of Irish travellers camping outside Llanelen just now. Do you have a connection with them?"

"Travellers? Just because I'm Irish, why would that mean I know anything about a group of travellers?"

"So you don't have any business dealings with them?"

Quinn's shoulders tightened in exasperation. "Look, my line of work is appraising fine art, and believe me, fine art is way out of their league. I know they trade in all kinds of commodities, but I doubt they'd recognize a valuable painting if they did manage to get their hands on one, so why would I be having any business dealings with them?"

"What if it wasn't a painting they got their hands on, but a valuable artefact? A cultural treasure, in fact."

"What are you getting at?"

Oh, no, thought Penny. I've probably said too much. If he thinks I'm on to him, he'll bolt. "It's just that a valuable chair was stolen from the Hall on Saturday night, in case you hadn't heard, and I was wondering if you think the travellers could have had something to do with it. But I guess not. They weren't even camped out there then. They didn't arrive until a couple of days later."

"I don't know anything about a chair."

"And you weren't up at the Hall yourself on Saturday night, I suppose?"

Quinn's eyes narrowed, and he leaned back in his chair and folded his arms. "What makes you think I was?'

Penny took the plunge. "A young man, Lane Hardwick, saw or heard something during dinner service, and someone threatened him that if he told anyone what he'd seen, they'd hurt him."

"I never threatened that boy." He unfolded his arms and hunched forward, reaching for his phone. Penny wasn't sure whether he wanted to use it or was just holding it for comfort.

She realised the uncomfortable conversation had gone as far as it could.

"Look, I'm going to go now."

"I thought you said you came here for lunch."

"I've lost my appetite."

He shrugged. "Suit yourself." She knew he was as glad to see her go as she was to be on her way.

She returned to the bar and slid a banknote across to the bartender. "Look, do me a favour. Give him a drink from me."

"Should I tell him it's from you?"

"No, you don't have to do that. He'll work it out for himself."

Chapter Twenty

The street was wet and slippery when Penny left the pub. She zippered up her jacket, put the hood up, and tucked her bag under her arm. She needed to find a café or sheltered place to make a phone call. When she reached the Spire of Dublin on O'Connell Street, a branch of an international chain of coffee shops beckoned from a nearby corner. She entered and, without stopping to order a coffee, found a seat in a quiet corner and rang Inspector Bethan Morgan.

"Oh, I'm so glad you answered," Penny exclaimed a moment later. "I'm in Dublin, and I've just spoken to Michael Quinn. I didn't want to say too much to him, but you need to talk to him. I'm sure he's involved in the theft of the Black Chair. I think he was the one who helped the gang of thieves by describing the layout of the house, and he was probably inside it on the Saturday night. He could be the one who threatened Lane. Whether he was involved in the death of Rhodri Phillips, I don't know, but he certainly knew about it." She listened, then replied to Bethan's question. "Because when I told him that a former student of his had been killed, his reaction was so muted. Now if I'd just been told that someone I used to know had been killed, I'd want details. How? When? That's how most people would react, wouldn't they? They'd say, 'Oh, no, that's terrible. What happened?' And yet Michael Quinn asked almost nothing. And besides that, he was in a pub, in Llanelen, the day after it happened, and everyone in the pub must have been talking about it. Now mind you, he's been drinking, so maybe his brain's befuddled, but I'm convinced he's involved in the theft and possibly the murder, so you definitely need to talk to him."

She answered a few more questions, then said, "He's in the Celt pub right now on Talbot Street. He'll be there for at least another twenty minutes. Can you ask the Dublin police to pick him up and hold him for you?" And then in response to Bethan's asking how she knew he'd be in the pub, Penny replied, "Because just before I left, I bought him a drink, and he should be taking his first sip of it just about now. He's not going anywhere for a bit." Penny then told her she'd be home late that night, said she hoped they'd talk soon, and rang off.

* * *

At closing time, she reluctantly descended the stone steps of the National Gallery of Ireland to find that darkness had fallen while she had been losing herself in vast collections of Irish and Continental European art, both classic and modern. The imposing building that housed the works was beautiful in itself, and the experience reminded her that as much as she enjoyed her life in Llanelen, cities offered cultural, artistic, and metropolitan experiences like galleries and theatres that she could not access in her quiet town, and remembering how much she'd enjoyed international travel in her twenties, she told herself she should do more of that. She promised herself she'd return to Dublin soon, stay longer, and see and do more.

She'd been so entranced by the beautiful collections that she'd almost managed to blot out the conversation with Michael Quinn, and now back in the real world, she decided to set it firmly to one side while she focused on getting herself ready for the ferry journey home. She'd passed a supermarket express on her walk to the Gallery, so she returned there and picked up a couple of sandwiches, a drink, and a bar of chocolate for the three-hour crossing. As she emerged from the shop, a taxi slowed and she hailed it.

After checking in at the ferry terminal, she was instructed to wait in the lounge until it was time to board. Penny walked down a short, narrow hallway that opened into a large, utilitarian waiting area. Just inside the door a hot beverage service had been set up, and she bought a coffee before finding a seat. Because this was an off-season, evening sailing, her fellow passengers were middle-aged or elderly couples and a few well-dressed men, professionals headed to Britain on business, perhaps.

There were lots of empty seats to choose from. She had just sat down and taken a sip of coffee when shouts and whoops of laughter coming from the doorway caused her and everyone around her to look up as two women, one blonde and one with dark hair, accompanied by three children, an older girl and two smaller boys, entered. The blonde woman's hair showed several inches of dark roots, and her puffy jacket that had once been white was open to reveal a pink top with a high-heeled shoe made of glitter stretched over an ample bosom. Jeans ripped at the thighs and knees bulged over her broad hips. The other woman, her dark hair scraped back in a severe ponytail that gave her face a stretched appearance, looked a few years younger, but not young enough to be the blonde woman's daughter. Both women had a hard, uncompromising look about them, as if they were used to being in charge and getting their own way.

"Sit the kids down and keep them quiet," the blonde woman ordered the girl in a thick Irish accent. "Look after your cousins while me and your aunt go out for a fag." The girl, who Penny estimated to be about fourteen or fifteen, took the two boys by the hands and led them to empty chairs while the women disappeared through a doorway on the far side of the room, letting in a cold blast of night air. The children were thin, their light-brown hair matted and stringy, and from where she sat Penny could detect a sour, unwashed odour. An elderly woman a few chairs closer to the children caught Penny's eye, raised a disapproving eyebrow, gave a light but clearly judgemental shake of her head, and moved to a chair further away from them. The children remained quiet and motionless until the women returned. The blonde woman opened a plastic carrier bag and handed the girl a can of fizzy drink and a small bag of crisps. "Here's your tea, and share it out with your cousins." Penny thought of the two sandwiches in her bag but decided not to offer them. The woman had such a domineering manner, Penny didn't think her gesture would be well received.

At last, the door from the outside opened and a man wearing an orange–and–lime green high-visibility vest motioned to the passengers that it was time to make their way to the bus that would transport them to the ship. After a short drive the bus pulled into the vessel's bowels and stopped alongside long lines of cars and lorries.

"Stay together now," the dark-haired woman shouted at the children as they left the bus. Penny followed them up a wide metal staircase for several floors to the main passenger deck. A section of the lounge near the entrance featured a cafeteria-style food service operation, serving hot meals and snacks, and beside it was a bar with a full selection of beer, wines, and liquor. A large area was given over to mixed seating arrangements, including theatre-style rows, tables and chairs along the windows, and banquettes with tables. Penny chose a small round table beside a window, although there would be little to see. The passengers dispersed around the lounge, and the women with the children chose a banquette across the aisle from Penny.

Several decks below, a low, rumbling vibration indicated that the engines were starting up. The ship shuddered to life and then slowly slipped away. Soon the twinkling harbour lights of Dublin disappeared into the rainy mist, and the ship was enveloped in the blackness of the open sea.

Penny closed her eyes. But just as she was about to drift off, the harsh voice of the blonde woman at the banquette cut into her solitude. "I told you, you cheeky beggar, no, you can't have fish and chips. You'll get something to eat when we get there." One of the small boys started crying. "You stop that right now, do you hear me?" the woman said. "Oh, I can't take any more of his mithering," she said to the girl. "Keep an eye on them while we get a couple of cans." The two women strode to the bar, once again leaving the girl in charge of the smaller children. Penny thought again of the sandwiches in her bag, but she didn't dare offer them to the children without their mother's permission. What if something in the sandwich caused an allergic reaction?

She opened her bag and withdrew the two books she'd bought at a bookstore on O'Connell Street. One was a history of Dublin and the other a heritage guide to its beautiful Georgian buildings. Not really in the mood for either and wishing she'd also picked up a magazine or a light, undemanding novel, she replaced them in her bag. The two women returned, set a couple of cans of beer on their table, and cracked them open. The girl looked at the drinks and then rested her head on her hand and closed her eyes.

Unable to bear it any longer, Penny pulled the sandwiches and chocolate out of her bag and approached the table. "Excuse me," she said to the blonde woman. "I brought these for the journey, but now I find I'm not hungry, so I wondered if the children might like them. It'd be a shame to see them go to waste." She held them out. The woman paused with her can of beer halfway to her lips and glared at Penny.

"Yeah, all right. Give them here," she said, setting down the can and snatching the packets out of Penny's hands. "There you go." She slid the sandwiches across the table to the girl, who closed a notebook in which she'd been colouring and moved it to one side. When her sketchbook was out of harm's way and her coloured pencils back in their case, she eagerly ripped open the plastic and cardboard wrapping and carefully tore each sandwich half into three equal pieces and handed the boys their share. Penny was appalled that all three children were allowed to eat without being taken to the lavatory to wash their hands.

"Thank you," the girl said in a small voice accompanied by a shy smile. She gazed up at Penny with a look of such gratitude in her dark-blue eyes that Penny was equally touched and alarmed that a simple gesture of offering a couple of sandwiches and a bar of chocolate could evoke such a response.

"You are most welcome," said Penny, with what she hoped was a smile that masked her true feelings of anger toward the mother. She glanced at the notebook the girl had pushed out of the way and realised that it wasn't a cheap commercial colouring book that she'd been working in, but an artist's sketchbook. "May I?" Penny asked. The girl nodded, and Penny picked it up. She looked at the sketch the girl had been working on, and then carefully flipped the pages back to reveal completed work. The pages were filled with hand-drawn and -coloured botanicals—roses, lilies, and chrysanthemums—their perfectly formed leaves delicately shaded and their petals so exquisitely vibrant Penny felt she could pluck one off the page.

"These are absolutely beautiful," Penny said to the girl, handing back her sketchbook. "You have a real talent. You'll be giving Redouté a good run for his money."

"Oh, you think so, do you?" snarled her mother. "Bloody waste of time, if you ask me."

"Bloody waste of time," echoed one of the small boys through a mouthful of sandwich, causing the other boy to laugh and spit a few crumbs onto the table. The girl's face collapsed and she lowered her eyes to the table, her fair hair hanging like a curtain to hide her face.

Seething, Penny returned to her seat, collected her belongings, and wandered into the darkened room off the lounge that had been set up as a small cinema. The film to be screened on this voyage was a period drama involving a shipwreck off the coast of Cornwall and an injured survivor who was given shelter in a lighthouse by a mysterious woman. While the music was stirring and the costumes and visual effects stunning, she couldn't follow the story line. She sat in the dark, her mind whirling as she thought about the artistic girl she'd just met and wondered what was happening with Michael Quinn.

About half an hour later she received a text from Victoria. LET ME KNOW WHEN YOU ON BOAT TRAIN. WILL PICK YOU UP AT JUNCTION.

Without waiting to see how the film ended, she left the screening room and returned to the main lounge. She took a seat facing the bow of the ship, and after a few minutes, the sound of light rain tapping against the windows lulled her into a light doze. When she woke, she could just make out lights ahead. She checked her watch. They should be arriving in about thirty minutes. She stood up, stretched, and went for a stroll around the lounge. Many of her fellow passengers were dozing, propped upright on chairs with their heads lolling back or sprawled out on two chairs pushed together. The two Irishwomen, a can of beer in front of each of them, talked louder than they needed to, and the girl sat across from them, her frail shoulders bowed as if by an invisible weight. She raised her sad eyes, half hidden by drooping eyelids, as Penny walked past. The two boys were nowhere to be seen, and Penny assumed they'd fallen asleep on the benches that formed part of the banquette seating arrangement.

A flash of light slashed through the endless darkness outside the cabin window. Then, another flash, and Penny realised they were sailing past the South Stack lighthouse, just off the northwest tip of the island of Anglesey. The ferry crossing was almost over, and the beacons of light were welcoming her home to Wales.

A short while later, the engine noise changed as the ship slowed to a stop, and after docking procedures that seemed endless, the call came to disembark. The passengers were once again boarded onto buses and driven to the terminal building adjacent to the Holyhead railway station, where a couple of British police officers scanned the arriving passengers. Penny hurried through the station to the platform to catch her train.

She climbed on board, found a seat, and just before it was due to depart, groaned inwardly at the sound of shouts on the platform indicating the women and their three charges were on their way. The girl entered first, looked up and down the aisle, and chose a table with facing seats about midway down the carriage. Oh, please, let them be quiet, Penny thought. It's late, everyone's tired, and we've all had enough of them.

She leaned back and closed her eyes as the train rattled and swayed across the island of Anglesey, crossed the Britannia Bridge over the Menai Strait to the mainland, and stopped at Bangor, where some passengers disembarked. Penny hoped the Irishwomen and children would be leaving there, too, but they stayed in their seats. At least they were quiet, and remained that way for the time it took to reach Llandudno Junction.

Followed by her now familiar travelling companions of the two women, each carrying a sleeping, floppy boy over her shoulder, and the girl trailing along behind, Penny climbed a set of stairs, crossed the bridge that spanned the railway tracks, and then walked down an identical set of stairs that led to the exit. She stepped through the doorway, placing her feet on a stone worn down in the middle by years of departing footsteps, and emerged into the station forecourt, where, to her relief, Victoria was standing beside her car, waving.

"I'm that glad to see you, I could hug you," Penny said as she placed her bag on the back seat.

"Let's not get carried away. You've only been gone a day."

"No, really, I am. And not to mention I'm starving. I bought some sandwiches to eat on the journey but gave them away, and after I'd done that, I realised it would look strange if I then bought something to eat from the food service place in the lounge. Although, really, why should I care what people I don't know and will never see again think?"

"You gave away your sandwiches? Why would you do that?" Victoria asked as they fastened their seat belts.

"There were some hungry kids and their mother didn't

look like she was going to get them anything to eat, although there was enough money for cans of beer for her. I felt sorry for them."

"Ah, that was nice of you."

As they pulled out of the car park, Penny twisted in her seat and looked behind them.

"What's the matter?" Victoria asked. "Do you think you've forgotten something?"

"No," said Penny. "I'm starting to wonder if I'm being followed."

"What makes you think that?"

"It's probably nothing, but the kids I gave the sandwiches to? They were with two women, and they got off at the Junction with me. That just seems a bit odd."

"Did anyone else get off the train with you?"

"An elderly couple."

"And were the elderly couple on the ship with you, too?"

"Yes."

"So how do you know the elderly couple weren't following you?"

Penny laughed. "I don't think they were up to it. No, it just seemed a coincidence, that's all. First the travellers pitch up in Llanelen, and now the women with the kids on the ship and train. I'm positive they're travellers."

"Well, maybe they're not following you at all but joining the rest of their people in Llanelen. They're still camped out near your cottage. Or maybe the women are going someplace completely different. Who knows?"

They were in the country now, and the road ahead was dark.

"Look," said Victoria. "It's late and you're hungry. You've probably got nothing in, or at least not much because you never do, so why don't you just come to mine for the night. I can make you something nice to eat while you have a shower, and then you can tell me all about it." She flicked on her turn signal and slowed down. "And besides, if you think you were followed, you probably shouldn't be alone in your cottage. In case you hadn't noticed, it's a bit isolated."

"I had noticed, and that's the second time in less than a week someone's told me that. But what about Harrison?"

"He's all taken care of. I was over to see him earlier. I even brought some work with me and kept him company after he had his dinner. We listened to some music and had a lovely visit."

Penny leaned back in her heated seat and, wrapped in the warmth of Victoria's car, closed her eyes. How wonderful to be met off the train and just be taken care of, she thought. There are times when you're exhausted, you've had enough of doing everything for yourself, and the thought of someone picking you up, taking you home, and making you a cup of tea sounds heavenly. "Yes," she said. "I'd love to go to yours. I'm shattered. For now, I just want a lovely warm shower, something quick to eat, scrambled eggs, maybe, and then bed. I'll tell you everything tomorrow. And thank you for picking me up."

"Can you at least tell me if you found out anything useful?"

But the answer would have to wait. Penny was fast asleep.

Chapter Twenty-One

"I hope you weren't worried that I was annoyed with you about taking time off work to go to Dublin," said Victoria the next morning as she buttered a piece of toast. "With Rhian back at work, there was no problem, and she was so grateful to you for trying to find out what happened to Rhodri, I couldn't possibly have minded. Anyway, it was only a couple of days. And I must say, your asking Rhian to come back to work was brilliant. I'm not sure I would have thought of that. You might not look it, but you really are rather clever." Penny smiled as she held up her cup and Victoria filled it with freshly brewed coffee. "I'm glad to see you're looking much better this morning," Victoria continued. "You were half dead last night."

"I always sleep really well in your spare room," Penny said. "That bed is heavenly."

"So tell me what happened. Was it worth it, going to Dublin?"

"I think so. I found Michael Quinn in a pub and bought

him a couple of drinks. I wasn't sure what to expect, but he's not doing well. I don't know where he's living, but he's drinking too much, and I don't think he's got a proper job. Does appraisals for an auction house, but it's not steady work. Anyway, I asked him lots of questions. He was evasive, but I'm quite certain he was in on the theft of the chair."

"What makes you think that?"

"He told me Emyr gave him a drink in the Ty Brith Hall library the day of the antique show, so he knows the layout of the downstairs. I'm pretty sure he was the one who guided the thieves to the Black Chair so they could steal it. And I think he was the one who bumped into Lane and threatened him if he told anyone what he'd seen."

"And Rhodri?" asked Victoria.

"Rhodri was a student of his, so he must have known him, at least a little, but I can't bring myself to believe he had anything to do with his death."

"Hmm. Well, I can see why you wouldn't want to think that."

"And then I rang Bethan to let her know where he was, and she was going to ask the Dublin police to pick him up and hold him for questioning. So we'll see what happens."

* * *

When the last client had left the nail salon, Penny tidied up and placed an order for a couple of new bottles of nail varnish. She did a walk-through of all the rooms, checking that everything was ready for the opening of business the next morning, said good night to Victoria, and let herself out the front door, locking it behind her. As she grasped the wrought iron gate and pulled it open, to her amazement, it swung silently and smoothly on its hinges.

"Hello," said a voice in the darkness, and out of the shadow stepped retired Det. Chief Inspector Gareth Davies.

"Is this your work?" asked Penny, indicating the gate. "It's lost its squeak."

"It has," he replied. "I'm only sorry it took me so long to get around to it. I told you a long time ago I'd sort it, and I finally made good on that promise."

"It's much better," said Penny. "Thank you."

"I just wanted to say good-bye," Gareth said. "I'm sorry we weren't able to get together for that cup of coffee, but I understand you were away."

"Yes, I was. You're here to say good-bye . . . you're leaving, then?'

"Contracts were finally exchanged this afternoon, so now that the house is sold, I'm off to spend a few days with my son and his family in Liverpool, and then back to Scotland."

"I'm glad it all worked out for you," said Penny. "I wish you every happiness."

"Would you like a ride home?" Gareth asked.

"No, thank you. I'm meeting someone for dinner."

With a questioning look he held out his arms, and she moved closer to him. He wrapped his arms around her, holding her against the soft wool of his navy-blue overcoat for a moment, and then released her.

He took a couple of steps back, then turned and walked away. The street lamp cast a yellowish light over his tall figure, but as he emerged out of its halo, he blended into the darkness and disappeared.

"Good-bye, Gareth," said Penny.

* * *

"Evening, Inspector." The waiter greeted Bethan and Penny at the entrance to the recently renovated dining room of the Red Dragon Hotel and showed them to a table. "Good to see you again. You haven't been in for a while."

Bethan acknowledged the greeting with a smile as the server handed her and Penny menus.

"I didn't realise how hungry I am," said Penny as she studied the menu. "I do this every time. Look at everything on offer and then order the same thing. I'll have the roast chicken with a jacket potato." Bethan opted for pasta, and after taking their orders and collecting their menus, the server brought Penny a glass of wine and Bethan a sparkling mineral water.

"Cheers," said Bethan, raising her glass.

"Cheers," Penny replied.

"Well, now," Bethan began. "As you can imagine, the chief constable wants that Black Chair found and returned to its owners in time for the visit by the Prince of Wales, and the people responsible for the death of Rhodri Phillips caught."

"Of course he does."

"And besides the chief constable demanding a result, the story is finally going to break tomorrow in the national media.

It's going to be everywhere, and reporters will be demanding to know what's being done. So I'm under a lot of pressure right now to get a result, and quickly."

"Yes, you are. So, tell me. Did the Dublin police pick up Quinn? What's happening with him?"

"They did pick him up, they talked to him, and rather to my surprise, he agreed to come back here to be formally interviewed, so that's one thing that's gone my way. Otherwise, it could have been a long process, not to mention the dreaded paperwork an extradition warrant involves."

"Has he admitted to his part in the robbery? Telling the thieves where they could find the chair?"

"Not yet."

"I'm convinced he did that. And if I'm right, what would he be charged with? Being an accessory, or something like that?"

"If he gave the thieves information used to plan a burglary, he could be charged with burglary, because he was part of it. But he could be in serious trouble. If he gave them information used to commit this burglary, he could be charged with murder."

"What! Murder! Oh, surely not. I can't believe he had anything to do with Rhodri's death."

"He may not be the person who actually killed Rhodri, but in law, there's this thing called secondary liability. It's complicated, but basically, if you help someone commit a crime, so in this case, robbery"—Penny nodded to indicate she was following—"and then if during the commission of that crime, another, more serious crime occurs—murder—you can be charged as an equal party in the second crime."

"Yikes. I never knew that."

"Well, we'll see what the investigation turns up, but our Mr. Quinn could find himself in very deep trouble, depending on what the CPS recommends."

"CPS . . . Crown . . ."

"Prosecution Service. They review the police investigation, then determine what the charges will be, and then prosecute in court."

"You know I want to help in any way I can."

Bethan let out a light, fluttery laugh. "Well, if you were to find out who killed Rhodri Phillips and were somehow able to recover the Black Chair, that would go a long way to solving my problems and would make the chief constable very happy."

"I'm sure it would." Penny took a sip of wine. "But your team is interviewing everybody who was at the Hall on Saturday night, so you must be getting a good idea of what happened."

"I've got the big picture, yes, but I'm still missing that one key piece that will make everything else fall into place. It could be that vital little bit of information that somebody has but doesn't even know they have or how important it is. I hope we'll get some leads from the interview with Quinn that will open up new lines of inquiry, but I need to make sure that I'm using all the resources available to me. And that includes you."

"So what would you like me to do?"

"Keep doing what you're doing. Keep your eyes and ears open and let me know immediately if something occurs to you. You know what I always tell people. No matter how trivial or insignificant a detail might seem to you, it might fit in with something we already know." The server appeared with their meals, and Penny asked for a second glass of wine. "It might be helpful if we reviewed what we know so far," said Bethan as she picked up her knife and fork. "What are your thoughts?"

"You used the word 'key.' I still think the key to Rhodri's murder is the chair, and when we find out who stole the chair, we'll find the killer."

"Or killers."

"Or killers. I talked it over with Jimmy, and as a reformed character, he had some good insight. He thinks the chair was stolen to order, probably for a collector because it's way too hot for the open market. It seems likely that Rhodri was killed during the theft. Rhodri was struck over the head with a rock or brick, most likely from the garden or walkway, so the thieves didn't come prepared to kill, and I doubt they intended to kill him, but maybe he got in the way somehow. We don't know yet what his role was. He might have been working for the gang, and maybe he knew too much and threatened to go to the authorities. Or maybe he tried to stop them and that's why he was killed. So I think we have to keep digging and find out as much as we can about Rhodri."

"We've talked to his family."

"Have you talked to his friends?"

"We're still trying to track down his friends. His mother doesn't seem to know anybody he hung out with, and if his workmates at the hotel know, they're not saying."

"I might be able to help you there. Eirlys mentioned that she went out with Rhodri a couple of times and on one occasion, he had two or three other lads with him. I don't know who they are. About the same age, but she described them as . . . what was the word she used? 'Rough.' In fact, she didn't like them at all, and although she liked Rhodri well enough, she decided not to see him anymore because of the company he kept. She said they seemed to have some kind of hold over him."

"I need to speak to Eirlys, then."

Penny nodded. "I thought you might, and I told her so. She mentioned this to me on Monday, and I probably should have passed it on to you sooner."

"That's all right. We've been busy enough with the people we already had to interview."

Penny nodded, then continued, "And we do have to consider there might be an Irish connection to all this. Michael Quinn is Irish. I think he was on-scene the night of the robbery to direct the thieves to the library, where they knew the chair would be. The travellers that set up camp near my cottage just after the theft are Irish. Is there a connection? Are they involved? Or is it just coincidence?"

Bethan set down her knife and fork and folded her hands. She gave Penny her full attention.

"And the one person who knows more than he's told us is

Lane. We don't know for sure if it was Michael Quinn who spoke to Lane in the hallway during the dinner party, but I think it was."

"Quinn might confirm that when we interview him."

"And we don't know what else Lane saw or heard."

"I gave him a few days to get himself together, and he's first on my list to interview tomorrow."

Their meal was interrupted a few minutes later by the ringing of Penny's phone. She pulled it out of her handbag and checked the number. "Oh, it's the nursing home. Must be about Jimmy. They wouldn't be ringing unless there's a problem, so I'd better answer it." She pressed the green button. "Hello? Yes, this is Penny." She listened, nodded a couple of times, then said, "Right. Can you tell him I'll be in to see him this evening? Thank you." She ended the call.

In response to Bethan's questioning eyebrow, she said, "Apparently Jimmy fell out of his wheelchair. He was shaken up a bit, but nothing's broken. Not an emergency. He's resting now. We can finish our meal, and I'll pop in to see him on my way home."

"I'll come with you."

They finished their main course and, by unspoken agreement, skipped dessert, settled their bill, and were on their way.

Chapter Twenty-Two

"I was pushed out of my chair," Jimmy insisted. "I didn't fall out of it, like they're saying. Someone came up behind me and deliberately tipped over my chair. I felt it happen."

"Do you have any idea who could have done that?" Bethan asked.

"No, because I was sat just inside the room with my back to the door, so anyone could have crept up behind me and done it."

"Was there anyone else in the room who might have seen what happened?" asked Penny.

"No chance. Everybody else was in the dining room having their dinner. I'd gone back to the lounge on my own to get my glasses. I'd left them on the table, and I paused for a moment to catch my breath just inside the room when it happened. One minute I'd just wheeled myself into the lounge, and the next, I was on the floor. I couldn't get up, and of course, the staff thought all the inmates were at dinner, so it wasn't until someone noticed I wasn't in my usual place that they came looking for me. So they got me back in the chair and then brought me here to my room and gave me my dinner on a tray in bed."

"Did you hear anything unusual just before this happened?" Bethan asked.

"No, I didn't," said Jimmy, "but then my hearing's not the best."

"And you're sure you have no idea who might have done this?"

"Well, to be honest, I hated to think this, because it's such a stupid thing to do, but I wondered if one of my mates might have done it as a bit of a prank."

"Oh, Jimmy," said Penny reaching for his hand. "I'm so sorry this happened. She leaned closer and examined his face. "I think you might have some bruising there, under your right eye. Are you sure you're all right? One of the carers told us you didn't want them to send for the doctor."

"No, no. I'm all right. Just a little shaken up, that's all."

Bethan looked at the wheelchair, and then Penny. "Would you mind sitting in the chair for a moment?" she asked.

"No. But why?"

Bethan pulled the chair out from the wall, positioned it in the centre of the room, and then inclined her head at it. Penny sat.

"Okay," said Bethan, grasping the handgrips. "Here we go." She tipped up the chair, quickly, and Penny started to slide forward. Bethan lowered the chair before Penny reached the point where she would have fallen out. "That took a fair bit of effort on my part." She spoke directly to Jimmy. "I doubt whoever did this was one of your mates."

"Someone younger and stronger?"

"That would be my guess." Bethan repositioned the wheelchair against the wall. "I don't think whoever did this meant for you to be harmed, but intended it as a warning. Have you done or said anything recently that could have rubbed someone up the wrong way or upset anyone?"

Jimmy shook his head. "I don't think so. I pretty much just mind my own business."

"Now, that's not quite true, Jimmy," said Penny. "Or at least not the way I see it. You're very social. Always talking to your fellow residents about one thing or another." She frowned. "Did you happen to mention that conversation we had about the stolen Black Chair to anyone?"

"I can't remember, but even if I did, it's not exactly a secret. For a couple of days, that's all anybody talked about. Everybody's worried about it and wants it found."

"Well, look, Jimmy," said Bethan. "My advice is that you take this incident as a warning, and it might be best if you steer clear of any conversation that could be considered controversial. It looks like someone has it in for you, so be careful. I hope you'll feel okay tomorrow." She gave Jimmy a reassuring pat on the shoulder and then turned to Penny. "I'm just going to check the visitor sign-in book to see who's been in and out today. When you're ready, why don't you meet me in the reception area and I'll give you a lift home."

Remembering the times she'd forgotten to sign in and the receptionist had been preoccupied and failed to remind her, Penny wasn't confident Bethan would find anything useful in the visitor log.

When Bethan had left, Penny turned her attention back to Jimmy. He looked frailer than the last time she'd seen him. Paler and thinner. She took his hand and they sat together without speaking. The bedside lamp cast a soft glow over him, and she found it strangely moving, just sitting there quietly with him. He closed his eyes, and his gentle breathing led her to believe he was asleep. She released his hand and got to her feet. As she stood, ready to tiptoe out of the room, he said in a low voice, "The police lady asked me if I heard anything unusual just before I got tipped out of my chair. I didn't. But now that I think of it, I did smell something unusual. It was the strong smell of tobacco. You know that stale smell of smoke you get off a heavy smoker? It was like that."

"Okay," said Penny. "I'll tell Bethan."

"So now I don't think it was someone who lives here," said Jimmy. "Nobody here smokes, because you have to go outside and most of us can't do that without assistance. And besides, most smokers don't live long enough to make it into a place like this."

"That's a good thought," said Penny. "Well, be sure to ring me if anything else occurs to you. I'll pop in and see how you're doing tomorrow. Try to get some sleep now."

She leaned over, lightly kissed his cheek as she gave his hand a reassuring squeeze, and then slipped out of the room.

Chapter Twenty-Three

Heavy rain lashing her windowpanes, accompanied by the howling of high November winds, awakened Penny during the night. She got up and looked out the window, but unable to see anything, she went back to bed, where she lay in the dark, snug in her cozy cottage, thinking. By morning the rain had stopped, and when she set off for town, all that remained of the night's storm was the dripping trees that flanked the road and dark branches brought down by the wind littering the verge. Through the light mist that drifted over the fields, she could just make out a fire in the travellers' encampment and shadowy human shapes moving toward it. The mournful barking of an unhappy dog disturbed the silence.

Not long after she passed the encampment, a small figure came toward her. As they neared each other, the girl's eyes darted anxiously in the direction of the encampment and then turned to Penny when they both stopped.

"Hello," said Penny with a gentle smile. "We meet again. How are you?"

"Grand, I guess," said the girl in the small voice that Penny remembered from the ferry. She wore a pair of trainers with holes in the toes, plaid trousers made of a flannel material, and a wooly jumper. Penny, in a lined, waterproof anorak, was warm enough, but not too warm. That child must be freezing, Penny thought. The two jugs of milk the girl was carrying hung loosely at her side.

"Are you staying at the encampment?" Penny asked. The girl nodded.

"Oh, sorry, I should have introduced myself. My name's Penny. Would you like to tell me yours?"

"Riley," said the girl. She gave no sign of wanting to move on and remained planted firmly in front of Penny. "When you saw my drawings on the boat, you said I'd give someone a run for his money. Redouté, I think you said." She pronounced the French name hesitatingly but correctly. "Who is he? Or she?"

"Oh, that's Pierre-Joseph Redouté. He was a French artist who lived a couple of hundred years ago and painted the most beautiful watercolours of flowers. Lilacs, carnations, and roses. Lots and lots of roses, in every colour imaginable. If you pop into the library in town, one of the librarians would be happy to show you a book filled with his paintings." As she warmed up to a topic she loved, Penny's smile was genuine, and for a moment, the girl returned it. And then, as quickly as it had appeared, it disappeared, replaced with a lowering of her head and a slumping of her shoulders. Realizing the girl might not be allowed to go to the library or might never have had the chance to visit one, Penny added, "Actually, I've got a small book of his paintings at home, and you'd be welcome to drop in to look at it. I live in the cottage just back there." She pointed behind her, and the girl raised her head to see where Penny was pointing. "I get a sense you really like drawing. Am I right?" The girl nodded. "I was really impressed by the work in your sketchbook. You have a great gift. You know, we have a little art group here in Llanelen. Sometimes we have a lecture by a visiting artist and sometimes we go rambling together, just to enjoy the fresh air and sketch. If you're stopping in Llanelen for any length of time, you'd be so welcome to join us. We're all older, of course, so it would be wonderful to have a young person join us. You seem to enjoy sketching botanicals, so we could go to Bodnant Garden. It's beautiful all year round, and even in winter there's lots of colour and I think you'd really enjoy it. We'd be happy to take you, if your mother agreed. I hope you wouldn't find us too boring."

"Oh, I'm sure I would love it," Riley replied. "I know I would. But my mother, she wouldn't let me. She thinks art is a waste of time. Well, you heard her."

"Sometimes people do think that," said Penny, biting her tongue before she could add, *people who don't know any better.* "But when it's something you love to do, well, you just have to do it, don't you? It's not even really as if you have a choice. It's so much more than just what you do, it's who you are. And we should all do what we're good at."

"That's it exactly!" exclaimed the girl. And then her face

dropped. "But that's not what they have in mind for me. We're here meeting with other traveller families to see if there's a potential husband for me."

"A husband! But you're only . . ."

"I'm fifteen," said the girl. "Traveller girls are supposed to get married when they're about sixteen. But I don't want to. It's an awful life. You're expected to clean and then have babies. I want to go to high school. And then I want to go to art school. At least I think I want to go to art school. Maybe a university where I could learn everything there is to know about plants. Where they grow, how they grow, all their names. Oh, that would be so wonderful."

"I . . . I don't know what to say," Penny said. She found herself in an awkward, uncomfortable position. While she didn't want to make a disparaging comment about the girl's traveller culture, at the same time she wanted to let her know that she supported her and found the concept of such an early marriage, and the denying of fundamental women's rights that most Western women took for granted, remarkable, to say the least, in the twenty-first century. "I've seen you walk by," the girl said. "I do know where you live. The cottage with the charcoal door."

"That's me. I can never decide what colour it should be, but fortunately I have a friend who's a painter—that's the decorator kind of painter, not the watercolour or acrylic kind, like us—so he changes the colour for me every now and then. One day, maybe, I'll find a colour I really like and stick with it. I'm thinking of a sage green next."

"That would work!" said Riley.

"Well, I'm sure those milk jugs are heavy, so I mustn't keep you, and I have to get to work," said Penny. "It was lovely to see you again." She hesitated, then added, "I hope you'll find a way to get the education you want and deserve."

As the girl moved away, something in the hedgerow caught her attention, and she set down the milk jugs and picked a late-blooming white flower, held it close to her face, and then tucked it in her pocket.

* * *

"Have you seen this?" Mrs. Lloyd placed a copy of a national newspaper, open to an inside page, on the manicure table.

Welsh treasure stolen

No leads yet on bard's chair

Eirlys, who was seated across from Mrs. Lloyd, peered at it, then handed it up to Penny, who was standing behind her. After reading the headline and scanning the rest of the article. Penny returned it to Mrs. Lloyd. "It doesn't tell us anything we didn't already know," she said.

"This article is not complimentary to our local police," said Mrs. Lloyd. "The reporter makes it sound as if the police aren't trying hard enough."

"Oh, they're trying hard, all right," said Penny. "The problem isn't though, as the headline suggests, that there are no leads. They've still got people they want to interview."

"They haven't interviewed me yet," said Mrs. Lloyd.

"They paid more attention to the waitstaff than the guests because no one left the dining room."

"What do you mean, no one left the dining room? Who said no one left the dining room?" said Mrs. Lloyd.

"Emyr did. When we were still in the library, just after we discovered the chair was missing, he said that to me, and then he said it again to Bethan later, in the sitting room. She was annoyed that he allowed the dinner guests to leave before the police could speak to them. He said none of the guests left the dining room during dinner service, so he assumed they couldn't have seen anything."

"I wish I'd heard him say that. I would have spoken up, because it's not true. I was in that dining room, and I ought to know. Someone did leave the room."

"Who? Who left the room?"

"Jennifer Sayles. Sayles? Is that her name? Emyr's lady friend, or whatever she is. I assumed she'd gone to the cloakroom."

"How long was she gone?"

"Oh, not very long. About as long as a woman would need to go to the cloakroom. Not so long as anybody would notice. I mean, nobody said, 'Where's Jennifer got to? She's been gone a long time, hasn't she?' So there was nothing out of the ordinary and nobody took any notice. Why would they? It was a dinner party and everyone was enjoying the delicious food and having a wonderful time."

"This could be really important. Can you remember when Jennifer Sayles left the room? At what point during the dinner?"

"I'm not sure, really."

"Was it during the starter, say, or . . ."

"Hold on a minute. Let me think." Mrs. Lloyd pulled her hands out of the soaking basin and held her wet fingers to her temples while she closed her eyes. A moment later she opened them and, with a quick apology to Eirlys, slipped her fingers back in the basin. "Yes," she said. "I've got it now. It was at the end of the starter course. The plates were being cleared and she wasn't in her seat, and the waiter asked me if he should take away her plate. I wasn't sure what to do, because what if she came back and wanted to finish her salmon? But then I thought, well, if that did happen, and she was that desperate for more salmon, Florence would have made extra servings, so I told the waiter he could take her plate away. And a couple of minutes later, back she comes, that Jennifer Sayles. And she didn't mind at all that her starter was gone. And then we moved on to the main course."

"And Emyr didn't notice she'd left the room, or he would have said," mused Penny.

"Well," said Mrs. Lloyd, drawing out the one-syllable word. "He was busy at his end of the table with the lady mayoress. She can talk the hind leg off a donkey, that one, and just try getting a word in edgewise. So he probably didn't notice Jennifer leave the room. Or if he did notice, maybe he told the police nobody left because he wanted to protect her? Maybe he was covering up for her, for some reason? Oh, I'm not saying he'd think she'd done anything wrong, nothing like that, but he might just want to save her the bother of the police asking her questions, and holding up her return to London. You know what the police are like."

"Oh, I do know what they're like," said Penny. "Mrs. Lloyd, you've been very helpful. I don't know just how helpful, but I'm going to call Bethan, and she'll likely want to speak to you soon." Penny dashed from the room.

"Look at her," grumbled Mrs. Lloyd to Eirlys. "I didn't even get a chance to reply." She shrugged. "Oh, well. I should be used to that by now. She always runs off when she's just had a brain wave. And to be fair, she's right a lot more times than she's wrong. I shudder to think of all the murderers who'd be roaming the streets of Llanelen today if Penny hadn't sprung into action. Right, then. If Bethan wants to talk to me, she knows where to find me. Now then, Eirlys love, what colour should I have today? You're always so good at helping me choose just the right shade."

"This is new in," said Eirlys, holding up a bottle of fuchsia-coloured nail varnish. "What do you think of this one?"

"It's a bit daring for me," said Mrs. Lloyd. "Oh, well, go on then. Let's live a little!"

Chapter Twenty-Four

"The bruising on your face is much more noticeable today, and there's some swelling around your eye," Penny said that evening as she peered at Jimmy's face. "Sometimes you don't feel the full effects of a fall until the next day." She set her handbag down, then dropped into the visitor's chair. "Has the doctor been in to see you?"

Jimmy shook his head. "The nurse had a look at me this morning and she said she'd check my face again at bedtime. She put me on the list for the next doctor's visit. That's tomorrow or the day after."

"Good. And what did you get up to today?"

"I stayed in bed most of the morning and then sat in the lounge for a bit this afternoon like I usually do, but people didn't know what to make of me." He raised a hand to the side of his face. "The men avoided looking at me and the women fussed over me. I had my tea in the dining room, but I felt uncomfortable. By then I'd just had enough of everything, so I came back to my room as soon as I'd finished." He let out a small sigh of defeat and resignation. "To be honest, I feel safer in here, with the door closed. Anyway, you said you'd pop in on your way from work, so I thought it would be better if we chatted in here. In private, like. But I think I'd like the door open now, if that's all right with you."

"I'm sorry you don't feel safe," said Penny as she rose and crossed the room to open the door. "But you're probably safer when you're with the rest of the group. Nobody would try anything when you're surrounded by other people. But it's good for us to visit in here so we can talk without fear of being overheard."

"Most everybody in the home is hard of hearing," replied Jimmy with a wan smile. "But there's some who can hear just fine."

"And the staff can hear just fine, too." Penny leaned forward. "Have you had a chance to think about whether you were asking questions or talking about anything that could be considered, well, sensitive? Anything to do with the theft of the Black Chair? And who might have overheard you? Did you discuss that with any of your mates? Maybe offered an opinion on what you think might have happened that showed a little too much insight?"

"I talked about it with you, didn't I?"

"That's right," Penny agreed. "Of course we did." Jimmy held out his hand to her, and she took it. "Isn't it strange that Bethan and I asked you last night if you'd spoken to anyone, and it never occurred to me to include myself."

A shadow falling on the hall floor outside Jimmy's room

caught their attention, and a moment later the figure of Mrs. Lynch filled the door frame.

"Evening, Jimmy," she said with a cheery little wave. "All right?"

"Yes, thanks," Jimmy replied. Mrs. Lynch gave Penny a tight-lipped smile and then continued on her way.

After a moment, Penny spoke. "Bethan said she didn't think any of your mates could have pushed you out of your chair, but do you think she could have done it?" She tipped her head toward the door.

"She might have been able to manage it physically, but she doesn't smoke. She said she gave it up a few years ago when she was diagnosed with a medical condition to do with her circulation that causes problems with the veins in her legs. And I got a really strong smell of cigarette smoke from the person behind me, remember."

"So you did. Does she get many visitors, this Mrs. Lynch?"

"She seems to have a close family. There's a woman who might be her daughter. Blonde, and looks older than she probably is. Got a hard look about her, like she's been ridden hard and put away wet. She's only been coming around in the past few days. And then there's a younger fellow; I'd say he'd be in his early twenties. Maybe a grandson? He's been coming to see her for a bit longer. And then there's a woman about her own age. Someone told me that was her sister and the reason Mrs. Lynch chose this home was to be close to her. She visits quite often, but to be honest, I don't think it'll be long before she's in here herself."

"You've still got your observation skills," said Penny.

"Well, there's not much else to do in here except observe," replied Jimmy. "People in here tend to take a keen interest in everybody else's business. I guess we see it as a form of entertainment."

"So," said Penny. "If we leave Mrs. Lynch and her sister out of it, one of the other two could have tipped you out of your chair last night. The blonde woman or the young man."

"They could have," agreed Jimmy. "But there's something about Mrs. Lynch that bothers me. My instincts are telling me something's not right. I don't think she's all she makes out to be."

"What do you mean?"

"Well, have you ever heard the expression 'You can't kid a kidder'?"

Penny wagged her head. "Hmm. I've heard it, but I'm not really sure what it means."

"It means something like, 'It takes one to know one.' And I recognize a thief when I see one."

Penny shifted in her chair and leaned closer to him. "What do you mean? Has residents' property gone missing?"

"Not that I've heard, and certainly nothing of mine has."

"Well, what then?"

"I could be wrong, but I've got this feeling about her. I think she's a wrong 'un. Apparently Mrs. Lynch used to be the housekeeper to some posh lord or somebody before her health forced her to retire. Always banging on about him, she is. 'Sir Tony' this, 'Sir Tony' that. And of course, nothing in here is up to her standards, because she knows how things should be done. Proper, like. But underneath that veneer of gentility, there's something else. Something coarse and unappealing. I think she came up the hard way, and I don't think she's as genteel as she'd like everybody to think she is.

"But here's what makes me think she's a thief. She's always on that mobile of hers in the lounge. I started paying attention, and from what I've been able to overhear, it's not the usual family chitchat, you know, having a natter about what the grandkids are up to. It's like she's running a business, and it's the same kind of talk I used to be involved in back when I was, well, let's call it working. She's always asking about times, pickup and drop-off points, telling people what needs doing and when—that sort of thing."

"What needs doing?"

"I don't have specifics, but she's giving orders. I got a sense of her being in charge. And she's quite secretive about it. If she thinks that someone's listening, she moves away."

"Maybe she's just trying to be polite and make sure her talking on her phone doesn't bother other people. And if it's privacy she's after, why does she make those calls in the lounge? Why not her room?"

"Because the telephone reception in the rooms is rubbish on the mobiles. Works better in the lounge, for some reason." He shifted in his chair and adjusted the blanket covering his knees as Penny remained silent. "What is it? Is something the matter?"

"Well, it's just that you've got me thinking. I might have said something I shouldn't have this morning," Penny said.

"Oh, what's that?"

"Well, there are travellers camping out down the road from me, and I met some of them on the ferry from Dublin. There's a girl, she's fifteen, and I got talking to her this morning. She told me she wants to finish high school and then go on to college, but there's cultural pressure on her to get married. She's fifteen, for heaven's sake! The conversation really bothered me. Anyway, I told her where I lived."

"Oh, I see," said Jimmy. "And now you're afraid you'll come home to find them squatting in your house or you've been robbed. She was probably told what to say to get you to feel sorry for her, so you'd give away where you live."

"I know their reputation, and what everyone says about them, so that's why I'm a bit worried. I hope nothing will happen."

"Just make sure you lock your doors, although even that's no guarantee. But they never stay in one place very long, so they'll probably move on soon."

"You're the third person to tell me that," said Penny, "about locking my doors. Which reminds me. I don't think I told you that your old nemesis, Gareth Davies, has moved away."

"I thought he'd already moved away. Scotland, wasn't it?"

"It was. And now he's really gone."

"For good?"

"For good. He was back for a few days to finalize the sale of his house."

"Well, as coppers go, he was all right. Not bent like some of them. Planting evidence to stitch you up whether you'd actually done the job or not. But at least he was honest. Good at his job, too. If he thought you'd done something, you probably had." He gave Penny a sly look. "And how do you feel about him going? No regrets?"

"I feel just fine. I want him to be happy. No regrets."

"I always hoped there'd be something between you two."

"You and everybody else. But it just wasn't to be."

"Well, if it's not there, it's not there," said Jimmy. "Whatever 'it' is."

Chapter Twenty-Five

The weather in North Wales in November is unpredictable. Some days are crisp and clear, filled with sunshine and blue skies, perfect for a brisk walk; others are overcast and gloomy, ideal for a leisurely hour curled up in front of the fire with tea and a scone, and a book or magazine. And still others offer up anything ranging from a fine mist to an outright storm, with high, blustery winds that whip up leaves from the pavement, and lashing rain. And often, the day can bring changeable weather with a mix of just about everything. Saturday was one of those days. It started out fine, as Penny walked to work, but over the course of the morning the day began to darken.

And unusually, Eirlys, who never missed a day and always arrived on time, was late. Penny completed the first client's manicure, then walked down the corridor to speak to Rhian at the reception desk.

"Eirlys isn't in yet, and she didn't ring to let me know she's not coming in. Have you heard from her? This isn't like her. I'm a bit worried, to be honest. I hope she's all right."

Rhian looked up from her desk, where she was checking off the contents of a box of products destined for the hair salon against their packing list. She crossed off an item, then gave Penny her full attention. "No, I haven't heard from her, and I agree, it isn't like her. She's always so reliable."

The door opened, and Penny's ten A.M. appointment entered. "Please call her," Penny said to Rhian as she prepared to escort her client to the nail salon, "and let me know what happens."

A few minutes later Rhian appeared in the doorway, and Penny excused herself from her client and stepped out into the hall. "She's terribly sorry," said Rhian. "She was out last night, things ran late, and she overslept. She said she'd be in as soon as she could."

Penny breathed a sigh of relief. "No, it's all right. Look, would you mind ringing her back? Tell her to take the morning off, have a shower, eat her breakfast. Tell her to take her time, do everything she needs to, and we'll see her when she gets here. I can manage, so there's no need for her to get all stressed about it. Goodness knows, she's covered for me so many times."

"She'll appreciate that. Being late for work is such a bad feeling when you're as conscientious as Eirlys is."

"True. I'm just glad she's okay." She met Rhian's eyes, as brown and dark and warm as coffee beans. "Well, I guess I don't need to tell you why."

We have the best staff, thought Penny, making a mental note to mention this to Victoria so they could do something special for the team for Christmas. Which wasn't that far off. Crikey!

By late morning, just as the weather was beginning to take a turn for the worse, Eirlys entered the nail salon to find Penny alone, making notes on one of the little cards they used to record what service a client received and what colour nail varnish she'd chosen. It saved a lot of bother the next time the customer came in and asked for the same colour she had last time. "I can't remember the name of it, but it was pink."

"I'm so sorry to be late, Penny," Eirlys said. "And it looks as if I made it just in time. The rain's really starting to set in now. I hope you weren't too busy this morning."

"Oh, we managed to fit everybody in," Penny smiled. "Anyway, it's not as if you're late very often. Everybody oversleeps from time to time. Good night out, was it?"

"Not bad," Eirlys said. "I really don't like a late night out when I have work the next day, but it was a mate's birthday party. Something interesting happened, though, that I thought you'd want to know about."

"Oh, tell me."

"Remember you were asking about those lads Rhodri Phillips was hanging out with? The ones I thought seemed rough and didn't like too much?"

"Yes, I do remember," said Penny.

"Well, I bumped into one of them last night and learned a little more about him. And not only that," she said, sliding her phone toward Penny, "I managed to get a couple of photos of him. You can't really make out his features because the light was so poor, but I did the best I could."

Penny picked up the phone and gave Eirlys an asking-for-permission look. When she nodded, Penny clicked on the camera icon and then opened the last photo in the roll. She walked over to the window and tilted the phone to get a better look. "So this is one of the young men who hung out with Rhodri?"

Eirlys nodded. "But I don't know his name."

"Well," said Penny, "Let's show this to Rhian and see if she knows him."

Rhian shook her head. "I don't know who he is, but my sister might."

Penny asked Eirlys to send the image to Rhian and copy her. "The police need to see this. I'll forward it to Bethan."

* * *

"It's Saturday night," said Penny as she and Victoria closed up the Spa for the day. "Bethan's had a long, hard week. I wonder if she'd like to join us for some comfort food."

"Good idea," said Victoria. "Let's ask her."

And so the two stopped off at the Co-op to pick up some good things for dinner. "Of course we don't have time to make anything from scratch," said Victoria, "like a chili con carne or a beef stew, but maybe we can find something that would do just as well."

"Or be almost as good," said Penny. She scanned the shelf of ready meals and then picked out a container and showed it to Victoria. "What about this? *Boeuf bourguignon.* And we could get a loaf of crusty French bread to go with it. My friends and I used to have that back in Canada after a day of skiing, and it really hits the spot on a cold winter's night. And maybe a crème caramel for dessert? Or a crumble?"

"Perfect," said Victoria. And so, laden with provisions for a hearty dinner, and more groceries besides for Penny to have on hand, they drove through heavy rain and a fierce wind to Penny's cottage, unpacked their shopping, set the table, and popped the entrée into the oven to warm through. When Bethan arrived, the three women took their places at the table, and Penny poured two glasses of wine.

"It feels so good to be off duty," said Bethan, "although with you two, I'm never really off duty because you always ask so many questions. So let's get that out of the way, and then we can enjoy our meal. We've spoken to Mrs. Lloyd and we're taking a closer look at Jennifer Sayles. And thank you for the photo you sent today of the lad that was the known associate of Rhodri Phillips. We've circulated it, and officers are on the lookout for him. They'll be dropping into the clubs tonight, just in case. It's all in hand, and that's all I want to say about that."

Victoria served up the main course, and just as she sat down, a loud knocking on the door startled them.

"Oh, who can that be?" said Penny. "Who'd be out on a night like this?"

The knocking came again, louder this time, demanding that the door be opened.

Chapter Twenty-Six

Although her face was obscured by the wet hair hanging over her shoulders in lank strands, Penny knew who it was. "Riley!" she exclaimed, reaching out to pull the girl into her small entranceway and out of the driving rain. "Come in. What are you doing out on a night like this? What's happened? Are you hurt?"

The girl was panting so hard she could barely breathe. Her ragged breath came in great, heaving gulps, and when she opened her mouth, no words formed and no sound came out.

"It's your friend," she finally managed to gasp before bending over, resting her hands on her knees and drawing another deep breath.

"What friend? My friends are right here," Penny said, gesturing at Victoria and Bethan, who had come to the hallway to see what was going on. Riley pointed at Bethan. "Her," she panted. "She's the one to help him. She needs to go. Right now."

"Help who?" Penny said.

"Your friend at the nursing home. I heard them talking.

They're on their way there now. I ran here to warn you. Oh, please, you've got to hurry." She was standing straighter now, although still breathing rapidly. Her eyes darted wildly from Penny to Bethan.

"Oh my God," exclaimed Penny. "Jimmy. They're after Jimmy."

Riley nodded.

Bethan grabbed her coat as she sprang for the door. "Penny, you're with me. Victoria, you stay here and look after this girl."

"Bookshelf. Redouté," Penny shouted to Victoria before chasing after Bethan, without bothering to grab her coat. In less than a minute they were in the police car and reversing out of the parking space in front of Penny's cottage. Somehow, between changing gears and steering the vehicle, Bethan managed to radio the station to alert them to what was happening and request that any officer closer to the nursing home go there immediately.

"What's Jimmy's room number?" she asked Penny. "Room one oh eight," Bethan barked into the microphone, repeating what Penny told her. "Bring a member of the night staff from the nursing home with you. If you have to break the door down, do it. Get into that room as soon as you can. An elderly resident's life may be in danger."

Just as they passed the site of the travellers' encampment, a white van shot past them at high speed, forcing them off the road and onto the verge. Bethan swore under her breath as she struggled to keep control of the vehicle. Penny twisted round in her seat and had just enough time to glimpse the purple writing on the side of the van. ROBERT SYKES WINE AND SPIRITS. "That's the same white van I saw parked at the Hall last Saturday night," Penny exclaimed. "The one Gwennie said was dropping off the complimentary champagne." Concentrating on her driving, Bethan did not reply.

After what seemed an eternity but was in fact just minutes, they pulled up in front of the nursing home, and Penny leapt out of the passenger seat and bounded up the stairs. Bethan shut down the vehicle, switched off the flashing lights, and raced after her. They burst through the doors and ran past the empty reception desk.

"Down here," Penny shouted, pointing to the right, indicating a hallway just before the now darkened residents' lounge.

"I know where his room is," responded Bethan. "I've been here before." They tore down the hallway, desperately hoping to find that a police officer had arrived before them and had the situation under control. The hallway was empty.

They slowed as they reached Jimmy's room, and Bethan wrenched at the door handle. It was locked. "Stand back," she ordered. She didn't body-slam the centre of the door, but one well-aimed kick from her sturdy police boot to the left of the door handle and the door splintered open with a loud crack. A man was bent over Jimmy's bed, holding a pillow, while a blonde woman hovered nearby shouting and swearing at him. As Penny and Bethan burst into the room, she directed her loud curses at them.

Bethan ignored her. "Put it down," she yelled as she dived at the man, grabbing him by his arms, wrenching him away from the bed and flinging him onto the floor. Holding his hands behind his back, she pulled a set of handcuffs from her pocket and secured him. The woman pushed past Penny, who was trying to reach Jimmy, and bolted out the door. Leaving the man sprawled on the floor, Bethan sprang to her feet and took off in pursuit. A moment later she returned with the woman and pushed her into a chair. "Don't you move," she said, keeping one hand on the woman's shoulder as she whipped out her phone and called for backup and an ambulance.

Jimmy, his sparse white hair sticking out on all sides of his pink scalp, had watched all this wide-eyed with Penny standing beside him, holding his hand.

"I kept them talking as long as I could," he said.

"You did great," Penny replied. "You kept them talking and distracted long enough to stay alive." She leaned over him, and they clung to each other in wordless relief until two uniformed police officers arrived, handcuffed the woman, and took the pair into custody.

Jimmy sighed, and then, using the side rails on his bed and with Penny holding him under his shoulders, he pulled himself into an upright position, then raised the head of the bed. When he was comfortable, he smoothed his hair, adjusted his blue-and-white-striped pajama top, and asked Penny to pour him a glass of water.

"Well, now we know who tipped me out of my wheelchair,"

he said as Penny picked up the jug of water on his bedside table. "Before that fellow tried to smother me, I got a good strong whiff of tobacco. I'm sure he was the one. And turns out you were right, it was meant as a warning to keep my nose out of their business."

He took a deep breath and leaned back against his pillows as Penny poured water into a glass.

"It's that Mrs. Lynch," he said as he straightened up a little, then took the glass from Penny's hand. After taking a slow sip through the bent straw, he handed the glass back to her and settled back down in his bed. "She was behind the theft of the Black Chair. I overheard her in the lounge on her phone today, talking about how they'd had to abandon the black goods, and when she caught me looking at her, she knew that I'd heard and that I knew. She organized the theft."

"Do you have any idea where she might be now?" Bethan asked.

"No idea. Halfway to Dublin, possibly, although she was still here at teatime."

"Let's hope she didn't get that far," said Bethan. She stepped out of the room and returned a moment later. "I've ordered officers to the travellers' encampment and requested a search warrant for the place, since that's where the white van was headed. And we need more officers for this building." A police officer approached her and said something in a low voice. "Check at reception," Bethan said to him. "There must be some night staff around, but where are they?"

The police officer returned a few minutes later with paramedics, and while one examined Jimmy, the police officers conferred in the corridor.

"He seems okay," said the paramedic, removing his stethoscope from Jimmy's chest. "Surprisingly okay, considering what he's been through." He then motioned to the police officers in the hall that they could come back into the room.

Jimmy insisted he was fine and refused to go to hospital. "You know what we're like, us old folks," he grinned at Penny. "We don't like a fuss."

"It's strange that we haven't seen any night staff," said Bethan. "I don't like it. We need the property searched."

"Try the room two doors down," Jimmy suggested. "That's Mrs. Lynch's room. I'll bet she summoned the night nurse to her room to lure her away from the nursing station, and when she got there, the woman and young man were waiting to overpower her, and they left her in there, then came in here to kill me."

"Was Mrs. Lynch in your room tonight?" Penny asked Jimmy.

"No, just those two."

"How's this for a theory?" said Penny. "The white van delivers the blonde woman—who, by the way, is Riley's mother—and the young man. I don't know who he is, but he looks like Rhodri's friend. The one Eirlys photographed in the club last night."

"Yes, he does," said Bethan.

"I don't know either of their names, though."

"Doesn't matter. We can get their names from Riley."

"So," Penny continued, "The van delivers the man and woman here, and they go to Mrs. Lynch's room. Mrs. Lynch summons the night nurse, but before she arrives, Mrs. Lynch leaves the room and hides, down the hall, let's say. When the night nurse comes to her room, the two overpower her and tie her up. Then, when she's safely out of the way and the reception desk is empty, Mrs. Lynch leaves the building and is driven away in the white van that passed us on the way here. The blonde woman and the young man then attack our Jimmy—the man who knew too much."

A police officer entered the room to tell them the missing night nurse had been found tied up in Mrs. Lynch's room and asked the paramedics to see to her. They returned a few minutes later saying she was unharmed, if a little shaken up, and was insisting on returning to the nursing station.

"Right, then," said Bethan. "I'm just going to take a look around Mrs. Lynch's room. And no, Penny, before you ask, you can't come with me. You stay here with Jimmy." She motioned to the uniformed police officer standing in the doorway.

Penny stayed by Jimmy's side until Bethan returned to let them know the police were wrapping up. After settling Jimmy in for the rest of the night and ringing Victoria to let her know she was on her way home, they prepared to leave. As Penny switched off the light to Jimmy's room, his voice came out of the dark.

"How did you know I was in trouble? How did you know to come here?"

"The woman who tried to kill you. Her daughter ran through the rain to my cottage to warn us that they were on their way here and that you were in trouble. If she hadn't . . ."

Jimmy did not reply. Penny quietly closed the door to his room, and she and Bethan made their way through the silent building, past the empty reception desk, and out the front door. The rain had let up, but without a coat, Penny shivered during the short walk to a waiting police car.

Bethan decided to return to the station and assigned a woman police officer to drive Penny home and remain in the cottage overnight.

"We can't take the chance that a member of the traveller community will come looking for Riley," she said. "It's too late to talk to her tonight, but we'll keep her safe until we can speak to her in the morning."

Once in her cottage, Penny took off her wet shoes and, with the police officer following, entered the sitting room to find Victoria reading in a wing chair. The only light in the room came from a small lamp beside her. Victoria held her index finger to her lips, then pointed to the sofa, where Riley was stretched out under a soft blue blanket, asleep, one arm wrapped protectively around the book of Redouté drawings.

"She could have had the spare room," whispered Penny.

"She fell asleep there, and I thought it best to leave her where she is and not disturb her," said Victoria. Penny gestured toward the matching wing chair, and the police officer sat down. "She had a bath," Victoria continued. "Her clothes were filthy, so I gave her an old nightdress of yours and I ran her clothes through the washing machine. They should be dry by morning, so at least she'll have clean clothes to wear when she leaves."

"Did she have something to eat?" asked Penny.

"She was ravenous," said Victoria. "And I'm sorry to tell you this, but she's eaten all your dinner." Penny smiled. "But that's not all. I caught a glimpse of her back and arms when she handed me her clothes for the wash. She's covered in bruises. Old greenish ones and fresh purple ones."

The police officer glanced at Riley's sleeping figure and opened her notebook.

A few minutes later, Victoria left for home and Penny went upstairs to bed, leaving the police officer to make herself as comfortable as she could in the wing chair with a blanket and a cup of tea. As Penny lay in the dark, her whirling mind going over the events of the evening, her thoughts tumbled over one another, demanding attention, then disappearing, to be replaced by others. Finally, she gave up, turned on her side, and drifted off into an uneasy, restless sleep.

* * *

She woke as a soft, grey light filtered under her window blind, signalling that a new day was about to begin. As the events of the previous night flooded her consciousness, she pulled on a dressing gown and went downstairs. The chair and sofa in the sitting room were empty, but warm, inviting smells were coming from the kitchen.

Riley, wearing her clothes that had been washed and dried

overnight, looked up from the table and gave Penny a shy smile backed by a mouthful of toast and marmalade. "There's a full pot of coffee," said the police officer. "I hope you don't mind we made ourselves some breakfast. Riley was starving, and I thought it best we eat here rather than going out."

"Yes, of course," said Penny. "I hope you found everything you need." She slid into a chair and pulled a slice of toast from the rack. "Have you heard from the nursing home this morning? Or maybe it's too early."

"I haven't heard from anybody yet," said the police officer. "May I have a word in private?"

"Of course," said Penny, putting down her toast and joining the policewoman in the sitting room.

"Inspector Morgan has asked that you not speak to Riley about what happened last night, or anything that led up to it. She's an important witness, and we don't want her recollection clouded or tainted," the policewoman said in a low voice. "We know the right questions to ask, in the right order, and we need to be the ones to ask them."

"Of course," Penny replied. "I probably shouldn't have mentioned the nursing home. Sorry."

"As soon as she's had her breakfast, I'm to drive her to the station, and we'll take it from there."

"What's going to happen to her?" asked Penny.

"Living arrangements, you mean?"

"Yes. With her mother in custody, I really hope she doesn't have to live with her aunt. She'd be nothing but an unpaid child minder helping raise her cousins. And that would be such a shame when she has ambitions for herself so far beyond that. She wants to go to school. She's eager to learn. She's got a bright, active mind and she's got so much talent."

The police officer shrugged. "Not for me to say. That'll be up to social services."

"I hope it won't come to that. I hope suitable private arrangements can be made for her."

The police officer glanced at the kitchen door. "I'd better get back to her. My instructions are not to leave her."

"And I'd better get dressed."

Penny rooted about in the front hall cupboard for a couple of spare carrier bags, then ran upstairs and changed into casual clothes. She then entered her spare bedroom, where she pulled out items from the cupboard and placed them in the bags.

When she returned downstairs, the police officer and Riley were preparing to leave. Remembering that the girl had arrived on her doorstep the previous night without a jacket, Penny took a dark-green jacket that she wore sketching from her cupboard and offered it to her.

Riley shook her head. "I can't take your coat."

"Yes, you can," said Penny. "You'll need it today." When Riley shook her head again, Penny said, "You can bring it back when you've got a warm jacket of your own. That'll give you an excuse to come back and see me." The girl grinned and reached out for the jacket. "And here," said Penny, holding out the carrier bags she had just filled with art supplies. "I thought you'd like to have these, and I hope you get a chance to use them. There are a couple of new sketchbooks, some pencils and some watercolour paints, brushes . . . everything you need to be going on with."

Riley's smile lit up the hallway.

"You're one of the best botanical artists I've ever seen," said Penny. "And you've got a brilliant future ahead of you. Wait a minute. Where's . . . ?" Her eyes turned in the direction of the sofa, and when she spotted what she was looking for, she sprinted across the room and picked up the Redouté book. "Here," she said, "Take this with you. I want you to have it. My gift to you. Let it inspire you."

As Riley started to cry, Penny reached out and wrapped her arms around her.

Chapter Twenty-Seven

On Monday morning, Penny paused at the site of the travellers' encampment. The caravans and vehicles were gone, but a massive amount of rubbish and litter had been left behind. She pitied the farmer who would have to spend precious time clearing it all up and then pay to leave it at the local tip.

The weekend storms had moved on, too, leaving behind a clear day. She filled her lungs with fresh, clean air and then walked on, determined to arrive at work in good time.

Just as she reached the Spa gate, Mrs. Lloyd emerged from the café, waved, and headed toward her.

"I was just on my way to see you," she said. "The police finally got around to interviewing me. I told them everything I saw and heard at the dinner party. Do you have any news?"

"There have been a few developments, actually," said Penny. Mrs. Lloyd's eyes widened as Penny described the events of the previous evening at the nursing home.

"Oh my lord. That's terrible. I do hope poor Jimmy is all right."

"Oh, I'm sure he will be. He's a tough old bird."

"He certainly is. Oh, and speaking of birds, I saw Dilys yesterday afternoon on her wanderings. On the riverbank she was, looking for her twigs and berries, I suppose. Honestly," laughed Mrs. Lloyd, "she looked like a flipping great jackdaw!"

"What do you mean?"

"Oh, she had this great black shawl thing wrapped around her shoulders, coming to a point in the middle of her back. It looked like a tablecloth." Mrs. Lloyd made sweeping motions around her own shoulders.

Penny laughed. "Remember that time she got hold of the quilt we were all looking for? She looked like a ghost moving across the landscape, so we followed her for miles, and finally we caught up to her and . . ." Penny stopped speaking and her head tilted slightly. "Sorry, Mrs. Lloyd, where did you say you saw her?"

"On the riverbank."

"And when was this?"

"Oh, didn't I say? I thought I did. Yesterday afternoon. Fairly late in the day. The café was about to close, and sometimes they mark down their baked goods at the end of the day, so I just popped in to see if they had anything on offer. Not that we really need more baked goods, what with the delicious things Florence makes. But it's always fun to look. Took home a couple of chocolate croissants, and Florence and I enjoyed them with our breakfast this morning. Made a nice change from my usual oatmeal. Oh, and this'll interest you.

There's a new staff member in the café! I don't suppose you've heard that . . ."

Penny touched Mrs. Lloyd on the arm. "Sorry, I've got to run. But thanks for the information about Dilys. It could be really important." She pushed open the Spa gate and hurried up the path that led to the front door.

"And she's off," muttered Mrs. Lloyd to Penny's retreating back. "It gets a bit unnerving when you're in the middle of a conversation and she suddenly gets one of her brilliant ideas and off she goes."

Penny entered the Spa and, with a vague good morning over her shoulder in the direction of Rhian, burst into Victoria's office.

"Can you leave that?" she said. "I've got to go someplace and I need your help."

Startled, Victoria looked up from her laptop. "Go where? I just got here. We've barely opened. Can't it wait?"

"No! And if I'm right, which I think I am, you're going to be so glad you were in on this."

"But what about . . . ?"

"Rhian can manage for an hour."

Victoria sighed. "Yes, I suppose she can. She always does. Why should this be any different than any other time?" She stood up. "I don't suppose I have any choice, do I?"

"Of course you do. If you don't want to come with me, I'll find another way." She turned to leave the room, but Victoria's voice stopped her. "And let you have all the fun? I don't think so. You talk to Rhian while I run upstairs and grab my coat."

A few minutes later they were in Victoria's car. "Where to?" she asked as she started it.

"The Hall."

"Can you tell me what this is about?"

"You'll see."

They rode in silence, and after Victoria had parked the car, they got out, and she locked it. "Back door?" she asked. "Is Gwennie waiting for us?"

"No," said Penny. "This way." Victoria followed her along the path that led to the terrace of workers' cottages. Smoke was coming from the chimney of the last one, and Penny pointed. "Good. Looks like Dilys is at home."

They reached the cottage, and Penny knocked on the door, although it was slightly open. She pushed on it gently and called out, "Dilys! It's Penny and Victoria. May we come in?" Without waiting for an answer, she pushed the door further open, and the two women stepped in.

"What's the point of asking if you can come in when you're halfway in already?" grumbled a voice at the far end of the darkened room. As their eyes adjusted to the gloomy interior, Penny and Victoria could just make out Dilys seated at the far end of the small room. They took a few steps closer and found her seated in a chair with a tall back, holding a mug on an armrest.

"Oh," gasped Victoria. "Is that it?"

"It is," said Penny. "And Dilys is going to tell us where she found the Black Chair."

"If you mean this beautiful old thing," said Dilys raising

her mug slightly, "it's mine. I found it in the woods where somebody dumped it."

"How did you get it here, Dilys? You couldn't have carried it here all by yourself."

"The boy helped me."

"The boy? Do you mean Lane?"

Dilys nodded.

"Well, I'm afraid you're not going to be able to keep it."

"Why not? I've only had it a day or two, and already it's doing wonders for my back."

As Victoria grinned, Penny told Dilys the story of the Black Chair—how it had been awarded posthumously to one of Wales's greatest poets and stolen from the dinner party at the Hall. "Everyone will be so glad to get it back, Dilys, you'll be quite the hero."

"So what happens now?"

"I'll ring the police and tell them it's here, and they'll take it away to be examined, and then it'll go back to its rightful home, Hedd Wyn's farmhouse. The museum at Yr Ysgwrn."

"Will I be in trouble, do you think?"

"In trouble? You mean for something like receiving stolen goods? I doubt it. But they'll want to know where you found it, so be prepared to give them as many details as you can." She looked around the room. "Now, where's the black cloth that came with it? What have you done with that?" Dilys pointed to a hook on the wall behind the door, where the cloth hung like a great sleeping bat.

"I suppose I have to give that up, too," Dilys said.

"The police will almost certainly want to test that cloth, and since it's now part of the chair's story, they should probably remain together. Of course that's not the cloth that covered the chair when it was at the Hall. The thieves must have provided that one."

Dilys heaved an unhappy sigh and then stood up. She ran a hand along one of the armrests. "I didn't have it very long, but I was getting fond of it."

"Actually, you did a good thing taking it in."

"How's that?"

"It rained last night. Heavily. And the night before. At least the chair was in your cottage, safe and protected. It's over a hundred years old, and a couple of days and nights out there could have ruined it."

"Well, yes, there's that, I suppose."

Penny looked around the room. "You know, in a weird kind of way, that chair looks right at home here, with all your other things." Dilys stood back, and the three of them contemplated the chair. Penny was right. In a Welsh cottage, with a flagstone floor and rough, whitewashed walls, surrounded by herbs and other botanicals, it did look right at home. And then, as she felt the beginning of an idea starting to take shape, she said, "Dilys, let me ask you something. If it could be arranged for you to have an apprentice, someone who wanted to learn about wildflowers and all the other plants that grow here, what would you say to that?"

"Depends on whether or not they like my herbal teas."

"Dilys, I hate to tell you this, but nobody likes your tea. The only person who likes your herbal teas is you."

Chapter Twenty-Eight

"You're thinking of Riley," said Victoria as they walked back to her car. "You're thinking Riley could live with Dilys and be her apprentice. I'm not so sure about that. For one thing, the place is barely habitable. And how would she get to school from way out here?"

"Hmm," said Penny. "I wasn't thinking about Riley actually living with her, more along the lines of tagging along with Dilys on her rambles, if she'd be interested. Dilys knows more about the flowers and trees in this area than anybody. And there's a lot to be said for Dilys passing on what she knows to a young person. She knows this area so well, and all its hidden natural secrets, it would be a shame if all that knowledge were to be lost. And to be fair, she can't keep walking and roaming forever."

"So you're thinking Riley might stay in the area. Surely social services will send her back to Ireland, to be with her relatives."

"They very well might," said Penny. "I have no idea how

these things work, but whoever makes that decision, and whatever decision they reach, I hope it's in Riley's best interest, and not what's easiest for them."

Penny rang Bethan to tell her where they could pick up the Black Chair, and she and Victoria walked on in silence until they reached the Hall's car park. "I wonder how Emyr and Jennifer Sayles are getting on," said Victoria as she unlocked the car. "The last time we saw them, at the Remembrance Day service, they looked on the verge of splitting up. I wonder if they've patched things up."

"That's a good question," said Penny. "Since we're here, why don't we share the good news about the chair with Gwennie and see if she has anything new to report?" When Victoria hesitated, Penny added, "I'm sure there'll be a lovely cup of coffee and possibly even a Welsh cake. Or if we're really lucky, a scone."

"Do you seriously think I'm so shallow that you can bribe me with a scone?" Victoria asked. The car chirped as she relocked it. "Well, come on, then. What are we waiting for?"

The dolphin-shaped door knocker clapped against its strike plate, and after a minute or two, Gwennie opened the door.

"We've got some good news," said Penny. "May we come in?"

"Oh, yes, of course. I was just about to sit down for an early elevenses."

She led the way down the familiar hallway to the warm, fragrant kitchen. Victoria and Penny exchanged a quick smile at the sight of a plate of freshly baked scones cooling on the counter.

"You'll have a scone," Gwennie said. "I baked extra today as a treat for the gardeners. This is the first day they've had complete access to the garden since the . . . well, you know. The police told them it was okay to take the tape down, so they did. Sad, really, that young man losing his life out there. I don't know that I'll ever be able to look at the walkway in the same way, thinking about him out there in the cold and the rain." The cups rattled slightly as she placed them on the table. "Well, go on then. I could use some good news. What is it?"

"We found the Black Chair!" exclaimed Penny.

Gwennie's face lit up. "Oh, that's brilliant! Mr. Emyr will be so relieved. How did you find it?"

"Well, to be fair, Dilys found it."

"Oh, her. And is it all right, the chair? Not damaged, I hope."

"No, it seems fine, but we're not experts. We've notified the police, and they'll be here soon to pick it up and interview her, so you're not quite rid of them yet, I'm afraid."

"Here? The police are coming back here?" She sighed. "Will it never end, I ask myself."

"They might want to ask you a few questions—if you saw anything suspicious over the past day or two. That sort of thing. And they'll park here, although it's Dilys they're coming to see."

"They're coming here to see Dilys?" Gwennie asked with a blank look.

"You didn't know she was stopping in the cottage that used to be her brother's?" Victoria asked.

Gwennie threw an exasperated look, combined with a mild eye roll, at the ceiling. "I doubt Mr. Emyr knows, which is the important thing. Still, she's a law unto herself, that one. Although now that she's getting older, her rambles are shorter and she's not ranging as far as she used to. I see her sometimes in the woodland, through the trees. Bent over, whacking things with her stick, picking up bits and pieces, although what there is to find, I have no idea. Acorns, maybe. I think Mr. Emyr's given up on her. He'll probably let her stay there until she dies. And if I know her, even death won't be enough to move her off the property. She'll be haunting those woods forever."

"Speaking of Emyr," said Penny, "We were wondering if you've heard anything more about Jennifer Sayles."

"No," said Gwennie. "Can't say as I have. She hasn't been back to the Hall since the dinner party. It's not my place, of course, to inquire into Mr. Emyr's personal life, so whether they've met up in London, I wouldn't know."

"Had they been seeing each other long before the dinner party, do you know?"

"Not that long," replied Gwennie. "Just a few weeks, maybe. Of course they've known each other much longer, seeing as how Jennifer was a friend of Meg Wynne Thompson's."

"Emyr's fiancée who died," Penny reminded Victoria.

"Poor Mr. Emyr. He hasn't been what you might call lucky in love," said Gwennie. "To be honest, I don't think they're particularly well suited, him and that Jennifer, and it seemed to me that she came on awfully strong towards him. She seems to be a very take-charge sort of person. Likes to be in control. So I was glad she didn't try to interfere too much with our arrangements for the dinner." She broke off a piece of scone and buttered it. "It was her idea to bring in a butler. Said it would be more in keeping with the way a dinner party would have looked a century ago and add a touch of class to the evening."

"This butler. Was he someone she knew?"

"Oh, I don't think so. I think she just went to one of those London agencies and was given a list to choose from, and she chose that fellow. He was all right. Seemed to know what he was doing."

"I expect there was a proper butler here at Ty Brith back in the day," Victoria remarked.

"Oh, yes, there was. I was only a girl then, but I remember him well. He made sure everything ran like clockwork. He adored Mrs. Gruffydd—that's Emyr's mother—and could never do enough for her. Old Mr. Booth, that was. Eventually he was pensioned off and given a cottage on the estate, taking all the impeccable old ways of doing things with him. He died a few years ago. Until the Remembrance Day weekend, we hadn't given a fancy dinner party in so long, and this one turning out so badly, with the death of that young man, makes me doubt we'll ever give another. There doesn't seem to be much point to this anymore." Her gesture to the rear of the kitchen, the butler's pantry and scullery, encompassed a long-gone way of life. "And Emyr, a single man, living here on his own. I wouldn't be surprised if he sold off this place. It really deserves to be a family home, but if that's not to be, then at least it could be turned into a boutique hotel or conference centre or some such." She took a mournful sip of coffee. "Anything to breathe some life back into the dear old place."

"And Lane," said Penny. "How's he doing? I hope he recovered."

"Oh, I just heard about him this morning from the head gardener," said Gwennie. "He's only gone and got himself a new job in the café. I hear he absolutely loves working that Italian machine. Making lattes and cappuccinos all day long. Happy as Larry, apparently."

* * *

"What do you think about Jennifer Sayles?" Penny asked on the drive back to town.

"I hadn't really given her any thought. She was just here, and then she wasn't."

"Interesting timing, though, from what Gwennie said about her appearing on the scene. It seems she got interested in Emyr around the same time he started talking about giving a dinner party."

Chapter Twenty-Nine

At lunchtime, Penny returned to her office and switched on her laptop. She typed in JSPR, and Jennifer Sayles's website popped up. Penny scrolled through it and once again read the brief biography, including the mention of Jennifer's parents: Jennifer Sayles is the younger daughter of Sir Anthony Sayles and his late wife, Cynthia (nee Richmond).

Sir Anthony Sayles. Sir Anthony. The name seemed vaguely familiar, but she couldn't remember anything about the man. And then she remembered she'd been about to Google the name when something had interrupted her, and she hadn't been able to actually do it. This time, she typed in his name and was shown a list of several choices. She clicked on the first one and was taken to a Wikipedia page with a detailed biography. She glanced at the photo at the right of the page and then turned her attention to the text. Comes from a long line of serving military officers . . . educated at Oxford . . . first in English and history . . . author

OF EIGHT BOOKS AND IS AN EXPERT ON THE FIRST WORLD WAR ENGLISH POETS SIEGFRIED SASSOON, WILFRED OWEN, AND RUPERT BROOKE.

Expert on First World War English poets? Then of course he would know about the Welsh poet Hedd Wyn and the bardic chair that had been awarded to him in 1917. Could Sir Anthony Sayles be the collector Jimmy had suggested would desire the Black Chair? And hadn't Jimmy mentioned that Mrs. Lynch had been the housekeeper to someone she referred to as Sir Tony? Sir Anthony? Penny's heart beat faster as she started to allow herself to think that she'd discovered the final, missing piece of the puzzle.

She examined the black-and-white photo on the screen of Sir Anthony. A formal head shot, taken by a professional photographer, it showed a serious-looking man with thinning grey hair and fine, distinguished features. She brought up more images of him, selected one, and printed it. She removed it from the printer, studied it, and then opened her desk drawer and removed a packet of coloured pencils. Selecting the chestnut-brown one, she colored in the hair and then drew a pair of round glasses.

She sank back in her chair, her chest rising and falling, as her mind raced, processing what she was seeing. Or rather, whom she was seeing. But she wanted confirmation. She reached for her phone and telephoned Mrs. Lloyd and asked if she might drop in for a few minutes, and when the answer was "Of course!" she slipped on her coat and hurried through the quiet streets to Rosemary Lane.

The net curtains parted to reveal a cheerful face as Penny walked up the front path. The curtain then dropped back into place, and Mrs. Lloyd opened the door before Penny had time to knock.

When they were seated in the sitting room, Penny took the document out of her handbag and offered it to Mrs. Lloyd. "Do you recognize this person?" she asked.

"Oh, my goodness," said Mrs. Lloyd, taking it from her. "You sound exactly like the police."

"Take a good look," said Penny, "and tell me if you've seen that man before."

"He does look familiar," Mrs. Lloyd said hesitatingly. "But I can't quite place him. I go so many places, and when you see someone out of context, it can be difficult to put a name to a face."

Florence entered the room, wiping her hands on a kitchen towel.

"Hello, Penny," she said. "Evelyn hasn't offered you a drink, I take it."

"Oh, I'm so sorry," said Mrs. Lloyd. "What am I like? What can I get you?"

"Nothing, thanks. I'm here on my lunch hour, so I can't stay long."

"Oh," said Florence, glancing at the paper in Mrs. Lloyd's hand. "What are you doing with that picture of Mr. Carson?"

Penny started. "Mr. Carson?"

"Oh, sorry, no, not Mr. Carson. That was the name of the butler in *Downton Abbey*, wasn't it? Not Mr. Carson. The one

we had at the Hall the night of the dinner. What was that fellow's name?"

"Carter," said Penny. "Mr. Carter."

"Yes, that's it." Florence held out her hand to Mrs. Lloyd. "May I see?" She examined the touched-up image, then looked at Penny. "You've coloured it in yourself and added a pair of glasses? Why would you do that?"

"Because in the original photo he's got grey hair, and he isn't wearing glasses."

"Oh, was he trying to look younger?" asked Mrs. Lloyd. "I wouldn't have thought age mattered in a butler. In fact, the older, the better. Up to a certain point, of course. Nobody wants doddery."

"Or," said Florence, "was this coloured hair and glasses meant to be some sort of disguise? I've seen people do that in films to change their looks."

"Yes, Florence, I think that's exactly what they were meant to do."

"Give it here," said Mrs. Lloyd. "Let me see that again." She peered at the picture. "Oh, so it is! That's the man who answered the door, took my coat, and showed me into the sitting room. Had a very erect posture, and looked very smart in his tailcoat. But tell me, Florence, how did you know that's who this was? I didn't think you'd met him."

"Oh, he wandered in and out of the kitchen, and while he wasn't terribly useful, as I recall he did help pour the champagne. And once when he was just standing around, I asked him to fetch me a platter from the butler's pantry and he

seemed unsure where it was, but Gwennie pointed him in the right direction."

"He was in the butler's pantry?" said Penny, thinking back to the door in the scullery that opened to the path where she'd found the gravely injured Rhodri Phillips. She'd accessed the scullery from the butler's pantry. Had Mr. Carter as well? "Can you remember when that was?"

"Yes, we were just coming up to the main course when I wanted the platter, so it would have been after the starter had been served." She settled into a seat beside Mrs. Lloyd on the sofa and plumped a cushion. "And Mr. Carter isn't really his name, then, is it?"

"No," said Penny. "His real name is Sir Anthony Sayles."

"Sayles," mused Mrs. Lloyd. "That sounds familiar."

"Because he's the father of Jennifer Sayles. Emyr's girlfriend. Although if she's still his girlfriend after this, I'll be very surprised."

"And speaking of names," said Florence, "Now that I think of it, Mr. Carson was the character from *Downton Abbey*, and isn't that wonderful actor who played him called Jim Carter?"

"Of course!" said Penny. "They would have their clever little joke."

"I wondered about him," said Mrs. Lloyd. "It crossed my mind at the time that there was something not quite right."

Of course it did, thought Penny. Now that we've unmasked him. But she asked, "What made you think there wasn't something quite right about him?"

"It was the white gloves, you see. He was wearing white gloves, wasn't he? A butler only wears white gloves when he's handling precious, delicate objects or cleaning silver. He would never wear them to answer the door or announce dinner. Footmen wear white gloves when they serve at table, the old-fashioned logic being that a butler's hands are cleaner than a footman's."

"Goodness!" exclaimed Penny. "How do you know all that?"

"I came across it in an old etiquette book I found in the spare room. It had been quite a few years since I'd attended a proper dinner party and I just wanted to brush up on protocol. When you see seven P.M. for eight on an invitation, you know it's going to be a bit formal, don't you? So when I saw this butler fellow wearing gloves to answer the door, I thought either he doesn't know what he's doing or he's not a real butler, for all his posh accent and cutaway coat. But then we all got swept up in the events of the evening, and it slipped my mind. And my etiquette book is at least thirty years old, so things might have changed and I could have been completely mistaken about the gloves."

"Of course!" said Penny. "He was wearing gloves so he wouldn't leave any fingerprints in the house."

"But why would he care about fingerprints?" asked Florence. "And why would he go to all that trouble to pretend to be a butler?"

Penny explained Sir Anthony's interest and expertise in World War I English poets, then added, "Jimmy said the chair was most likely stolen for a collector, and I think that collector was Sir Anthony. I suspect that Emyr happened to mention to Jennifer Sayles that the chair would be at Ty Brith Hall, she realised instantly that her father would be interested, and they decided to steal it. So Jennifer Sayles made sure she got an invitation to the party, and they cooked up the scheme to have her father on hand playing the role of the butler."

"But why did he need to be there?" asked Mrs. Lloyd. "Surely he wouldn't do the job himself. Wouldn't they have hired a gang?"

"Yes," said Penny. "There was definitely a gang involved. I don't know enough about him, but he might have wanted to be on hand to reassure himself that everything went according to plan."

"Or maybe he just couldn't wait to get his hands on that chair," said Florence. "Gloves or no gloves."

"And the question is," said Penny, "did he want that chair enough to kill for it?"

As Mrs. Lloyd let out a little gasp, Penny glanced at her watch and then leaped out of her chair. "I've stayed longer than I should have. I must get back to work. But there's one more thing. Mrs. Lloyd, didn't you take some photos just before the reveal of the Black Chair went so badly wrong? May I see them?"

"Yes, of course." She picked up her handbag, retrieved her phone, and handed it to Penny.

Penny flicked through the photos until she came to the one she was looking for, and using her thumb and forefinger, she enlarged it.

There, standing against the wall, hands clasped in front of him with Jennifer Sayles by his side, was the butler.

"Why, Mr. Carter," said Penny. "You're not wearing your gloves."

Mrs. Lloyd leaned in looked closer.

"So he's not. Why do you suppose that is?"

"I don't know yet, but we're going to find out." She handed the mobile back to Mrs. Lloyd. "Did you give this photo to the police?"

"Yes, I did. They asked everyone who took photos that night to send them in."

"Good. Well, I must run. I'll talk to you later."

"Let us know what you find out, won't you," said Florence, as she closed the door behind her.

Chapter Thirty

"That's the man you're looking for."

Penny slid the marked-up image of Sir Anthony Sayles across the coffee table in the Spa's quiet room to Inspector Bethan Morgan, who studied it for a moment, then sat back in her chair.

"Even though I'm not one for speculation," Bethan said, "I'd like to hear your theory. Tell me what you think happened."

"All right. But as you say, it is just a theory. I'm not saying it happened this way, but it could have."

Bethan nodded. "Go on. I'm all ears."

"Right. Here goes." Penny tapped the image with her forefinger.

"His name is Sir Anthony Sayles and he's an expert on World War I English poets. And the Black Chair is one of the greatest artefacts with a continuing connection to an outstanding British poet of that period, Hedd Wyn. Because he's Welsh, he may not be as well-known as the best English poets of the period, but he's right up there with them, and he deserves to be. His being awarded the bardic chair in 1917 is a testament to that.

"When Sayles's daughter told him that the chair would be at Ty Brith Hall, he recognized a golden opportunity to acquire the chair and he simply had to take it.

"So he asked his former housekeeper, Mrs. Lynch, if she 'knew people' who could help, and she brought over a few from Ireland, including her own daughter and grandson, the two who tried to kill Jimmy when they realised he'd worked out that they were involved in the theft.

"Mrs. Lynch planned the theft and assembled the people needed to pull it off. But a vital piece of information was missing. They knew from Jennifer Sayles that the chair would be on display in the library, but they needed to know how to get to the library, and more importantly, how to get the chair, and themselves, out of the house, quickly.

"Her grandson, who knew Rhodri Phillips from Bangor but wasn't at the university with him, remembered he was from Llanelen, and asked him if he knew anybody familiar with the layout of Ty Brith Hall. And Rhodri, a former student of Michael Quinn, knew that he'd been at the house in the spring for the taping of the antiques show. Eirlys mentioned that the Irish lads seemed to have some kind of hold over Rhodri—possibly he owed them money for drugs—so he provided the link to Michael Quinn, but under duress," Penny continued.

"And Michael Quinn agreed to help," said Bethan.

"Yes. For the very old reason that he needed the money. His life is in a downward spiral. He's lost his job, his wife, and his home. And he's drinking too much. So yes, he agreed to help by drawing a floor plan, showing the location of the library, and the best way to access it and then get out of the house. He probably thought that would be the end of his involvement, but I'm certain he was there on the night, although I don't know why he would have to be." She toyed with the handle of her coffee mug. "I don't suppose Lane was able to corroborate that it was Quinn who frightened him in the hallway?"

"No. We've tried speaking to him a couple of times, with and without his mother present. He's just not able to bring himself to tell us what he saw. And Quinn hasn't been forthcoming, either. He arrived back yesterday and I questioned him last night. After we showed him university records, he had to agree that Rhodri was in one of his classes, but he insists he didn't know him outside the classroom and had nothing to do with him personally." Bethan then prompted Penny to continue where she'd left off. "Let's move on to the night of the crime. What was meant to be a foolproof robbery while the guests were in the dining room and the staff were busy in the kitchen went pear shaped."

"Yes. I believe that over the course of the day and into the evening, Rhodri Phillips began having second thoughts about what was going to happen and his part in it. When he helped me light the candles just before the guests entered the dining room, his hands were shaking so badly I had to take over and finish up for him. He might have realised he'd got caught up in something that sounded fine in the planning stages, but now that it was about to go down, he recognized what a deadly serious matter it really was, and he was getting cold feet.

"So following that train of thought, after the starter course was served, and while the servers were hanging about waiting to clear the table and bring in the main course, the chair was spirited out of the house and Rhodri tried to prevent the thieves from loading it into the white wine merchants' van. It was raining quite heavily then, and Sir Anthony, possibly seeing it all slipping away from him, intervened, grabbed the rock, and hit Rhodri to silence him, but probably not intending to kill him. He might even have slipped on the wet paving stones as I did, hitting Rhodri harder than he meant to. When I noticed later that the butler's clothes were wet, I didn't really think anything of it. People had been going in and out all evening to use their phones or smoke."

"And the chair?"

"At first I thought that because a young man died during the commission of the robbery, Sir Anthony could no longer tolerate the idea of having the chair in his home. It would be one thing to possess a stolen artefact but quite another to possess a stolen artefact linked to a murder.

"And then I realised that's exactly why he had to abandon the chair, but it wasn't because of his finer feelings. It was a catch-22, you see. He had to attack Rhodri to get the chair, and then he realised he couldn't keep the chair because he'd killed Rhodri. If the police discovered—as I did—that Sayles posed as a butler that night, well, that would raise questions, and it wouldn't take much to get a warrant to search his house, and of course they'd discover the chair and he'd be the prime suspect in Rhodri's murder. So after all that planning and expense, it was all for nothing, and he had to let the chair go. He just couldn't risk it."

"That would have been incredibly difficult for him."

"Oh, absolutely. I think the chair was kept at the travellers' encampment for a few days until he could bring himself to tell Mrs. Lynch to arrange to get rid of it. He probably didn't think he needed to tell her to do so in a responsible way, like leaving it outside a police station, or at least somewhere where it would be out of the weather, so she took the easy way out and told her grandson and his mates to dump it, and that's what they did. It seems incredible to us that someone would do that to a valuable artefact, but as Jimmy said, thieves often don't care about the well-being of the stuff they steal, they just care about the money it will make for them. And I know this is true. You can find all kinds of examples of stolen, priceless artwork kept for decades in the most appalling conditions."

"And the gang had already made their money off Sayles. Sill, at least the chair wasn't destroyed, so that's something to be thankful for," said Bethan.

"Yes, we have Dilys to thank for that."

"'Well, you've certainly given me a lot to think about. Looks like I'm off to London tomorrow to interview Sir Anthony and Jennifer Sayles," said Bethan. "It would be nice to have the gloves he was wearing, but chances are pretty slim we'll find them. He or his accomplices would have disposed of them."

"You never know. If they were thrown out the window of the vehicle when they were driving off, Dilys might pick them up in her wanderings. It wouldn't hurt to ask her to keep an eye out for them. And if she's already found them, she'll still have them. She keeps just about everything, and uses most of it herself. I wouldn't be surprised if you saw her actually wearing them."

"Well," said Bethan, "thank you very much for all this, but we've got no real evidence to support any of it, and while your explanation of the theft of the chair sounds plausible, I'm not convinced about Sayles attacking our victim. Rhodri was struck with some force, which indicates the attacker knew the victim. I'd say the motive was personal; there was something going on between the killer and Rhodri. And speaking of motive, that's what we need. When you know the motive, you understand the full mosaic of the crime."

Chapter Thirty-One

Over her bowl of oatmeal the next morning, Penny's thoughts turned to Michael Quinn, who, despite his denials, she believed had been at the Hall on the night of the robbery. Why? What had brought him there? If his role had been to submit a diagram showing the layout of the ground floor, he'd done that. Knowing that a robbery was going to take place at the Hall, surely he wouldn't have risked being there while it was in progress unless he had a really good reason to do so.

After rinsing her bowl and spoon, she reached for her phone and scrolled back in time until she came to images she hadn't looked at since that day she'd learned Michael Quinn was married. How could she ever have been attracted to him? Of course, he'd looked better then, not nearly so seedy as when she'd seen him in Dublin, but still he was the same person, then as now. Or was he?

If only Lane would or could tell us what he saw, she thought. He might be able to place Quinn inside the Hall on the night Rhodri was murdered. And as her next step came clear to her, she copied a couple of images that clearly showed Quinn's face to move them to the front of her camera roll.

She set off for work a little earlier than usual, to leave time to pick up a cup of coffee, and just as she'd hoped, when she entered the café, Lane was behind the counter working the coffee machine.

"Morning, Penny," he beamed at her. "What can I get you?"

"Morning, Lane. You're enjoying your new job, I see. I'd like a latte, please." She said nothing to break his concentration while he measured out the coffee, tamped it down, and poured milk into a jug ready for the steamer. When her coffee was ready, he handed it to her, and she paid the woman behind the cash register. As there were no other customers waiting to be served, she asked Lane if she could have a word with him.

"Sorry, Penny, not right now. This is the breakfast rush. Too busy."

"It's all right, Lane," said the woman at the cash register. "You can take five minutes." Penny nodded her thanks, and Lane stepped out from behind the counter. "Let's just sit over at that empty table, shall we?" Penny said.

"What did you want to ask me? You'll have to be quick, because I have to get back to work."

Penny got out her phone. "We really need your help, Lane," she said. "The investigation into the death of the young man who died up at the Hall is stalled. We need you to help get it going again." Lane frowned. "If you could help bring justice to this young man, you'd want to do that, wouldn't you?"

Lane didn't respond, but an encouraging flicker of something like agreement flashed across his face, so Penny continued, "Now, you told me before that someone told you not to tell anybody what you saw or heard in the Hall just before you dropped the tray or you'd get hurt, but what if I told you that the man who said that to you is now in police custody and he can't hurt you? And I know it's hard keeping a big secret. Wouldn't it be nice if you could just get rid of that burden so you don't have to carry it around anymore?"

A look of vast relief marked Lane's face, replaced almost immediately by a pained frown. He held up his hands to the side of his face and said, "I just want it to stop. I don't want to think about it anymore. I don't want to be asked any more questions."

Penny held out her phone to him.

"Let's get this over with then, once and for all. Tell me, is that the man you saw in the hallway outside the library at Ty Brith Hall the night of the dinner party?"

Lane's eyes slid to her phone and then darted back to meet Penny's. He nodded slowly. Penny looked at her phone and then back at Lane, her mouth making a little round O of surprise. She'd scrolled back an image too far and shown him the picture of Rhodri Phillips. "Lane, that was the young man who died that night."

"He was in the hall," Lane said. "With the other one."

"What other one?"

"The other man. The older one."

Penny thumbed to the picture of Michael Quinn. "This man?"

Lane nodded.

"And what were they doing? Were they talking? Did you hear what they were saying?"

"The younger man, he was angry. He used bad words."

"I'm amazed nobody heard all this going on. Were they shouting, or talking loudly?"

Lane nodded. "The older guy, he said, 'Keep your voice down.'"

"And did you a get a sense of what they were arguing about?"

"The younger man, he said, 'I want my paintings back,' and the older man, he sort of laughed and . . ."

"Sorry, Lane, don't mean to interrupt, but the younger one said, 'I want my paintings back.'"

"Yeah, and then this woman in a blue dress appeared out of the dining room, and she told the younger man to go back to the kitchen, and then she went to the loo and then the older man saw me, and he told me not to say anything to anyone, and then he put his hand underneath my tray and knocked it out of my hands. Like this." Lane demonstrated with a strong upward swing of his right hand how his tray had been upended. "It all happened so fast. But I don't remember how I ended up on the floor."

"You probably slipped on some spilled champagne," said Penny. "But tell me . . ."

But before she could frame her next question, asking Lane if the older man had used the word "grand," the door opened and half a dozen men in work clothes, high-visibility jackets, and heavy boots walked up to the counter. Lane glanced at his boss, who tipped her head at the coffee machine. Penny's time was up.

Chapter Thirty-Two

"Rhian said I'd find you in here," said Victoria as she switched on the light to the Spa's quiet room. "What are you doing sat here in the dark all by yourself?"

"Thinking. This is the first chance I've had to relax all day, and I just needed a few moments to myself." Penny smiled up at her friend. "But I'm glad to see you. I haven't been here very long, but it must have got dark without me noticing. It gets dark so early now."

Victoria held out three envelopes. "Emyr dropped off these invitations for the opening of the new visitors' centre at Yr Ysgwrn and the unveiling of the restored Black Chair. One is yours and the other two are for Mrs. Lloyd and Florence. I thought you wouldn't mind delivering them on your way home."

Penny tucked the invitations in the pocket of her jacket. "Of course I don't mind. Oh, they're going to be thrilled beyond belief."

Victoria dropped into the chair opposite Penny. "So what have you been thinking about?"

"Rhodri Phillips. And something Lane said."

"What did he say?"

"He said he overheard Michael Quinn and Rhodri arguing, and Rhodri said, 'I want my paintings back.'"

"So Quinn has paintings belonging to Rhodri?"

"It sounds like it."

"Poor Rhodri. Died so young. All that unfulfilled promise. Who knows what kind of artist he might have become? You said yourself how talented he was when we saw that painting of his in Rhian's sitting room."

"Yes, he was," said Penny, as a vague idea that was slowly becoming a motive began to take shape at the back of her mind.

"I've just had the most terrible thought. What if Michael Quinn also recognized how talented Rhodri Phillips was? And then managed to get his hands on some of Rhodri's paintings? And because nothing drives up the value of art like the artist being dead, he . . ."

"Oh, God, are you saying he killed him for his paintings?"

"I don't know," said Penny in a low voice. "But that would be a motive. All he'd have to do is hang on to the paintings for ten years or so, while Rhodri's reputation is established, and with his connections in the art world, Quinn could give that a helping hand. Then with the paintings in demand, Quinn produces the ones he's got and they're worth an awful lot of money. And he's had plenty of time to create a legitimate provenance for them."

She sighed. "But problem with that is, as soon as Quinn surfaced with the paintings, interest would be revived in Rhodri's murder, and being in possession of the paintings, Quinn would put himself right in the frame. So either he wouldn't be able to sell the paintings, or if he did, they'd point to him as being involved, somehow, in the crime. And it wouldn't take the police long to unravel it."

"Well, there'd be a certain poetic justice in that," commented Victoria.

"Quinn denies knowing Rhodri outside of the classroom, so we'd have to prove that they knew each other. Any ideas?"

"I'm afraid not, but then I don't know the man as well as you do."

Penny let that remark pass. "And there's one other thing that bothers me. If Quinn had already given the thieves a map of the ground floor of Ty Brith Hall, showing them where the library is so they could locate the chair, why was he even on the scene? You'd think he'd have wanted to be safely out of the way in Dublin when it went down."

"I'm afraid I don't know the answer to that one, either. Why don't you ask Jimmy? If anybody'd know, he's your man."

After tidying the magazines on the coffee table, Victoria stood up. "Come on. It's time we all went home." She reached up to the floating shelf and switched off the battery-operated lights on the artificial candles. Then, pausing to admire Penny's watercolour painting of the Spa, she reached up with both hands, straightened it, and took a step back to check her work.

"Better?" she asked Penny over her shoulder.

Penny's eyes widened, and a huge grin broke across her face. "Much better!" she exclaimed. "You've done it! I've got to ring Bethan." Penny dashed from the room. leaving Victoria to close the door behind them.

"What's your street number?" Penny asked Rhian when she reached the receptionist's desk.

"Number thirty-eight Station Road. Why? What's happening?"

"Ring your mother and tell her to expect the police. And then go home to be with her."

"The police! Oh, God, what's happened?"

"Your nephew's painting. If I'm right, it'll prove who killed him."

Rhian reached for her phone, and a moment later in her office, Penny did the same.

Chapter Thirty-Three

An hour later, Penny entered Jimmy's room. Seated with a bright red rug over his knees, he greeted her with a cheerful smile and gestured for her to sit. She sat on the edge of the bed, leaving the visitor's chair for Bethan, who was to join them as soon as she could.

"Something's been bothering me, Jimmy," Penny began.

"Fire away."

"If Michael Quinn had already given the thieves a map showing the layout of the ground floor of Ty Brith Hall and marked the library where they could find the chair, what was he doing in the house on the night of the robbery? Surely he'd done his bit."

"Oh, he had," agreed Jimmy. "He was there as insurance. You see, the thieves would have wanted him there in case the chair wasn't where it was supposed to be. What if, for example, at the last minute Emyr decided the chair should be on display in the sitting room instead of the library? Plans would have to be changed to accommodate that, and presumably this Quinn fellow could have led them to the chair in the new location. They couldn't take the risk of wandering about looking for it, could they?"

"No, of course not."

"He was probably paid half his fee when he delivered the map, with the rest due on completion of the job," Jimmy added. "As the incentive to ensure he showed up."

"Oh, right, well, that makes sense."

A nervous silence settled over them as they awaited the arrival of Inspector Bethan Morgan. Finally, she entered the room and Jimmy and Penny turned expectantly to her. Penny could read nothing in the policewoman's inscrutable face.

"Well, don't keep us in suspense," said Jimmy.

Bethan's face lit up with a broad smile. "You were right, Penny. Michael Quinn's fingerprints are on the Rhodri Phillips painting in his grandmother's sitting room. And what's more, the painting is in the same style as several recovered earlier by Dublin police. We didn't realise they were painted by Rhodri Phillips.

"I've just come from interviewing Michael Quinn, and once we put it to him that the painting proves that he had a relationship with Rhodri, we have a witness who can place him at the scene of the crime, and we can demonstrate that he had a strong financial motive to kill Rhodri, he confessed. He says he was drunk and angry, and he may have been, but that's no excuse. There was a lot of self-pity in his statement, but I don't think a jury's going to have a lot of sympathy for him."

She stood up. "So well done, you two. Now, I must be on

my way. I've got a night filled with paperwork ahead of me. Can I give you a lift, Penny?"

"No, thanks," said Penny. "I'll sit with Jimmy a little longer, and then I've got to call in at Mrs. Lloyd's."

* * *

Mrs. Lloyd gently lifted Florence's ginger cat from the sofa, set her on the floor, and invited Penny to sit. "White wine is it? Or would you prefer an aperitif? Sherry? I'm just pouring one for Florence."

"White wine, please," said Penny.

After handing Penny her glass of wine, Mrs. Lloyd sat in a comfortable chair that faced the sofa, pressed her hands together, and leaned forward slightly.

A moment later as footsteps in the hall signalled Florence was on her way, Mrs. Lloyd picked up the glass of sherry, and when Florence was seated, she handed it to her. Both women were dressed in rather old-fashioned attire: Mrs. Lloyd in a tailored navy-blue dress accented with her favourite pearl necklace and Florence in a plaid skirt, with a white blouse, over which she wore a white apron.

"Well?" said Mrs. Lloyd.

"There's so much to tell, I'm not sure where to begin," said Penny.

"At the beginning, of course," said Mrs. Lloyd.

Penny summarized everything for them. How Emyr had mentioned to Jennifer Sayles that he planned to show the Black Chair at his dinner party; how she'd told her father, Sir

Anthony Sayles; how Mrs. Lynch had planned the theft but it had all gone terribly wrong when Rhodri Phillips confronted Michael Quinn, demanding the return of his paintings. How Lane Hardwick had witnessed them arguing in the hallway, and how Rhodri had made the fatal error of following Quinn outside and, in the heat of a searing moment, been struck and left to die on the walkway.

"At first I thought Sayles was the killer," said Penny, "because the two crimes were so closely linked. And when the Sayles's heist of the Black Chair became tangled up with the murder of Rhodri Phillips, they realised they were in such deep trouble they could not keep the chair, so they were forced to abandon it."

"Oh, how that must have hurt," said Florence, without the slightest trace of sympathy in her voice.

"Still," said Penny, "the chair's recovered and safe, and the thieves and the killer of Rhodri Phillips are in custody. And there might even be a happy ending in store for Riley, the young traveller girl. I want to help her get the education she wants so badly. I've arranged for her to spend some time roaming about with Dilys, who will teach her all about the plants and trees, and just now Jimmy said he'd like to help pay for her university. But there are still lots of details to be worked out, including where she'll board while she goes to school and guardianship, as she's still a minor."

"Oh, that's lovely," said Florence.

"Yes, it all seems to have ended well," said Mrs. Lloyd. "I'm sure the young man's family will be happy to know the full story of what happened to him that night, and the chair's where it belongs, and in time for the visit by the Prince of Wales. I'm sure he'll be very keen to hear all about what happened to it."

"Oh, he will," said Penny. "And now for the real reason I came here." She reached down for her handbag.

"There was an unfortunate mix-up over your last invitation, so I was asked to hand-deliver these to you." She gave Mrs. Lloyd and Florence each a stiff white card.

"What is it?" asked Florence.

"Read it," said Penny.

"I haven't got my reading glasses," Florence said.

"I'll read it," Mrs. Lloyd. "Let me see . . . 'Mr. Owain Jones, chairman, Snowdonia National Park Authority, cordially invites you to a reception to celebrate the restoration of Yr Ysgwrn, home of the bardic poet Hedd Wyn, in the presence of HRH The Prince of Wales.'" She lowered the card, blinked, and then picked it up again and repeated, "'in the presence of HRH The Prince of Wales.'"

Her bright-blue eyes twinkled as she clasped her hands together and let out a rapturous "Oooh!"

"We're going to need that etiquette book," said Florence.

* * *

Although winter had taken hold of the landscape, a lush green carpet still covered the rolling hills surrounding Yr Ysgwrn, home of the renowned Welsh poet Ellis Humphrey Evans, better known by his bardic name Hedd Wyn. A flock of Welsh mountain sheep grazed in the pale afternoon sunshine, safe behind their stone walls and taking no notice of the steady stream of visitors. The word that sprang into Penny's mind as she gazed at the tranquil scene that Hedd Wyn himself would have known a hundred years ago was peace. And that was so fitting, she thought, as the poet's bardic name meant Blessed Peace.

Penny, Victoria, Mrs. Lloyd, and Florence approached the traditional farmhouse, built from local dressed stone with a slate roof from a nearby quarry, and crossed the threshold, stepping back into the early days of the twentieth century.

In a small, whitewashed room that would have once been the parlour, flanked by wreaths of poppies, was the Black Chair, looking none the worse for its recent adventure. A Snowdonia National Park Authority official stood beside it, and when the room had filled, she explained the history of the chair, omitting its recent theft and the arrest of Sir Anthony Sayles and his daughter, Jennifer, for their part in it.

Beside the chair was an Oxo tin.

"What's that doing there?" Mrs. Lloyd asked.

"That's the tin in which Hedd Wyn's nephew kept all the little bits that fell off the chair over the years," said the guide, "so when the time came to restore it, the original pieces could be reattached." The guide smiled and then gestured toward the door. "If there are no more questions, I'll have to ask you to move on, so others can view the chair. Please enjoy your visit to the rest of the house and then make your way to the visitors' centre. You must be there fifteen minutes before the reception begins."

After a tour of the farmhouse, which, although modest, was filled with a warmth and closeness that spoke of grueling work balanced by the love of a large family, the women made their way to the new visitors' centre, which had been converted from an old agricultural outbuilding into a bright, modern space with a tearoom, shop, and museum.

The exhibition space filled up with invited guests, and when excited whispers of "The prince, he's on his way" swept through the room, all heads turned to the entrance. A moment later the Prince of Wales, accompanied by a few dignitaries and a couple of local officials, entered. He was introduced to various people in the crowd, and then approached Penny and her friends.

"And this is Penny Brannigan," said an aide. Penny dropped a small curtsy, and the aide said something in a low voice to the prince.

"Ah, it's you we have to thank, is it?" he said. "Well done."

The party moved on to the person on Penny's right.

"Have you come far?" asked the prince, extending his right hand to Mrs. Lloyd.

She let out a small, muffled squeak, but the words wouldn't come. For once, she was speechless.

Acknowledgments

The Black Chair is real, as is the background story told here of poetic achievement during a time of war, loss, and remembrance.

It was inspiring to view the iconic Black Chair that had been awarded posthumously at the 1917 National Eisteddfod to the great Welsh poet Ellis Humphrey Evans (Hedd Wyn) and uplifting to explore Yr Ysgwrn, the beautifully preserved farmhouse where he grew up. Thank you to Sylvia and Peter Jones for making all this possible during an unforgettable day out. My thanks to them, too, for applying their excellent proof reading skills to this work.

My thanks go to Eirlys Owen for her assistance with background material on Bangor University and for her expertise in Welsh language usage and spelling. It should be noted that for plot purposes this book mentions a course in art history that the university does not actually offer.

This book is dedicated to Carol Lloyd, a reader who became a friend, and I thank her for her encouragement over the years.

# Acknowledgments

I am grateful to Matt Martz, publisher, Crooked Lane Books, for giving the Penny Brannigan mystery series its new home, and to Jenny Chen, Ashley Di Dio, and Sarah Poppe for making the book magic happen. The delightful cover illustration is the work of Scott Zelazny and he has my admiration for capturing the elements of the story.

Thank you to my agent, Dominick Abel, for his guidance and literary acumen.

And finally, as always, heartfelt thanks to Lucas Walker and Riley Wallbank for their love and support.